# MIDNIGHT MISCHIEF

When Cassandra heard the scratching on her door, she assumed it was her sister, so she opened the door without putting on her dressing gown.

It was Adrian. She regarded him blankly until he moved past her, closed the door, and turned the key in the lock, pocketing it.

She hardly knew whether to be angry or laugh. "Adrian, you can't . . ." she began, but was silenced as she found herself enfolded in his arms. The kiss was long and lingering, and he released her only to carry her to the bed.

"Adrian, stop this," she said as firmly as she could. "You can't suppose I mean to allow you to ravish me?"

"I won't *ravish* you," he promised, laying her on the bed tenderly. His eyes were very dark and glittered as his pupils caught the light. Looming over her, he reminded Cassandra of a great bird of prey . . . about to descend. . . .

ELIZABETH HEWITT who hailed from Pennsylvania, now lives in New Jersey with her dog, Maxim, named after a famous romantic hero. She enjoys reading history and is a fervent Anglophile. Music is also an important part of her life; she studies voice and all of her novels for Signet's Regency line were written to a background of baroque and classical music.

# THE
# ICE MAIDEN

*by*

*Elizabeth Hewitt*

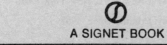

A SIGNET BOOK

**NEW AMERICAN LIBRARY**

SIGNET TRADEMARK REG. U.S. PAT. OFF. AND FOREIGN COUNTRIES
REGISTERED TRADEMARK—MARCA REGISTRADA
HECHO EN CHICAGO, U.S.A.

SIGNET, SIGNET CLASSIC, MENTOR, ONYX, PLUME, MERIDIAN
and NAL BOOKS are published by NAL PENGUIN INC.,
1633 Broadway, New York, New York 10019

First Printing, June, 1988

1   2   3   4   5   6   7   8   9

PRINTED IN THE UNITED STATES OF AMERICA

# 1

$C$ASSANDRA Tilton lowered her eyes and folded her hands in her lap, composing herself in the proper attitude of a young lady about to receive an offer of marriage. She had no doubt of Sir Matthew Bourne's intent, for she fully recognized the signs of an imminent proposal. As well she should; she had received five similar declarations in the six years since she had made her curtsy to the polite world.

"In short, my dear Cass," Sir Matthew said, coming to the end of a catalog of her womanly virtues, "any man who would not find in you the ideal wife must indeed be blind or a fool."

He was standing a little away from her by the fire, one hand resting negligently on the mantel, quite obviously striking a posture. Cassandra forgave him the affectation for she knew that however confident Matthew might be of success, it was only natural that he feel at least a trace of self-consciousness. She was grateful that he had not fallen to his knees to beg for her hand, for the would-be lover who had last done so had felt the sting of her amusement, which she had not been able to quite suppress.

There was no doubt at all that Sir Matthew's suit would prosper, either in her mind or in his. Though theirs was not a passionate love match, they held each other in regard and shared similar tastes and interests. In breeding and in fortune they were also well-matched; between them, they were connected to most of the politically and financially powerful families in the realm. Their mating was nothing short of dynastic and was heartily approved and encouraged by both her family and his.

"You may think me overnice in my notions of propriety, Cass," he continued, at last crossing the room to sit beside her on the brocade sofa, "but I would not have been easy in my mind if I had not spoken first with Tilton and had his assurance that he would approve of my suit. It needs only you to smile on me, fair lady, and my happiness will be complete." He took one of her hands and held it in a firm, possessive grasp.

Cassandra wondered why it was that men seemed to think it necessary to couch their offers in flowery language; in her experience it was always so. There was a dancing light in her dark green eyes that might have given her thoughts away, but her smile was encouraging and Sir Matthew noted only that. "Give me your pledge, dearest Cassandra," he said, his tone more assured than pleading, "and make me the happiest man on earth."

Cassandra knew quite well what her answer would be, but she did not answer him directly. "Since I am four-and-twenty, and Harry has nothing at all to say to my marrying," she said, her manner gently quizzing, "I can only assume that you spoke first with my brother to bind me to any promise I might make. With Lord Hallerby, you know, I cried off before the banns could even be called."

Matthew's smile was a bit mechanical, for though he did not hold it against Cassandra that she had earned the reputation of a jilt, he did not think it a matter for lightness. "You were a green girl then and did not know your mind," he said, with the barest quelling note in his tone. "I trust you will be sure of the answer that you give to me." Cassandra looked away from him and perceptibly withdrew at these words, and for the first time his confidence wavered. There was a moment of uncomfortable silence between them and then he said, "If I am to receive my *congé*, my dear Cass, you needn't concern yourself with expressing the usual sentiments about the honor I have done you. Just tell me so directly."

Cassandra met his eyes for a moment, gave him a brief smile, and removed her hand from his clasp. "It is not that, Matthew," she said to reassure him. "You *do* honor me by asking me to be your wife, and it would be my very great delight to accept your offer. But there is something we must speak of before I can accept your proposal."

He was a bit surprised by this unexpected element. He had not supposed she would qualify her answer to him. "You mustn't tease yourself with odd notions, my dear," he said understandingly. "You must allow me to convince you that we shall deal excellently together."

"I hope you may, Matthew," she said sincerely. "I know you are aware that you are not the first man who has offered marriage to me." Her smile was self-mocking as she thought of her succession of suitors. "I say that without conceit, for I know it is my purse as well as my person that attracts so readily. I have no regret for the offers I refused, but in my first Season I was betrothed twice, and twice cried off, and for these I do bear regret, though for very different reasons."

Matthew took her hands in his again and pressed them to show that he understood. "It is exactly like you to feel your youthful follies, but I assure you it is unnecessary. I do not regard them."

"But I do, Matthew," she said, faintly impatient at the interruption. "I did Lord Hallerby a great disservice, for I accepted his offer for all of the wrong reasons, and repented of it almost instantly. He, however, was quite sincere in his affection toward me, and I know I hurt him grievously."

"You did not intend so."

"But I did give him pain, nevertheless. And with Ned Tarkington it was much the same, but in that instance I gave myself equal pain. I was very much in love with him when I accepted his offer. Telling Ned that I could not after all be his wife was the most difficult thing I have ever had to do."

Matthew nodded, his gray eyes expressing his compassion. "It was calf-love, of course. You needn't be ashamed of it. It is to your credit that you came to realize it before your mistake became irrevocable."

Cassandra bit back the tart recommendation that he allow her to speak for herself without assuming that he knew her mind. "It was more than calf-love," she said with a touch of asperity. "Had Mr. Tarkington not proven by his consistent and unrepentant faithlessness and dissembling that the strength of his attachment did not equal mine, I should certainly have become his wife."

A small frown creased the baronet's brow. "Are you telling me that you are still bound by that attachment, Cass?"

"No," she said so firmly that there could be no doubt of it. "I have been cured of that some time since. But I have a fear—a natural one, I think—of making a similar mistake again. If we are to be married, we must both of us be certain of our minds and know precisely what it is we wish for, both from this marriage and from each other."

"I have no doubt at all of it," he said with gratifying readiness. "I have already told you that I believe you are everything that I have ever wished for in a wife, and any marriage entered into with sense and consideration surely cannot but succeed."

It was what she wished to hear, coinciding with her own beliefs, and she felt a sense of relief at his reassurance. She wished she might have no doubt at all of their future together but her history made her cautious, and caution, for her, bred doubt.

"And you, Cass?" Matthew prompted when she remained silent.

Matthew did not make her pulse race as Ned Tarkington had done, nor was he the heir to a dukedom, as was Lord Hallerby, but she had no need to marry for money or position, and pulse-fluttering passion had brought her more pain than pleasure. Cassandra smiled and said, "If you will have me, Matthew, I should be honored to be your wife."

Matthew at once embraced her and lightly kissed her. Cassandra was prepared to accept his further advances, which her experience had taught her to expect, but this token of his regard appeared to satisfy him, at least for now. He sat back, took out his watch, and said in a rather matter-of-fact way, "I would like us to be wed from Bourne Hall before the end of the summer, if you are agreeable." When she acquiesced, he nodded, rising. "I had best be off then. I have an appointment with Castlereagh at eleven. No doubt you are anxious to share our happiness with your family," he added.

Cassandra, a little nonplussed by this unloverlike behavior, stood as well. "Yes. Sarah is here to visit with Livia, and she and Livy will both be pleased by our news."

"Then by all means I would not keep you." He took her hand. "I wish I had the time to speak with Lady Fareland myself. Please take her my regard. I know she has been my friend in this."

"Sarah never misses an opportunity to extol your virtues," she agreed with just a hint of dryness in her tone. Sarah's constant encomiums on Matthew's character and assets had been the one thing that had nearly put Cassandra off the match.

Matthew bowed over her hand and then surprised her again by turning it over and bestowing a gentle kiss on her palm. He could be the lover if he chose. "We shall do very well together, Cass," he said, and left her.

Since Sir Matthew was a friend of long standing and the Tiltons did not stand on ceremony with him, Cassandra allowed him to find his own way out and turned her own steps in the direction of the small parlor at the back of the house where she knew she would find her sister and sister-in-law.

It was unprofitable to compare Matthew's proposal

with the others she had received, but the thought would not be banished. Tarkington and Hallerby had been all exuberant passion, pressing kisses on her until she was breathless, and even her rejected suitors had exhibited more emotion than Matthew had done, but since it was her wish to marry a temperate man, she knew it was unjust in her to complain. And in fairness, she had to acknowledge that her affection for Matthew was based on friendship rather than passion. Yet her vanity was piqued by his phlegmatic response.

As Cassandra approached the morning room, Sarah, Countess of Fareland, opened the door of the ladies' parlor jut enough to see into the hall. When she saw that it was Cassandra and not another false alarm, she threw back the door to its fullest extent and waited in obvious impatience for her sister to come into the room. "Well," she demanded, "did Bourne come up to scratch? You don't seem especially pleased," she added after a quick search of her sister's countenance. "It would be the most infamous thing ever if he did not offer for you when we were all expecting it so." Another thought occurred to her. "Never say that you have refused him!"

Cassandra smiled at her sister's frowning outrage. "You are always saying that you despair of my ever being respectably settled," she said, deliberately hedging to quiz her elder sister. "I have thought myself at times that I am simply not destined to marry."

Cassandra was generally reckoned the great beauty in the family, but Sarah possessed the same thick bronze-colored hair, green eyes, and rose-petal complexion as her sister. In her first Season she had been extolled by one suitor, who had witnessed her in a temper, as "magnificent." She seldom missed an opportunity to live up to this judgment, and now she raised her chin, swelled her chest, and straightened her carriage before exclaiming, "You did not! This is too bad of you, Cass. If you will not think of yourself, you should think of us. Are we to have you on our hands forever? No Tilton has ever been left on the shelf."

Livia Tilton, an attractive brunette in her own right, but cast in the shade by her beautiful sisters-in-law, was seated at a worktable. She glanced up from the fancywork which was occupying her attention and said in her placid way, "Nonsense. Cass is roasting you, Sally. Sir Matthew spoke with Harry before he saw Cass, and she knew why he was come to see her. She need not have received him if she didn't wish to accept his offer."

"But she just said . . ."

Cassandra put a hand on her sister's shoulder. "I beg your pardon, Sally, I shouldn't tease you, I know, but you are such an easy fish to land. Of course I have accepted Matthew's offer."

Lady Fareland warred between indignation and relief. The latter won and she sat in a chair across the table from Livia and picked up her needlework. "Perhaps the question should be whether or not you will go the distance," she said tartly. "Until a priest has actually declared you bound, I, for one, shall not be easy."

"Nor I," Cassandra agreed amiably, and sat in another empty chair drawn up to the table. "I think I was at least a little serious when I said I was not sure I was destined to marry. Who knows? Perhaps my personal devil will come upon me again and I shall cry off this time too."

"You are a great fool if you do," Sarah said unequivocally. "You should be grateful that Matthew is generous enough to overlook your history. You publicly humiliated two of the finest prizes on the marriage market and have whistled I don't know how many other excellent offers down the wind. I am sure I cannot see what so many men find to admire in you; you have no regard at all for their feelings. You are young yet and have pretensions to beauty, and I suppose you think that you have still a thousand hearts to break, but it is not so, I promise you. If you pull your tricks again this time, even the fortune hunters will look at you askance, and then where will you be?"

"Doomed to spinsterhood, I expect," Cassandra said with unimpaired good humor as she sorted through the assorted skeins of silk spread out on the table for the colors that she liked best. The light of battle sparked in Sarah's eyes, and Livia sent Cassandra a look which was clearly imploring. Cassandra put down the silks and sighed. "You needn't fear it, Sally. Even I know that another jilting would not easily find forgiveness in the world. I should find myself ostracized by men, pitied by women, and cast off by my family."

Livia gave her a warm smile. "The last isn't so. You are welcome to remain with us for as long as you should wish, my love. Neither Tilton nor I would wish you to feel other than that this is your home."

"You do her no kindness to encourage her," Sarah admonished as she plied her needle with angry stabs.

Cassandra ignored her sister and said, "You are the kindest creature, Livy, but I am four-and-twenty and I know it is time that I had my own establishment."

"Aren't you going to tell us what he said to you?" Sarah asked. "For someone who has just received an offer of marriage from one of the most eligible men of the *ton*, you show a remarkable lack of elation. You were not so indifferent when Tarkington proposed."

Livia, fearing that Sarah's remark might open an old wound for Cassandra, said quickly. "But that was different. It was Cass's first offer and she was quite young and . . ."

"And I was in love with Ned," Cassandra finished. "I hold Matthew in affection and respect, but I won't pretend it is a love match."

"I am sure it is better for you that it is not," Sarah said, laying aside her work and leaning toward her sister for emphasis. "People of our order have much to consider when we marry. We must consult our heads rather than our hearts."

Cassandra rested her chin in her hand and said in

dulcet accents, "Was it your head that advised you to marry Fareland, Sally?"

Since it was well known in the family that the Farelands had scarcely spoken a civil word to each other since the ink had been dry on their marriage lines, the question was incendiary and Livia stepped in to prevent open battle from breaking out between the sisters. "When I married Harry I consulted both," she said. "It was my great good fortune that we were well-matched as well as in love. But you have not told us what Matthew said, Cass."

Cassandra shrugged. "All of the usual things. I should have blushed for the compliments he paid to my person and character, but I fear I am past the age of taking such things to heart or being readily confused."

"Well, you are certainly not past the age of celebration. I have spoken with Harry," Livia said, gathering up her silks, "and we agreed that we must have a ball in honor of your betrothal."

"You'd do best to wait to make sure it isn't another false alarm," said Sarah caustically. "We have so many friends in common with the Bournes, it will be mortifying to have to face them if Cass cries off again."

"Cassandra knows her mind, or she would never have encouraged Matthew," Livia said quellingly as she rose. At that moment Lord Tilton came through the door and was informed by his wife of the happy news.

The viscount at once expressed his pleasure to Cassandra. "He will make you a fine husband, Cass," he said. "His fortune is more than the equal of yours, so there need be no concern on that score, and though we touched on the subject of settlements only briefly, since he had not yet had your answer, I can assure you that he is all that is generous."

Sarah and Livia exclaimed favorably at these words, but Cassandra found nothing particularly laudable in them. Matthew was a rich man who could well afford to be generous, and in any case, she brought to him a fortune of her own that was far from contemptible.

"He could not be otherwise," she said with a notice-able lack of inflection, and added, "I am glad you are pleased for me, Harry. It is you and Livia who are generous to have a ball in my honor."

"I was about to ring for Dodkins and Mrs. Waite so that we may begin our plans at once," Livia said. "A fortnight, I think, will give us ample time to plan the ball. I hope everyone is not quite weary of your news in that time," she added, smiling.

"Oh, in Cass's case I wouldn't concern myself with that," Sarah interposed. "Hope rather that the won-der of Cass embarking on yet another betrothal will have died down by then."

Livia again started toward the bell-pull, but the viscount put a hand on his wife's arm to stay her. "If you don't mind, my love, I wish to have a word with you before you see Dodkins and Mrs. Waite."

It was clear from his tone that he wished to be private with his wife, and Cassandra immediately made an excuse to leave, but Sarah remained. Cassandra reflected as she closed the door behind her that it was exactly like her elder sister not to take the hint that her presence was not required.

It was decided that the ball would take place on the last Friday in April, and within only a day or two the efficient Livia, with the aid of her sisters-in-law and her very capable staff, had matters well in hand. The invitations were out and the orchestra, florist, and extra staff had been selected and commissioned to provide their services for the ball. It was short notice, for the Season was at its apex, but for the Viscountess Tilton, whose connections and influence were so ex-tensive, all things were possible.

By Tuesday morning of the week of the ball, little remained to be done except the physical labor of dec-orating the ballroom at Tilton House and the prepara-tion of the elaborate dishes that would be served both at the select dinner before the ball and at the buffet supper which would be laid out for all the guests at midnight.

The task of visiting the florist and selecting from his samples which blossoms would adorn the ballroom fell to Cassandra. She was in the hall drawing on her gloves when her elder sister arrived and demanded to know the purpose of her excursion. Cassandra groaned inwardly, for she feared that Sarah would insist on accompanying her, and the fear proved not unfounded.

"I only need return this book to Livia and then I shall join you," Sarah said as soon as she learned her sister's purpose.

"It is not at all necessary, Sally. Surely you have your own plans for this afternoon."

Sarah would not allow this to be a consideration. "I have a fitting for the dress I am to wear for the ball, but other than that, nothing that signifies, and we may stop at Madame Celeste's when we have finished with the florist. If I do not go with you, you are sure to make a mull of it, choosing flowers because they are pretty rather than practical."

"And what is wrong with that?" Cassandra demanded. "It *is* my ball."

"But Tilton is paying for it, and you needn't tell me he can well afford it—it is no excuse to be wasteful. I shall be but a moment."

Cassandra resigned herself to her fate and in a very few minutes they were enclosed in Lady Fareland's crested town carriage headed toward the fashionable Mr. Tobridge's glasshouses.

"You should be very grateful to Harry that despite all he has to worry him, he takes the trouble to think of you," Sarah said as the carriage pulled away from Tilton House. "I only hope you do not again betray the trust of your family, as you have done in the past, by scorning our every effort to see you suitably established."

Cassandra, who had no intention of allowing herself to be drawn into a discussion of her past mistakes, said quickly, "What has Harry to worry him? Livia mentioned only the other day how pleased he was by his bailiff's reports this past quarter, and everyone is in good health as far as I am aware."

Sarah gave her a brief condescending smile. "My dear, surely you noticed how upset he was the day that Bourne proposed to you."

"He was a little distracted," she agreed, "but it could have nothing to do with Matthew, for I know Harry completely approves of the match."

"He is upset because of the duke, of course."

There were exactly twenty-six dukes in the realm, but in this context there could be only one that would be of concern to the Viscount Tilton. "I had heard that Portland was doing much better."

"The Duke of Portland is an old man, Cass," Sarah reminded her, "and frankly I think it is for the best. He has not been well for much of the time since he became prime minister, and if it weren't for his cabinet and able men such as Harry, I don't know what would have become of the government. As if it weren't enough that poor Mr. Fox died so untimely, now we may lose another great man as well. Whom they shall find to replace him and what shall become of the government, heaven alone can say. Hannah says that she is sure that the king will send for Mr. Canning, but Harry says it is not likely and it shall probably be Mr. Perceval who succeeds the poor duke."

"Hannah would very well like it if it were Mr. Canning," Cassandra said dryly. "He is her cousin by her mother's first marriage, and she doubtless hopes he will continue to advance her husband, as he did in the first place by giving him a position in the Foreign Office. McInnes was languishing as a *very* undersecretary in the Horseguards before Mr. Canning became foreign secretary."

"Why should Mr. Canning not help Freddy?" Sarah demanded a little defensively. Hannah McInnes was her closest friend and confidante and she would brook no criticism of her, even from Cassandra. "Freddy is a very capable man. Everyone says so."

"When he is sober, perhaps, but that isn't often."

"That is unfair. Most gentlemen drink more than is good for them, including Harry, I am sure. Why, only last Thursday at the Conningby rout several of the men were quite castaway, and Lord Burryton had to go outside to be sick."

It was as well for the sake of peace between the sisters that the carriage stopped at that moment before Mr. Tobridge's shop and prevented Cassandra from responding, for she frankly disliked Hannah McInnes, who she considered encroaching, and in her opinion the Honorable Mr. Frederick McInnes was nothing short of a sot. She could scarce recall a social occasion when he was not at least a bit up in the world, and at most parties he could be counted on to become totally disguised before the evening ended. For all she knew, he was a model of sobriety when attending to his duties at the Foreign Office, but once or twice Harry had made a comment that made her think it was not always the case.

"It won't do for you to say such things of Freddy now, whatever you may think," Sarah said to her just as they were about to enter the shop. "Since Hannah is Matthew's stepsister, he is very soon to be a close connection of yours."

Cassandra was well aware of this, but forbore to make the comment that most families could boast a few dirty dishes. They were greeted at the door by Mr. Tobridge, and the subject was allowed to drop. Cassandra's business at the florist's was concluded quickly and satisfactorily with a minimum of interference from her sister, and they went from there to Madame Celeste's.

It was not uncommon for gentlemen to frequent the fashionable modiste's, either in the company of their wives or to order something particularly fetching for those ladies that held their hearts if not their names. A small room had been set aside for them to avoid embarrassing encounters with friends of their wives or, worse, with their wives themselves. But now and again, a gentleman with nothing to fear wandered into the principal room, which was tastefully decorated to resemble as closely as possible a gentleman's withdrawing room and with little about it to proclaim it a shop.

While Lady Fareland was discussing the detail of her overdress with one of Madame Celeste's assistants, a tall, well-favored, and well-formed young man with gently curling flaxen hair and eyes of a particularly arresting shade of blue came into the room. Perceiving Cassandra seated on a spindle-legged chair in the far corner of the room, he went over to her immediately, his unstudied, wholehearted smile further enhancing his attractiveness.

Cassandra looked up at his approach and returned his smile. Though she regarded him now with unruffled serenity, she could well recall when the approach of Ned Tarkington had had the power to make her heart turn over within her.

"My dearest Cass," he said, taking her hand with a courtly flourish and planting a warm kiss on it. "I only heard your news yesterday, or I should have called before now. Caro's increasing again, you know, and she's always so sick with it that she thought it best to return to Berkshire, and I accompanied her to see her well-settled. Bourne is to be the lucky man, I see. With all my heart, I wish you well of him. I know you will make him the best of wives."

Sarah, hearing Ned's voice, turned and came over to greet him. "Do we see you at Cass's ball, Ned?" she asked as he dutifully bowed over her hand.

"Of course," he replied with a smile that made it seem as if pleasing her were his sole concern. "Although I shall have to send my regrets for dinner. I am already promised to Berkley Craven, who is giving some of us dinner at White's for Adrian Searle that evening."

"Searle?" Sarah's brows went up in surprise. "Is he finally returned from Spain then? I heard he was all but living as a native and wasn't likely to return."

"Portugal," Tarkington amended. "And actually,

he is latterly come from Brazil, where he was attending the Braganzas, who, you know, have gone into exile there. He has been back a month or two, I believe, but he's spent most of it with his family at Dunwhittie."

"And he is fixed in town now?" asked the countess, who like most hostesses was ever interested in securing personable young men to make up her numbers. "I shall certainly tell Livy, for she will wish to send him a card to her ball. A dinner cannot last the whole night."

Cassandra listened to this exchange with interest. Though she was acquainted with the Marquess of Dunston, she had never met his younger brother, Lord Adrian, and knew him only by repute. A friend who did know him once described Lord Adrian to her as the most beautiful man she had ever set eyes upon, but as Cassandra had been totally enraptured of Ned at the time, she had not credited the encomium. "Do you know Lord Adrian, Sarah?" she asked.

Sarah responded with a condescending smile. "*Everyone* knows Lord Adrian, or at least everyone female. He is quite a favorite with our sex. He is fatally attractive, you know. But you do not, do you? He was with the Viceroy in Ireland the year you came out, and it was the following that he left for Spain."

"Portugal," Cassandra corrected automatically. Scenting a possible romance, she added, "Did he go by choice or was it due to his 'fatal attractiveness'?"

"The devil fly away with Searle," Tarkington said, laughing, but with an underlying note of annoyance. He did not much like all of the attention going to another man, even one who was absent. "He got into his share of scrapes in his salad days. What high-spirited young man does not? But there was no scandal, open or hushed, that I am aware of. It's just a career for him. Most younger sons, however highborn, have their own way to make in the world. I heard from Emily Cowper that Livia has ordered bolts of watered silk to drape the ballroom," he added to turn the subject.

Sarah did not follow his lead. "The Dunstons much prefer life at Dunwhittie," she said to Cassandra, "which is so near to Bath that they needn't be entirely out of the world living in Somerset. Annabelle Dunston is *enceinte* at last, I am told. The Dunstons had all but given up hope of a family, and her interesting condition may put Lord Adrian's nose out of joint. He is his brother's heir, you know."

"The Dunstons are both fairly young," Cassandra pointed out. "He could not have counted on it."

"Nevertheless, they often do. I only hope Lord Adrian has not become brown with the Brazilian sun. 'Twould be a pity if he has. It is the contrast between the fairness of his complexion and the darkness of his hair and eyes that makes him appear so striking." Madame Celeste approached her to call her to mind of the purpose of her visit, and Sarah excused herself and followed the fashionable modiste into another portion of the store to view the progress of her gown.

Tarkington's laughter was just a little forced. "Well, Searle's fame precedes him. I only hope he may still live up to it."

Cassandra's laugh was quite genuine. "No you don't, Ned. You never did like competition. You hope he is as brown and weathered as a raisin."

"Actually, it is a matter of indifference to me," he said with a quick smile before his expression changed to one of concern. "Cass," Ned said, dropping his voice to a confidential level, "I want you to know that I really do wish you happy with Bourne. I don't know him well, but if he is your choice, I am sure it is a good one."

"Thank you, Ned. It *is* my choice and I haven't any doubt it is a good one."

Unexpectedly, he took her hand and brought it to his lips. "Dearest Cass, I hope this means that your heart is finally at peace. I know enough of Bourne's circumstances to know that it is an excellent match in the eyes of the world, but I hope it is more than just expedience for you. It would lie heavy indeed on my heart if I thought that it was only resignation behind this step."

Cassandra's brows knit for a moment in puzzlement, and then cleared, her mouth turning up in the hint of a smile. "Are you suggesting, Ned, that I am past my prayers? I thank you for the compliment, sir. I am marrying Matthew because it is what I devoutly wish to do, not because he is my last hope."

"You know that isn't what I meant," he said, his voice still low, but intent. "You have a loyal heart, my lovely, and I have long feared that I had done it irreparable harm."

"Do you mean that you were concerned that I would spend the rest of my life wearing the willow for you?" she said, open laughter now lurking in her eyes. "How little you know me, after all."

He squeezed her hand and let it drop. "You were ever one to keep your own counsel, Cass, but I want you to know that I have not been insensitive to the deep hurt you suffered at my hands. I understood why you became betrothed to Hallerby scarcely a fortnight after my betrothal to Caroline was announced, and I must always be grateful that you did not go through with it. It would sorely trouble my conscience if I thought your betrothal to Bourne was of a similar nature."

Cassandra marveled a little at his vanity, and more so at her willful blindness that had failed to recognize it when she had loved him so. "You may rest easy on that score, Ned. It is not."

A remarkably pretty young woman wearing a basted gown of gold-shot green satin came out of the fitting area and said, "Isn't it perfect, Neddie? Madame has promised that I shall have it early next week."

The young woman was unknown to Cassandra, but she was definitely not Caroline Tarkington. Cassandra smiled with self-mockery. Naively, she had not questioned what Ned would be doing in the shop of a fashionable modiste when he had just told her that his wife was in Berkshire. Though the accents of the young woman were refined, Cassandra had no real doubt of her origins or her trade. Cassandra neither waited nor expected to be introduced to her. She picked up her reticule from the table near her chair. "In the end, at least, I have always been guided by my good sense," she said, and with a haughty lift to her brows, added, "It is a pity that Caroline was not similarly led."

He was not in the least abashed. "It is not at all what you are thinking, Cass."

"No," she said sweetly, walking toward the fitting rooms. "Knowing you, I am sure my imagination is not the equal to the truth."

He opened his mouth to reply, but her back was already to him, and the young woman was demanding to know who Cassandra might be in a slightly less-educated voice than when she had first spoken.

As she joined her sister in the fitting room, Cassandra silently congratulated herself for the good judgment she had shown by not wedding Ned Tarkington. It was obvious that her assumption that marriage would not reform him, as he had claimed, had proven correct. She was absolutely certain that Matthew would never do anything to subject her to such humiliation, and felt confirmed in her belief that he was exactly the sort of husband that she wished for.

Her belief in this remained steadfast through several unsatisfyingly brief and unromantic visits from her betrothed, the continued encomiums on his virtue from her elder sister, and the tiring bustle that not even the best-run households can quite escape at the approach of an entertainment to which well over three hundred guests have been invited.

# 2

*I*N spite of the short span of time from when the invitations were sent out until the night of the ball, the majority of the invited guests attended. This was due in part to the general popularity of the Tiltons, who moved in the first circles, and also in part to curiosity. Cassandra's previous engagements, which had ended unhappily, and her persistent refusal to take up any of the other hearts which had been laid at her feet had gained her the reputation of a care-for-nobody. This made it an occasion of special interest both to those who wished her well-settled and to those who declared cynically that Bourne was as likely as his predecessors to share their fate.

Guests for the ball began arriving almost as soon as the company at dinner had quitted the dining room, and standing at the head of the receiving line with Matthew, Cassandra felt her hand would be quite chafed if one more man wishing to express his gallantry brought it to his lips. She was at last freed from this duty when the orchestra was ready to begin and she and Matthew were required to lead the dance.

As the ballroom and her dance card filled rapidly, she soon ceased to regard dancing as a respite from duty, and seized the opportunity to cry off from a promise to stand up with an old friend. She made a slow progress out of the ballroom, which was so crammed with people that there was barely room in the center of the room for the sets to form. The hall outside the ballroom was only marginally less crowded, and Cassandra continued on until she reached a side

hall which led to a number of anterooms. She saw
Livia standing in conversation with a few people and
headed toward her, realizing only after she had com-
mitted herself to joining them that Hannah McInnes
was one of their number.

Cassandra knew that her dislike of Matthew's stepsister was unreasonable, for Hannah had never been
anything but kind to her, but Cassandra could not like
her, even for Matthew's sake. Matthew had confided
in her that much of Hannah's ambition, social for
herself and political for her husband, was the result of
a wretched childhood she had spent with her then
widowed mother as a poor relation in the home of
cousins who had treated mother and daughter as un-
paid servants. Cassandra could pity Hannah McInnes,
but feel no sympathy for her; she thought the older
woman too pushing and relentless in attaining her
ends to allow for compassion.

The advancement of her husband's career was listed
high amongst Mrs. McInnes' goals and she could be
counted on at any entertainment such as this, where
not only the cream of the *ton* but also most of the
power within it could be found, to fix her interest
where it would do the most good toward achieving this
aim. She did not disappoint her detractors this night.
Standing with Hannah and Livia were Mr. Perceval,
the chancellor of the exchequer, and Lord Moreville,
who was second only to Mr. Canning in the Foreign
Office.

"Of course Freddy supports the Portuguese Legion
that was formed last year," Hannah was saying to
Lord Moreville as Cassandra approached, "but he agrees
with Mr. Alistar that Perponcher is not the man to
head it, whatever Castlereagh might say."

"I believe that the general has the support of Wellesley as well as Lord Castlereagh," Mr. Perceval said in
his quiet way, which belied the power vested in him.
With Portland failing rapidly, he was virtually prime
minister and actually resided at No. 10 Downing Street,
for many years the home of the prime minister.

"Whatever private opinion might be, I feel we must bow to their superior knowledge of the man and the circumstances."

Gently as this was spoken, it was clearly a set-down, but Hannah showed no sign that she knew she had been snubbed. "Yet I believe that Mr. Canning does not precisely disagree with Mr. Alistar, and since Lord Strangford remains in Brazil with the Portuguese court, surely Mr. Alistar must be considered the principal authority on the Portuguese."

"From the prospect of behind a desk, most certainly," said Moreville with a definite note of testiness. Cassandra came up to them and he took her hand at once. "Allow me to tell you again, Miss Tilton, how much I envy Bourne. You will be the most beautiful hostess in the War Office and will doubtless do much good for your husband. If I were Castlereagh I would forbid the match for fear of the competition."

Cassandra responded in kind, very glad to turn the subject. Since McInnes had been appointed the special assistant to Mr. Alistar last year, his wife's capacity for discussing Portuguese politics and the campaign in the Peninsula was limitless, and in direct proportion to Cassandra's boredom with the topic.

While Cassandra exchanged light banter with Moreville, Mr. Perceval excused himself to his hostess. When, a few minutes later, Lord Moreville did the same, Hannah, deprived of her quarry, left them as well.

"I am so glad you came when you did," Livia said to her sister-in-law. "Moreville is well-known for the sharpness of his tongue and I think he must have soon said something to penetrate even Hannah McInnes' thick skin."

"I rather doubt he could," Cassandra replied cynically. "One would have to be shockingly ill-bred to set her down. Perhaps that is why she and Sally get on so well together."

"I know Sally can be trying, but there isn't any harm in her," Livia said. "But I am all out of patience with Hannah McInnes' constantly encroaching ways.

She likes to compare her interest in her husband's career with Georgiana Devonshire's efforts for Mr. Fox, but she really has no idea how to go about winning influence. If McInnes ever stands for Parliament, he will win only if she promises to kiss those who do not vote for him."

Cassandra responded to this with a peal of laughter that rang and sparkled like crystal and caught the attention of one of two men who had just achieved the top of the stair. Lord Adrian Searle looked in the direction of the sound, and by a fortuitous parting of the company, caught sight of Cassandra. He placed a hand on his brother, Lord Dunston's, shoulder to halt him.

Dunston followed his brother's gaze and saw Cassandra. "Don't bother to cast your black eyes in that direction," he advised the younger man. "That's Cassandra Tilton. Her betrothal to Matthew Bourne is the reason we're here tonight."

A faint smile touched Searle's lips. "I've always thought Bourne a bit too toplofty. I daresay a setdown would do him a world of good."

"Not a bit of it," returned the marquess. "Bourne's a good man. Castlereagh quite relies on him at the War Office. You dislike his soberness because you are too rackety by half. Though," he added, lowering his voice a little, to avoid being overheard, "he's reason enough to be puffed up in his conceit at having won the Ice Maiden. It's odds on at White's that she'll send him packing before he gets in sight of the altar. It's her usual style." Some friends came up to the brothers to greet them, particularly Adrian, who had been little in society since his return from Brazil, and the conversation passed to general topics as they entered the ballroom.

But as soon as he could, Adrian brought the subject back to Cassandra, asking his brother to elaborate on his remarks. "You *are* interested there, aren't you?" Dunston asked suspiciously.

Adrian had led a quiet life by choice since his return, but now the prospect of the chase was not without appeal, particularly if there were some special challenge attached to the prize. "Let us say curious," Adrian replied. "Why is she called the Ice Maiden?"

Sighing in resignation because he knew that if he did not give his brother the information he sought, Adrian was quite capable of discovering it elsewhere, Dunston gave him a brief history of Cassandra's previous betrothals as he knew of them, and her reputation as a breaker of hearts. "I don't claim to know Miss Tilton's mind, but the general opinion is that this betrothal is a political rather than a love match," he finished. "The lady apparently hasn't a heart to give. Or to break," he added as he caught the speculative gleam that came into his brother's eyes. "You don't mean to make scandal for us, do you, Adrian? I wouldn't want Annabelle upset in her condition."

But his brother was not the man to give away his counsel too readily. "My dear Gerald," said Adrian mindly, "you must rid yourself of the notion that giving birth is unique to your wife. She will do far better without you forever fussing over her, which is why she was so adamant that you return with me to town." The marquess opened his mouth to protest at this, but was forestalled. "No need to fly into the boughs, dear boy. I only give you the hint for your own good." He then gave his brother a quick disarming smile and turned away in the direction he had last observed Cassandra.

Shortly before midnight, during a break in the music while a new set was being formed, Cassandra and Matthew escaped to a somewhat less-crowded corner of the room. It was natural for them to wish a little time together on this occasion, but Lady Fareland was not of a sensitive nature and had no compunction about bringing their *tête à tête* to a quick end.

"I knew exactly how it would be," Sarah said to Cassandra as she came to stand beside her. "The whole world has come to stare at you, Cass. It might have been best if you had not made a public show of your betrothal."

Matthew looked a little taken aback, but Cassandra was too used to her sister's outspokenness to be perturbed. "But then Livy would have been denied the triumph of this ball, which I think must be the success of the Season," she replied. "I don't believe I have ever before seen this many people in one room in my life. It is certainly a shocking squeeze. I wish I could leave just to find air to breathe that I don't have to share with half of London."

"The ball is in your honor and it is your duty to accept the good wishes of Livy's guests until the last of them are gone home," her elder sister admonished. "What would people think?"

"I am sure you concern yourself unnecessarily, Lady Fareland," Matthew intervened. "Cassandra is only roasting you. She would not be so unmindful of her obligations."

Cassandra searched the company while he spoke, and then said musingly, "Do you know, I believe I saw Lady Oxford just now. I thought she was gone out of town with her husband, but I am certain it was her going out onto one of the balconies with Fareland."

Lady Fareland paled visibly but her pallor was quickly replaced by an angry flush. Not even bothering to excuse herself, she left her sister, heading in the direction of the tall windows that ran along the entire east wall of the ballroom.

"That was unkind of you, Cass," her betrothed admonished.

Cassandra knew that it was, but she was unrepentant. Sarah, who had married for position, had made a sad mull of her own life, but this never prevented her from informing others how they should conduct theirs. Cassandra's reply to him was an indifferent shrug. "I haven't any idea if Lady Oxford is here, but Fareland has been making sheep's eyes all night at Mrs. Carteret, so he is hardly blameless."

"I was referring to the fact that your careless words

clearly upset your sister," he said a little sternly. "I know you are not as close as sisters should be, but you should be mindful of the fact that Lady Fareland is your elder sister and therefore deserving of your respect as well as your regard."

Cassandra stared at him for a moment in mute astonishment. She was not unaware that Matthew had an occasional inclination toward priggishness, but she was not only surprised but also displeased by his presuming to correct her. "I fear that neither my regard nor my respect is readily compelled," she said frostily. "Both must be earned."

There was sufficient pointedness in her last words to bring faint color to Bourne's countenance. "Surely there is a sense of responsibility toward one's nearest connections that is a hallmark of good breeding."

It was Cassandra's turn to color. "There is a great deal of insincerity and insipidity that is masked as good breeding," she said tartly, and turned and left him abruptly before her tongue got away with her.

The color was still high in her cheeks as she made her way through the ballroom. She schooled her expression to hide her displeasure, but she had only as many words as civility demanded for those who would have caught her attention as she crossed the room to go out into the hall. It was nearly time for supper to be served in the anterooms directly across from the ballroom, so there were even more people to be found in the hall than there had been when Cassandra had visited it earlier.

Hot, tired, angry, and perhaps more concerned than she wished to admit that a cloud had cast a shadow over her betrothal, she made her way down the stairs to the next floor, which was less populated. There were a number of people standing about talking, but there was no one with whom she was particularly acquainted, and some were virtually unknown to her. She walked over to a window embrasure at the end of the hall and was left to sit in solitude, which was exactly what she needed to regain her composure.

Cassandra was not blind to the fact that Matthew was a bit pedantic at times, but she would not allow this defect to outweigh his many virtues, except at moments like this, when doubts which she generally had no difficulty keeping at bay escaped to prick at her.

She would not allow these self-made demons to torment her, though. If she could not quite persuade her mind to more profitable channels, she could at least force it into indifferent ones. None of the people nearest her faced her directly or paid her the least heed, so she was able to observe them frankly without rudeness. Based on gestures and little snatches of conversation that drifted her way, she gave each person she focused on an identity of her own invention, which more often than not was entirely outrageous, and thus she teased herself back into spirits.

She was about to bring her respite to an end when she saw a man quite unknown to her come into the hall and proceed in her direction. He paused to exchange a word or two with several people, and finally joined a small group fairly near to her. This appeared to be his goal, and Cassandra felt a faint stab of disappointment, which she immediately dismissed as absurd.

The man was tall, athletically formed, and perhaps some thirty years of age. His hair was a rich, deep brown, thick, with a natural wave that was not precisely curl. Even at a distance, Cassandra could see that his eyes were that very dark brown commonly called black, and his complexion was of a fair quality that any woman would have envied. Though she had never set eyes on him before, she knew for a certainty who this paragon must be. But Sarah was wrong, Cassandra decided. It was *not* his coloring which gave Lord Adrian Searle his reputation for masculine beauty, it was his exquisite, perfectly composed features, and the way his wonderful eyes sparkled and snapped with the emotions that passed through them. Just so must Adonis have looked, or the great King David.

His beauty fascinated her; her eyes were drawn to him, not against her will, but without need of it. He was facing her, but did not appear to notice her until he suddenly raised his head a little and looked directly at her. Adrian Searle was not unaccustomed to stares; usually it only required his acknowledgment of such rude behavior for the starer to be properly set down. But Cassandra, when he caught her eye, returned his gaze levelly, neither turning away in confusion nor smiling her encouragement, which some bold young women of a certain character were at times inclined to do.

Adrian's route was circuitous, but seeking her out had been his goal from the moment he entered the hall. Fortunately, he was acquainted with several of the other people in the hall, but even if all had been strangers to him, he would have found some means of delaying his approach to Cassandra. The delicious little games of dalliance were his forte, and just as her reputation and unavailability had quickened his interest with the spice of challenge, so he meant to arouse in her, at the least, curiosity, at the best, an equal attraction. He knew she had noted him as soon as he had come into the hall, and now, as he held her eyes with his own, he knew as well that his stratagem had succeeded.

He acknowledged her with a faint amused smile and returned his attention to his friends. But only a few moments passed before he excused himself and walked toward Cassandra.

She watched him approach and noted that he moved with such grace that he almost seemed to glide as he walked. He came to stand quite close to her so that she was very conscious of his physical presence, which was precisely what he intended. "You were staring, you know," he said severely. "A missed lesson in deportment, perhaps?"

"Possibly," she replied, and though her voice was steady, her pulse was not. "I slept through many of them."

He laughed, a silvery sound, which, Cassandra thought cynically, she might have expected. But her cynicism aside, she felt a faint shiver of elation run through her, as if some special treat were in store for her. It was not a new sensation; she had felt it with Ned Tarkington, particularly in the early days of their courtship. But Ned was merely handsome in comparison with Adrian Searle, and Cassandra knew from that bitter experience just how shallow beauty can be. "I suppose I am staring because you are very beautiful," she said baldly and entirely without commendation.

She startled an expression of blank surprise from him. His interest was quite genuine now, and he no longer regarded her merely as a challenge to be met. "And you are direct," he responded after only a moment's check. "And also quite beautiful yourself. We should marry and have divinely exquisite children."

This parry, which was designed to raise a blush from her, went wide of the mark. Her smile was caustic. "They should probably throw back to an earlier generation and be quite hideous. Besides, I am already betrothed."

"Yes. To Matthew Bourne. I am not without hope."

Cassandra laughed at his daring. "At least that is refreshingly different from the sentiments expressed by our other guests. Is it arrogance or champagne?"

He shook his head and smiled. "Claret, if anything. But I thought you preferred plain speaking," he said with mild complaint. "It isn't fair to change the rules of the game without telling the players."

"Are we playing a game, sir?" she asked archly, not acknowledging that she knew his identity.

"The oldest one in the history of man," he said outrageously, untruthfully adding, "And you made the opening move by trying to stare me out of countenance."

Her jaw nearly dropped at the audacity of his words, for he was skirting outright impropriety, but instead of taking offense, she laughed again. "Well, perhaps I did," she concurred unaware that he had deliberately sought her out. "But I should think it is no unusual thing for a woman to stare at you."

"Unfair!" he cried at once. "If I say that you are right, you will accuse me of conceit, but if I disagree you will think I mean it as a reproach."

She shrugged. "You have already set me down for staring at you," she reminded him. "I did not regard it."

"By God, you are something out of the common way," he said, speaking his thought aloud. The light in his dark eyes was impish and infinitely amused. "You have a quality that far surpasses commonplace beauty."

"What is that?" Cassandra asked, a little more eager than she wished to be.

He shook his head. "The definition is elusive, I fear," he said quite truthfully. "It may be style, or perhaps it is humor."

"And you discerned this in the space of a few minutes' conversation?" she asked, her tone disbelieving.

"I discerned it across the hall."

"You have more than beauty to recommend *you*, as well, I see," she said dryly.

"You say the word 'beauty' like an epithet," he objected. "You count it a fault, I think."

"It is certainly not a recommendation."

Certainly no woman had ever said that to him before. He tilted his head as if to better regard a curious specimen. "No? What is, then?"

"Character," she replied without hesitation.

"Does the one preclude the other?"

"That has often been my experience."

"Then I paid you no compliment when I told you you were beautiful."

"Nor I you."

He grinned in appreciation and leaned a little forward so that his face was disturbingly close to hers. For one startled moment she thought he was going to kiss her. In fact, it was very much what he wished to do, but for now his only purpose was to beguile. "My dear Miss Tilton, you intrigue me greatly," he said, his voice a caress.

"It was not my intent," she assured him, a little sharply. Her heart had begun beating quite rapidly. She stood to give herself a moment to regain her composure; she would not for the world have allowed him to see that he had unsettled her. "Mama warned me against speaking to men who were unknown to me, but I did not perceive the danger here in my brother's house. I fear it *must* be the champagne in my case."

"And a sad want of breeding in mine?" he quizzed, retreating a little. "Shall we return to the ballroom so that I may discover a mutual acquaintance to present me to you? I am acquainted with your betrothed, but I don't think that would do."

Cassandra meant to snub him for his impertinence, but in spite of herself she smiled. "No, I don't think it would."

"I am Adrian Searle," he said, "and I promise I shall find someone to perform the office before the night is out. Do you know my brother, Dunston?"

"Not well enough," she said repressively. "You have been out of the world for some time. Your task may be harder than you think."

"Then I am not unknown to you?" he said, picking up on her words with a quickness that she found disturbing.

"I have heard your name mentioned, I believe," she replied with feigned indifference.

Adrian was too perceptive not to realize that she had been playing her own game with him. It did her no harm in his regard. He smiled slowly and said, almost as if to himself, "Why is it that the best women always cast their lot with the dullest dogs?"

Cassandra stiffened and moved a little away from him. "Do you refer to Sir Matthew, my lord?" she said coolly.

His smile grew in response. "But it is quite your fault, you know, for you set the tone for plain speaking. You cannot blame me if I find it contagious. It is a delight to say what one thinks in company where dissembling is generally the rule."

"You are a cynic, my lord."

"So are you. You see, we are well-matched."

Cassandra looked beyond his broad shoulders and saw that the others in the hall had gone upstairs to supper. "I must return to our guests," she said with sufficient coolness in her tone to have discouraged most men.

But Adrian was not at all disheartened. He nodded understandingly. "Bourne would not like it, I suppose, if he knew how you were occupied."

"You flatter yourself, my lord."

"Perhaps I do," he replied, and once again closed the distance between them so that they were nearly touching. He did not really intend to kiss her, not this time at least, but the attraction was irresistible.

Cassandra's heart was beating like a hammer in her breast but she regarded him with a calmness that it took all her skill to maintain. Heavy lids dropped over his eyes, and his lips touched hers so briefly that she was almost unsure it had happened and scarcely knew how to react.

There was the sound of footsteps on the stairs above them and he moved away from her. Cassandra's fingers ached to box his ears for his arrogant presumption, but she contented herself with casting him a fulminating glare before she left him. She reached the foot of the stair just as Matthew reached the landing.

"There you are," Matthew said, a faint note of annoyance in his tone. "Sarah was concerned and sent me to find you. Supper has been laid out this half-hour, and everyone has been asking for you. We have a duty to our guests."

Cassandra had quite forgotten their earlier argument that had led her to seek the refuge of the window embrasure, but at these words her anger at Adrian abated and was redirected toward Matthew. "Then I wonder that you neglect them to look after me," she

said with considerable sharpness. "It is quite unnecessary, you know." She started up the stairs to prevent
him from coming into the hall. Adrian remained in the
embrasure, and she would have preferred it if Matthew did not know of his presence.

But the hope was forlorn. Matthew descended the
few remaining stairs to meet her and chanced to glance
in precisely the direction of the window. Matthew saw
the other man and halted. "Who is there?" he asked,
and Adrian, seeing that there was nothing else to be
done, stepped out of the shadows.

"Good evening, Bourne," Adrian said, approaching
them without haste. "I fear it was I who kept Miss
Tilton from her duties for a few minutes to wish her
well of your marriage."

There was a short and not entirely comfortable silence. Cassandra felt the urge to rush into the breach
with explanations, but her good sense told her that it
would make matters worse rather than better. "I had
heard you were returned from your duties in Brazil,
Searle," Matthew said, his voice level, "but I thought
you in Somerset and didn't expect to see you tonight."

"Lady Tilton was kind enough to send me a card,"
Adrian replied with equal formality, "but I fear I have
repaid her hospitality by arriving late and keeping
Miss Tilton from her responsibilities. I had best find
Lady Tilton and suitably express my repentance. I
would not wish to be denied the privilege of calling at
this house," he added with a quick provocative flash
of his dark eyes toward Cassandra. He nodded to
Bourne, made Cassandra a bow that she felt was mocking, and went up the stairs before them.

Cassandra directed her steps to follow him, but Matthew's hand on her arm arrested her. He regarded her
for a long, unnerving moment. "I was not aware that
you were acquainted with Searle," he said. "What
were you discussing with him?"

"The folly of vanity," Cassandra said, her eyes steady
on his.

His brow knit as if in puzzlement, but he did not

pursue the matter. He gave her his arm and they went up the stairs toward the sounds of the gathering. "I am aware," he said, his voice low so as not to be overheard, "that more latitude is given to women who are promised in marriage, but it is hardly sensible for you to open yourself to unnecessary criticism. You may not be aware of it, but Searle has a certain reputation where women are concerned, and neither your credit nor mine would be enhanced if it were known that you spent time in private conversation with him."

"And is it my credit or your own that concerns you, Matthew?" she asked, looking up at him as they reached the top of the stair.

Matthew looked at her for a moment as if he were not sure how to answer, and then said, "My concern is for you, of course."

"You needn't have any," she assured him, her tone crisp. "It was a mere chance encounter and I have no wish to pursue the acquaintance." Even as she said the words, she knew they were untrue.

Adrian proved as good as his word and shortly after supper he was presented to her in proper form by Andrew Estcourt, the brother of one of Cassandra's particular friends. As they exchanged the usual words of greeting, their eyes spoke quite differently to each other. Cassandra could not refuse to know him without cause, and she could certainly not refer to his earlier audacity, but curiously, she was more amused than offended. Her one satisfaction was being able to inform him that she was not free to dance with him for the remainder of the evening.

He saw that it gratified her to reject him and could not really blame her for wishing to pay him out for his presumption. The bow he made to her was again more than a little mocking, and he said quite softly, for her ears only, "Point to you, I think."

Cassandra's expression was serious, but her eyes were not. "Oh, no, my lord. I quite concede it to you."

Ned Tarkington came up to her to claim her for the

set that was forming, and exchanged perfunctory greetings with Adrian. The two men, unquestionably the most handsome in the room, sized each other up instinctively. Like game cocks, Cassandra thought as Ned led her away.

Ned demanded to know how she was acquainted with Adrian, and without waiting for an answer, proceeded to inform her that she would be a great fool to encourage interest in that direction.

"Why do you suppose I would?" she asked, smiling, but inwardly annoyed.

Ned's responding smile was insufferably knowing. "It was quite clear from the way he looked at you that he will need little enough encouragement. I wouldn't say that Bourne is the jealous sort, but he won't much like it if you get yourself talked about because of Searle."

"You presume a great deal, Ned," she said, more gently than his impertinence deserved.

But he did not regard the affront. "I think of myself as a brother to you, Cass, and I only tell you this for your own good."

Cassandra bristled, but held her tongue, knowing that argument was futile. Ned could be counted on to think as he pleased, whatever she might say, and ever since the days of their betrothal, had taken it upon himself to be her unsolicited mentor. But Cassandra's good humor steadily deteriorated throughout the remainder of the evening, fueled not only by Matthew's correction and Ned's unwanted advice but also by the sight of Hannah McInnes in earnest conversation with Adrian on one of the little sofas set against the wall. Hannah's interest in Lord Adrian was certainly clear to be read in her expression, and when later Cassandra observed them joining a set that was being formed, she felt a twinge of disappointment that he could be so easily taken in by so obvious a woman as Hannah McInnes. It was no concern of hers how or with whom Adrian Searle chose to amuse himself, but she could not deny that she was piqued. It tarnished, somehow, her own encounter with him.

Hannah was too ambitious to be other than discreet—she was no Lady Oxford—but it was an open secret in their circles that her reputation could not bear close examination. Hannah's choice of lover was usually a man of power or position who would be likely in some manner to advance her husband politically or herself socially, but Adrian, as far as Cassandra was aware, could do neither. But he *was* beautiful. Even the most calculating female might be excused for casting out lures to him with no better cause than the strength of his physical attractiveness.

When the ball was finally over in the early hours of the morning, Cassandra felt quite differently than she usually did after an evening of pleasure. The dance exhilarated her, and conversation with friends she generally found quite stimulating, but tonight she felt curiously unsatisfied, with a sense of expectations somehow not met, yet it had been in every respect a most successful evening. She supposed it was a natural feeling of letdown after so much preparation for the ball, but that answer did not satisfy her any more than the evening had.

Yet, as she sat up in bed in her darkened room, there came into her mind a picture of Lord Adrian Searle, and though she tried to deny it, she knew that he was responsible for her odd humor. She wished she might dismiss him from her thoughts, but she was too honest with herself to deny that, despite his arrogance and audacity, she felt a strong attraction toward him. This in itself in no way concerned her; she had felt similarly toward a number of handsome, dashing young men since her first Season, but only once before had her peace been cut up, and that time her heart had suffered a similar fate. She had no intention of allowing it to happen again. But her dreams were as treacherous as her thoughts, troubling her with visions of a man with black eyes who swept her into his arms and kissed her until she was breathless.

# 3

*C*ASSANDRA went down for breakfast later than her usual hour the following morning, but the Tiltons had risen later as well and were still at table when Cassandra entered the breakfast room. She saw at once from their troubled countenances that something was amiss. There was a footman in the room replenishing a platter of cold ham when Cassandra came into the room, so she exchanged only the usual morning common-places with Harry and Livia until the servant had gone. "You are looking quite blue-deviled this morning, Harry," she commented as she put a plate containing some of the fresh-cut ham on the table and sat down. "Has one of our guests run off with the Tilton Rubies? You are glum enough for it to be that."

The only purpose of her flippancy was to tease a smile out of her brother, but it fell flat. The viscount pushed away his nearly untouched plate. "Michael Alistar was murdered last night," he said.

Cassandra stared at him, not really crediting his words. "You are joking, Harry. You must be! Alistar was here last night. I stood up with him, in fact."

"I wish I were joking," he said in a flat tone. He stood up, pushing his chair back with some force. "Damn! I count it my fault. I knew he was a bit foxed; I shouldn't have allowed him to insist on walking back to his rooms."

"You must not say so, Harry," Livia said in her quiet way. "He was his own master, and he quite refused to allow you to call our carriage for him."

"Yes," said Harry impatiently. "I have told myself that, and also that there were others that left before and after him, making a similar choice, and arriving home, I presume, without taking any harm. But Alistar is dead, and he was a friend of mine. It shouldn't have happened."

Livia and Cassandra exchanged glances. Harry was not the sort of man to do violence to his feelings. Cassandra got up and went over to her brother, who was standing by the window facing down into the street. She put a hand on his arm, and when she was not rejected, she was encouraged to say with gentle and sincere concern, "What happened to him, Harry?"

"He was set upon and robbed and murdered by footpads." The words were spoken with a dull finality.

It was, unfortunately, a common occurrence, for the streets of the city were virtually lawless after dark, despite the efforts of the watch to keep crime in some sort of check. It was a rare week that went by that some notice was not read in the papers of brazen robberies and occasional murders, and at times these misfortunes even occurred to acquaintances, but Michael Alistar had been a friend of the Tiltons', and his tragedy could not but affect them. Cassandra felt tears sting her eyes, but she blinked them away, not wishing to further upset her brother. "I am so sorry, Harry. It is worse, I know, that it should have happened when he had just left us, but Livy is right, it is not fair to blame yourself. It is a terrible thing, to be sure, but neither is it an uncommon thing, and it might have happened at any time."

"It was not so common as you might think," Harry said bitterly.

Cassandra was surprised by both his words and his tone. "What do you mean, Harry?"

But the viscount ignored her question. He shrugged off her arm and went back to the table, sitting heavily and drinking off the remains of his coffee. "Alistar wasn't castaway by any means, but he was up in the world enough to make easy prey. If he wouldn't have the carriage, I should have gotten one of the others who left when he did to walk with him to his door. Petersham left about that time, and so did Searle and Carteret; any one of them might have done so without going much out of his way."

"If he was not utterly castaway, he would only have resented your interference," Cassandra pointed out. "Confess, it never even occurred to you to ask anyone to accompany him home."

Harry gave her a slightly twisted smile. "No, it did not," he admitted. "But, damme, how I wish it had."

Livia got up and went over to her husband to place a kiss on his forehead. "You must stop teasing yourself, Harry. It is not like you and it certainly won't accomplish anything except to make you wretched."

Harry took her hand and kissed it, and Livia, speaking with the determined briskness of one tending a sickroom, declared her intention of seeing to her household duties.

Neither Harry nor Cassandra followed her. Both sat motionless, the one lost in his thoughts and the other speculating on hers. "Harry, what was uncommon about Alistar's death?" she asked in her forthright manner.

The viscount was clearly annoyed by her query. "Please, Cass, don't give your imagination rein. My remark meant nothing, and you would best please me if you put it out of your head." He, too, then made an excuse and left the room.

Harry was too good a diplomat and politician not to know that curiosity fed on evasion, and Cassandra, unconvinced by his words, supposed that it was his distraction over the death of his friend that had made him so careless. In the political circles in which she and her family moved, there was always hushed talk of espionage and the infiltration of spies, but Cassandra had never taken any of it very seriously. She had no notion if this was what Harry had hinted at, but it was a chilling thought to imagine that a French agent, and a murderous one at that, had infiltrated their own circles. She ruminated in this vein for several minutes before realizing that she was doing just what Harry had advised her against: giving her imagination rein. She took herself in hand and did put it out of her mind. In her distress for her brother and Mr. Alistar's family, Lord Adrian Searle was also put out of her mind, which was all to the good for her peace.

On the following day Matthew arrived in Berkeley Square to escort Cassandra and Livia to Hookham's Circulating Library, and it was he who referred to suspicions concerning the death of Mr. Alistar. It was a fine day near the end of April and, as the distance to the circulating library was not far, they elected to walk. They passed a narrow lane leading off Colechester Street, and Sir Matthew pointed toward it with his cane and said, "It was just there that they found poor Alistar." Livia shuddered and refused to turn her head in the direction Matthew indicated, but Cassandra regarded the passageway with frank curiosity. "One wouldn't expect footpads to journey so far west," Matthew continued, "but that is the account that is given, so I suppose it must be so."

"No doubt the robbers were hoping for a fat wallet," Livia said, and added with a faint pleading note, "Can we go on, please. Surely it is vulgar to be staring in this morbid way."

They continued on, but Cassandra said, "You don't believe it was footpads, Matthew? What do you think really happened?"

But Matthew, having reawakened her curiosity, was not going to satisfy it. He said with seeming unconcern, "Oh, I suppose it probably was footpads. I understand his body was stripped of everything of any value, but there has been talk that is difficult to ignore."

"I have heard nothing," Livia said firmly, with an admonishing look toward Sir Matthew.

"Such as?" demanded Cassandra.

Matthew gave Livia a reassuring and faintly condescending smile and patted Cassandra's hand, which he held in the crook of his arm. "It is only the affairs of politics, nothing to concern yourself about."

Cassandra withdrew her hand abruptly, stung by his patronizing tone. "My brother is a politician, as was my father," she said sharply. "Political affairs have always been of concern to me."

Matthew seemed genuinely surprised that he had offended her. "My dear, I meant no affront to you. I am only saying that it is the merest gossip and therefore should be disregarded, not repeated."

"Then you should not have spoken of it at all," Cassandra said reprovingly.

Matthew acknowledged the rebuke with a slight chilly bow of his head. "As you say. I pray you will forget the matter entirely."

Livia, an unhappy witness to this exchange, saw with relief the facade of the library and at once began to speak of the books she hoped to find there. Matthew and Cassandra tacitly lay down their cudgels and took her lead, discussing their own choices. Once inside the library they went their separate ways, dictated by their separate tastes.

Cassandra was browsing through the latest novels which the clerk recommended to her, when a man came up quite close to her, excused himself, and reached in front of her for a book. She was engrossed in a passage that had caught her notice and did not even look up, but only moved a little to allow him the room that he needed. But after another minute had passed, the same thing occurred and this time she did look up directly into the amused black eyes of Lord Adrian Searle. The effect of her awareness of him was immediate and almost physical, as if her heart had missed a beat. He was as handsome to behold in the harsh light of day as in the more flattering candlelight, and Cassandra, though she deplored it, could not quite dispel the effect his attractiveness seemed to have upon her. "We meet again, Miss Tilton," he said in his soft but resonant voice.

"And again by chance, my lord," she said with

marked coolness, and then pointedly turned a little away from him to return to the perusal of her book. The snub was certainly intentional, but when he left her without further comment, she felt a stab of disappointment and was put out of patience with herself.

She put the book back on its shelf and sought out Livia, who was happily searching through the latest volumes on housewivery. Matthew was standing near to her in a waiting posture. He smiled as Cassandra approached. "Did you find what you were seeking?"

"No, I could find nothing at all," she admitted. "It would seem I am not in a humor to be pleased today."

"I fear I was similarly disappointed." He motioned toward a nearby table on which a number of books were piled. "But Lady Tilton means to make up for both of us, I fear."

"Perhaps we should leave at once then, before we regret not bringing the carriage," Cassandra suggested with a laugh.

Livia protested and Matthew assured her that he had already made arrangements for a servant to pick up her selections after they had returned to Tilton House.

"If we are to remain until Livy has gone through every book on the shelf," Cassandra said, to quiz her sister-in-law, "perhaps I should use the time studying improving sermons to regain my temper."

Adrian came from behind one of the high-stacked shelves and paused for a moment to enjoy his observation of Cassandra and her betrothed without being noted. What he felt as he regarded them he recognized as a rather primitive desire to cut out his rival and secure for himself the female of his choice. Amused with himself, he nevertheless knew at that moment that it was precisely what he intended to do.

"Have you lost your temper, Miss Tilton?" he asked, coming up behind her and at last making his presence known.

Cassandra turned almost reluctantly and Matthew nodded a greeting to Lord Adrian and said, "Miss

Tilton was expressing her disappointment at not being able to find any book to please her."

Searle's expression showed surprise. "Indeed? The one you were holding when we spoke a moment ago, Miss Tilton, is thought to be quite excellent. I have it on the best authority that it is expected to be quite the rage this Season."

To her astonishment and dismay, she felt color steal into her cheeks, as though she had been meeting him secretly and was now caught out in it. She had no doubt his intent was to discompose her, and he had very nearly succeeded. Though her tone was no more than civil, there was just the hint of an edge to it to show her vexation. "I was not aware, my lord, that you had a knowledge of such things or I would have certainly sought your advice."

"I developed my taste for novels while in Portugal," he said conversationally, unperturbed by her displeasure, which he had deliberately provoked. "Though I suppose it is indiscreet of me to say so, the Portuguese court is the dullest in Christendom, and even the fantasies of others are something to while away the time on sultry afternoons."

"I thought politicians had intrigue to keep them occupied," she responded tartly.

Adrian glanced toward Matthew, then smiled at Cassandra. "I am sure you are right, but I am not a politician, you see. I am, or rather was, a diplomat."

"Really? I perceive little difference."

"It is small," he acknowledged, "but distinct. Politicians ruffle feathers and diplomats smooth them. Is it not so, Sir Matthew?"

"There is always a need for servants to sweep up the debris," Matthew replied levelly.

Adrian acknowledged the hit with an appreciative grin, pleased, rather than not, that his adversary could show steel of his own. "And what is a diplomat but a public servant?"

Livia, who as a politician's wife was as adept at diplomacy as any sitting ambassador, said, "Does your knowledge extend to cookery books, Lord Adrian? I cannot seem to make up my mind amongst these."

Adrian duly examined the books and chose one without hesitation. Looking up, he caught Cassandra's skeptical gaze upon him. "I do know that it is a good book on cookery," he said, almost apologetically. "I found that a steady diet of Portuguese cooking was not to my taste, and cookery books were a part of my reading that I might persuade my chef in Lisbon to attempt my favorite dishes."

"I am sure the wives of your colleagues were only too happy to be of assistance," Cassandra said with false sweetness.

His expression was quite grave, but his black eyes danced with amusement. "Yes, the women of the court did not hesitate to show me every kindness."

Once again Cassandra's fingers itched to leave their mark on his impudent face. She turned to her betrothed and bestowed on him her most dazzling smile, though it was not for his benefit that she did so. "Perhaps we should be leaving, Matthew. We are to attend Mrs. Lytten's *al fresco* luncheon this afternoon and I must change before we leave."

Adrian accepted his dismissal with good grace. He had proven to himself that Cassandra was not indifferent to him, and that was enough to please him for the moment. He turned his attention to Livia. "Do you attend as well, Lady Tilton?" When Livia assured him that she did, he added, "Then I hope I shall have the pleasure of meeting you there." He made a very pretty bow for the ladies, but there was a promise in his smile that was for Cassandra alone.

Cassandra scarcely knew whether she looked forward to the afternoon with dread or anticipation. Though she had chosen to be angry at Adrian's impertinence, the truth was that he amused her as much as he infuriated her, and she rather enjoyed locking swords with him. In spite of the warnings of her common sense, she wanted to meet the challenge she saw in his

eyes. If only he were not so confoundedly attractive
and had the power to set her pulse racing, she would
have had no qualms about encouraging his friendship.
But she was not just out of the schoolroom and knew
that it was dalliance at the least that he wished for,
and very probably more. She certainly had no intention of allowing herself to be seduced, but given the
strength of her attraction toward him, she knew she
would be very foolish to be off guard.

She also had no wish to create unnecessary difficulties between her and her betrothed. Although Matthew had said nothing to her about meeting Adrian at
Hookham's, she fancied that he was quieter than usual
on the way home. Matthew might not be given to
displays of jealousy or suspicion, but she knew that
Ned was right when he warned her not assume that
Matthew would make a complacent husband.

Though Adrian Searle had been away from England
and society for over six years and had only returned to
town from Somerset for less than a week, there was
not a fashionable or exclusive party to which he did
not possess an invitation. As Sarah had said, attractive, amusing, and personable young men were sought
by every hostess, and Adrian was a favorite with most
women. Not even Livia was immune to his charm, and
when she discovered that his brother had again returned to his estate in Somerset, and Adrian had come
alone to Mrs. Lytten's, she did not hesitate to invite
him to join their party when they sat down on pillows
spread out on the grass to partake of the cold luncheon picnic-style. Cassandra watched him enthrall
her sister-in-law with his tales of the bedraggled landing in Brazil of the Portuguese court, the mad queen,
the ineffectual regent, his Spanish wife, who was in
disgrace for intriguing against him, and life in general
in the Brazils. All of his anecdotes were amusing, but
never cruel.

He conversed with equal ease on matters entirely
domestic and social, and when Matthew, tiring of what
he privately classified as women's talk, engaged him in

a discussion of the current situation in the Peninsula and what Wellesley could expect in the way of help from the Portuguese people in his attempt to defeat Bonaparte's imperialist ambitions, it was quite clear that Adrian's opinions and information were the result equally of firsthand experience and intelligent, considered thought. By the end of the day Cassandra was forced, almost against her will, to revise her opinion of the younger brother of the Marquess of Dunston: he possessed substance as well as flash.

Yet her feelings toward him were unstable and swung constantly between a desire to know him better and an equal desire not to burden herself with an acquaintance that was likely to cause her as much vexation as it did pleasure. He did not remain with them for the entire afternoon, and when she next saw him he was with Hannah McInnes again, their dark heads together, laughing and obviously well-pleased with each other's company. His manner toward Cassandra had not been at all flirtatious while he had sat with her, but she supposed that if she had given him any sort of encouragement it would be she who was the object of his gallantry instead of Hannah. Cassandra felt somehow both pleased and disappointed that she was not.

She and Livia sat beneath a large tree, their conversation desultory, and Cassandra's eyes, though she would have sent them in another direction, kept returning to Adrian and Hannah, who were close enough to be easily observed, but far enough away so that her scrutiny of them was not obvious. She saw him lift Hannah a little so that she could pick a choice bloom from the flowering tree they stood beside, and it seemed to her that he held on to Hannah's waist longer than was dictated by necessity or propriety.

Livia had followed her gaze and now said, "It would seem that La McInnes is setting her sights on Lord Adrian. She was casting out lures to him before he left for Portugal, but I don't think he paid her much heed then. Perhaps this time she'll snare him for her court."

"I expect she will," Cassandra said with patent indifference. "Her heels are round enough."

"Cass, you really should not say so. I know she is the sort who likes to have men dangling after her, but I know nothing more to her discredit."

"Yes, you do. You just refuse to listen to gossip."

"Because it *is* gossip, and therefore entirely unfounded."

"Not entirely."

"Well, maybe not," Livia conceded, "but I don't hold with furthering idle talk. Do you know," she added thoughtfully, "I felt a little concerned before that perhaps Lord Adrian was taking an interest in you. It was a bit particular that he sought you out at Hookham's and then again almost as soon as we had arrived here."

Cassandra was idly weaving several strands of grass together. "I don't know how you can say so," she said without looking up. "You invited him to join us, and all his attention while he sat with us was given to you."

"But his eyes were often on you, particularly when you were not attending."

"And now they are on Hannah," Cassandra said with a faint shrug. "He is not discriminate in his choices, I fear, so I take his notice as no special compliment."

"Which is just as well, I suppose," Livia said. "I know your betrothal to Matthew is not a love match, but I doubt he would like it if you permitted Lord Adrian to single you out for his attentions."

"Of course I would not!" Cassandra replied a little more sharply than she intended. Hearing her own thoughts aloud was disconcerting. She rose and shook out her skirts.

Livia looked up at her sister-in-law and dimpled. "I wonder if any woman could completely resist Searle if he made a push to attach her. You know that I quite dote on Harry, but when Lord Adrian smiles in that certain way, even my heart begins to beat a little faster."

"I was cured of my fascination for a pretty face years ago," Cassandra reminded her, and left Livia to find Lady Fareland, who had come with a party of her own.

She was in no particular hurry, and as she crossed Mrs. Lytten's handsome gardens, laid out with deliberate informality to appear quite natural, she stopped several times to converse with friends. She had just left Maria Sefton and her charming daughter and was walking in the direction of the rose garden, which grew with apparent wildness, when Adrian fell into step beside her. She was a little startled and her inward response to him as she accepted his arm was not as indifferent as she would have led her sister-in-law to believe.

She had decided it would be best to keep him at a distance, but his address was such that within a few minutes she was smiling at his amusing chatter and before much longer partaking in a conversation with the ease of long acquaintance. His wit was dry, but she preferred that sort of humor, and a telling comment he made about a much-publicized debate on a recent bill before Upper House made her laugh outright.

"That is much better, Miss Tilton," he said approvingly. "Laughter suits you."

"Flirtation, it would appear, suits you," she said, casting him a glance through her thick lashes that might itself have been described as coquettish.

"Yes," he acknowledged without hesitation. "I find it a pleasant diversion."

"One you no doubt learned from the ladies of the Portuguese court on those sultry afternoons."

"Oh, no," he said, his expression solemn. "I suppose I refined my skills in Portugal, but I was reasonably well-versed in the art before I received my appointment to the court."

"No doubt it was a requirement of the post," Cassandra suggested dryly.

He laughed. "It is a diplomatic tool, of sorts. Whenever it was the feathers of a female that required smoothing, I was usually the one called upon for the task."

"Is vanity also a tool of diplomacy?" she asked archly.

He was genuinely surprised, but her words stung a little, for he knew that his wish to make her fall at least a little in love with him despite her betrothal to Bourne was arrogant in its assurance that he could readily do so. "I hope I am not vain," he said slowly. "I do try to be honest, though. I know that women find me attractive. I would be falsely modest to pretend I'd never noticed it."

"Or a complete idiot. Are you also honest enough to admit that you use your attractiveness to your purpose?"

She had scored another hit. There was only the barest hesitation before he spoke. "Yes. At times I do," he said simply.

She had expected only more banter in answer, and it was her turn to be surprised. She halted and faced him a little. "Well, that *is* honest. What is it you want from me, my lord?"

"To know you better."

She could not read the expression in his dark eyes, which caught the sunlight filtering amongst the trees and reflected it back to her. "Why?"

Neither complete honesty nor seriousness was a usual part of flirtation, but once again he answered her in that vein. "Because I think you are very beautiful and delightful, and from the moment I first saw you I wanted to kiss you."

"You did," she said, and was astonished at her own coolness.

His smile broadened appreciatively. The game was again afoot. "Ah. I thought we were pretending that hadn't happened," he said. "That wasn't the way that I wanted to kiss you."

Cassandra was momentarily speechless. She felt a sensation run through her that forced her to repress a shiver. "I am betrothed," she said at last, pleased with the firmness in her voice.

"So you told me that night, and I admit that it nearly put me off. But I abhor waste. You can do very much better than Bourne, you know."

"Such as you?" she asked sardonically.

He smiled again and shook his head. "I told you I was not vain. You won't catch me out that easily. I believe that's Lady Fareland sitting on the bench with Mrs. McInnes, is it not?"

Cassandra was a little startled by this abrupt change from dalliance to the matter-of-fact. "Yes, it is. I'll draw off Sarah, shall I, so that you can show off your expertise to a more appreciative audience." As soon as she said the words, she saw the speculative gleam come into his eyes and wished she had held her tongue. She turned from him and walked toward her sister, leaving him to follow her.

The next few days were exceptionally busy for Cassandra, as certain preparations for the wedding, which was to take place in August, had to be seen to, as well as the selection and ordering of her bride clothes. Several parties were also given by friends and associates of Matthew and Harry to honor her betrothal, and these, though they were often, by nature of the company, somewhat dull political affairs, were dutifully attended. She had little time for thought of Adrian Searle. As he also moved in the same circles, she saw him frequently, but they were seldom in one another's company for more than ten minutes together.

He did not so much as enter her mind as she dressed in a green silk gown with an ivory gauze overdress that brought out the color in her eyes, for a soiree being given by Lady Jersey for a hundred or so of her particular friends, but when Cassandra entered Lady Jersey's well-packed rooms, she realized, as she looked about the company for friends, that she was searching for his tall, athletic form.

Harry and Livia were attending a different party

and Matthew had an earlier engagement that would
cause him to arrive late, so Cassandra went to the
party in Sarah's company, along with Freddy and Hannah McInnes. Both Sarah and Hannah were a dozen
years Cassandra's senior, but still rightly retained their
titles as accredited beauties, and as the three entered
the principal saloon, they caused a considerable stir.
The Tilton sisters with their bronze locks catching and
reflecting the light from the faceted chandeliers and
Hannah with her raven-black hair and warm brown
eyes were perfect foils for one another, and an admirer hailed them as the three Graces.

Freddy commented wryly that he had no desire to
find himself cast as Pan and went off to seek the
conviviality of the card room. It was early in the
evening and he had not yet fallen into his usual state
of intoxication, but Cassandra was not sorry to see
him leave their party. On the carriage drive from
Tilton House he had sat beside her and had several
times found excuses to touch her in ways that were
both familiar and unnecessary.

For once Adrian did not appear to be present, and
Matthew had not yet arrived, so Cassandra contented
herself by indulging in light flirtations with one or two
of her other admirers, who, in Matthew's absence,
were quick to attach themselves to her. Her hostess
came and sat with her for a bit to quiz her about her
plans for the wedding, and Sarah, seeing them from
across the room, hastened to join them.

"When I saw Silence fasten herself upon you," she
confided to Cassandra when Lady Jersey had left them,
"I left poor Sir Arnold in mid-sentence to rescue you."

Cassandra raised her brows. "Did you? Why?"

"You know what she is. She is forever trying to
ferret out one's secrets."

Cassandra laughed. "I don't think I have any. The
whole world knows the worst there is to know of me."

"With your unfortunate past, there will always be
the suspicion that there is more." Only a brief flash
passing through Cassandra's eyes showed she was an-

noyed, and Sarah did not notice it. "It would take only an unguarded word or action to have every tongue in town wagging about you again."

"You refine too much upon it," Cassandra assured her, her tone a bit clipped. "With all the speculation about poor Mr. Alistar, no one has given me or Matthew a second thought."

It was a successful diversion. "Livia told me that Harry has been in a pelter about it," she said, her tone taking on a shade of eagerness. "I have heard it said that the authorities are not entirely satisfied that it was footpads who set upon him. Has Harry given you any hint of what he suspects?"

Cassandra let her eyes roam about the room. "People are saying a great many stupid things," she said repressively. "Very probably it was nothing more than what it seemed. He was certainly robbed, and most likely killed entirely by accident."

"Yes, but Emily Cowper told me that she had it from no less a person than Lord Bathurst that because of Mr. Alistar's sensitive work for the government, they cannot rule out the possibility of a French Element." Cassandra had heard similar things any number of times in the fortnight since her betrothal ball and had determined not to pay the least heed to such unfounded rumors, but her obvious unwillingness to participate in idle speculation did not prevent Sarah from allowing *her* tongue and imagination to run free. She never really required more than an audience, and it was not until she realized that Cassandra was not even pretending to listen that she finally broke off her monologue and looked to see what was the object of her sister's interest.

It took no more than a moment to discern. Matthew and Adrian, both of whom appeared to have only just entered the room, were standing near to the door engaged in conversation. Cassandra regarded them with a rapt interest of which she herself was quite unaware.

"I do hope you aren't going to be foolish, Cass,"

Sarah said with such a sharp, clear note of warning
that Cassandra reluctantly gave her her attention.

Cassandra had to repress an exasperated sigh. It
seemed the whole world was intent on warning her
away from Adrian Searle. "I hope so too," she said
with a faint smile, "but there are many ways to be
imprudent. Did you have a particular one in mind?"

Sarah had returned her gaze to the two men by the
door. "He is the most beautiful creature I think I have
ever beheld," she said, a bit wistful. "I would have
thought that you would have learned your lesson with
Ned. If you are a moth to that particular flame, you
will singe your wings for certain."

"Do you think so, Sally?" Cassandra said, her tone
dulcet. "Then I shall have to practice my flying skills
to see that I don't get burned."

She got up and went over to Matthew and Adrian.
She returned Adrian's greeting in a perfunctory way
and immediately gave her attention to her betrothed.
"I did not hope to see you so soon, Matthew," she
said, looking at him as if he were the sole source of
her delight.

But the effort was wasted, as Matthew answered her
with a literal explanation of his early arrival. Cassandra
did not want to look at Adrian, whose eyes she knew
were upon her, but she could not resist the draw and
was paid out for her weakness by the quizzing smile
lurking in his dark eyes, for he was not at all deceived
in her purpose.

"At least you have gotten away early," she said,
interrupting Matthew's account, as she cast Adrian a
darkling glance. "With your business concluded, you
may indulge yourself in pleasure for the remainder of
the night."

Matthew smiled temperately. "You may regard my
visit to Downing Street as merely business," he said,
"but I count myself as having been profitably engaged."

"How very dull," she said with a bright smile. "It is
possible to be too respectable, Matthew. You must
take my word on it." With this she turned her smile on

Adrian and, hooking her arm into his, led him into the room.

Adrian was mildly surprised at her action, but scarcely displeased. The look that he gave her was wickedly amused. "Was that wise?"

"You have been telling me so."

"Yes, but I didn't think you paid me any heed. I think he is a bit of a toad, but I suppose I should not say so to you."

"No, you should not," Cassandra replied, but without any noticeable rancor.

"I don't know why it is that everyone who gives a party these days declares it a success only if there are so many people in one room that it is suffocating on even the pleasantest evenings," he said. It was a calculated opening, but also the truth. "There won't be a shirt point left standing before the night is half over."

"There is a terrace looking out on the garden at the other end of the room," she responded daringly, and more favorably than he had dared to hope.

It was not a particularly warm night, and the doors were open less to entice guests onto the terrace than to provide a little ventilation in the crowded room. As they stepped out onto the terrace, he drew her a little to one side so that they could not be easily seen from inside the room.

"I would not have counted on Bourne to prove my benefactor," he remarked as he sat against the balustrade. "Am I to be used to arouse his jealousy? I do not precisely object, you understand, but I wish such things to be clear so that I may know what is expected of me."

Cassandra gave him a catlike smile and said, "No. He was being tiresome, and needed a set-down. You served my purpose well enough."

"And that serves me for my conceit," he said, laughing, and then was suddenly serious. "Why don't you like me, Cassandra?" he asked, using her given name for the first time.

She did not object to the familiarity. "I don't dislike

you," she said with perfect honesty. "But I have no intention of becoming your latest conquest."

His tone held a touch of cynicism. "What would you know of my conquests? Gossip perhaps, but old gossip, and surely you would not hold against me the sins of my salad days."

"You are a self-confessed rake, you know."

"I am?"

"You admitted to me that you use your attractiveness to ensnare the unwary of my sex."

"Not at all!" he said as if offended. Then he bestowed on her a roguish smile. "Only the wary ones."

"Such as Hannah McInnes?" she asked with a bit of waspishness.

"I have known Hannah since my first Season," he said, commendably hiding the satisfaction her words gave him. If she disliked his attentions to Hannah McInnes, then her interest in him must be greater than she acknowledged. He added musingly, "You don't approve, do you? Or is it just me you disapprove of?"

Cassandra ignored the last of this. "Is she one of the sins of your salad days?"

He gave a short, sardonic laugh. "No. She was sleeping with my brother at the time. She was also trading shamelessly on the fact that she was an occasional mistress to one of the royals, though I forget which one it was now. There are some things I don't care to share," he added dryly.

She raised her brows in disdainful surprise. "I wonder you were so particular. It doesn't seem to concern you that I am promised in marriage to another."

"But we are not yet lovers."

Not even Cassandra's celebrated coolness was equal to his deliberate provocativeness. He had gone beyond the line of what was proper, but she knew that insult was not his purpose. He was challenging her. "Nor shall we be," she replied icily, but with just a hint of unsteadiness to betray that he had disconcerted her.

But it did not escape his keen perception. He stood straight and gently embraced her. She might have broken away from him if she wished, but she stood in the circle of his arms, meeting the challenge, fearful of the consequences, but determined to see it through. He bent his head and kissed her, lightly at first, and when she did not object, the kiss deepened and lasted until they were both rendered breathless.

He was more moved than he had expected to be. He lifted his face from hers and drew her tight against him. "The moment I set eyes on you, I wanted you." His breath was warm against her cheek and the closeness of him was intoxicating. He kissed her, gently again, and reluctantly released her.

Her eyes met his and after a moment she said very quietly, "We had better go inside."

"Cass . . ."

"I am not an unseasoned girl, nor a lightskirt," she said with a calmness that was only surface deep. "I won't allow myself to be seduced and I won't accept your *carte blanche*." She turned and left him as abruptly as she had left Matthew only a little earlier, but with very different cause.

# 4

———————————————•———————————————

CASSANDRA returned to the saloon without making any effort to be discreet, but her return was unremarked. While in the room she spoke with a number of people, but had she been pressed to give an accounting of her conversations, she would have found it impossible. She was the epitome of cool, poised elegance, fully living up to her sobriquet, but inside her was a seething turmoil caused by her recognition of her own desires. With every fiber of her being she had wanted the fulfillment his kisses promised.

Little shivers of an emotion she chose not to define ran through her when she thought of it, and so she pushed it from her mind. Gradually, with the performance of the commonplace, her equanimity returned in some measure. But she had had enough of Lady Jersey's soiree and unobtrusively searched the room for her sister to see if she could persuade her to leave, though the hour was still early.

She did not find Sarah, but she found Freddy McInnes coming out of the card room and asked him if he had seen Lady Fareland. Freddy's earlier sobriety had deteriorated somewhat but his manner was still quite coherent and he informed Cassandra that he had seen Sarah head toward the supper room in the company of Lord Moreville. It wanted more than an hour to supper and Cassandra did not think much of this, but nevertheless went down to the ground floor, where two rooms had been opened to make one and tables were set out laden with food for Lady Jersey's guests.

The room was completely empty. The servants, no

doubt having completed their tasks to make supper ready, had returned belowstairs to await the time for supper to be served. Cassandra walked into the room to be certain it was empty. A door leading into a further room was slightly ajar, and impulsively she walked over to it and opened it, though no light shone out and she did not really expect to find her sister there. But she did.

Sarah was half-sitting, half-lying on the sofa and she was not alone. The position in which she was discovered with Lord Moreville might most politely be described as compromising. The illicit couple, startled by the sudden light pouring into the room, sprang apart as if a shot had been fired between them.

Cassandra scarcely knew whether to be amused or dismayed. Without a word she shut the door and went back into the supper room. As she was about to quit it, her brother-in-law strode into the room with purpose. He checked when he saw her. "Cass," he said curtly, "is Sally with you?"

"No," Cass responded quickly, once again calling on reserves she scarcely knew she had. "I believe I last saw her going into the card room with Hannah."

Charles Fareland seemed a little surprised by this. "Did you? I just saw McInnes and he said he saw her come in here with Moreville."

Cassandra inwardly cursed the helpful Mr. McInnes. "You know what McInnes is," she replied disdainfully. "No doubt he thought . . ." She broke off abruptly as she heard the door behind them open and turned to see Sarah step unheedingly into the room.

Husband and wife faced each other and Sarah's face drained of all color. "Moreville's in there, I suppose," Fareland said, his voice tight and clipped.

Sarah seemed incapable of speech. She made a small sound that might have been taken for protest or denial, but her husband ignored her and pushed past her into the room. It proved to be quite empty.

Both women stood as if rooted to the floor. When Fareland returned to the supper room, not precisely mollified, but looking considerably less prone to violence, Sarah visibly sagged with relief. Her husband came up to her and took her arm none too gently. "Sarah and I will be leaving now," he said to Cassandra. "I would be obliged to you if you would make our excuses to Lady Jersey."

Though Cassandra wished to leave as well, nothing would have persuaded her to make a third on their drive home. She murmured some sort of agreement, and Sarah, avoiding both her eyes and her husband's, docilely permitted him to lead her from the room. Cassandra sat on one of the small chairs that lined the perimeter of the room, but she was given no opportunity to digest the events she had witnessed. Freddy McInnes strode into the room and sat down beside her.

"I never would have involved you if I'd guessed Fareland would happen along just after," he said without preamble.

"You sent us both here deliberately," she accused, and he did not deny it.

He smiled with cynical amusement. "Let us say I owe Moreville, and now I am in some measure paid out."

"And Sarah, did you owe her as well?" Cassandra demanded coldly. He shrugged with elaborate unconcern, and Cassandra did not bother to hide her disgust. "Tilton told me you were not a fool, but I think he was mistaken. Moreville is the most powerful man in the Foreign Office after Canning. He'll never recommend you for Alistar's position now."

Again the shrug, this time accompanied by a short, bitter laugh. "He never would have anyway, and I've never said I wanted it. It's all Hannah's idea, you know. She thinks I'll be foreign secretary one day, but I'm just a civil servant. I haven't even a seat in the House, and try as she may, she hasn't been able to beg, cajole, or sleep her way to one for me, though God knows she's left no stone—or sheet—unturned."

Despite his vulgarity, for the first time her distaste

for the man beside her lessened. She knew firsthand the bitter pain that went with that sort of betrayal. But her sympathy was short-lived. Seeing the softened expression in her eyes, he seized the opportunity to gather her awkwardly into his arms. Cassandra was so startled that he nearly succeeded in his attempt to kiss her, but in short order he found himself embracing air and his face was smarting with the stinging imprint of her hand.

"For the sake of your wife, who is the sister of the man I am going to marry, we will let this incident pass," she said, her voice hard and cold. "But if you ever attempt to touch me again in any way, I shall not hesitate to inform Matthew, who will not overlook the insult even to spare Hannah."

She left him at once to return to the main saloon, determined now to leave as quickly as she could. Her sister was gone, she had no wish to return home in the company of either of the McInneses, and it would have looked odd to the point of causing comment if she had left alone while Matthew remained, so she had little choice but to seek him out, though she was still out of charity with him for his prosiness.

When she did find him it was in the principal card room, where he was engaged in a game of whist. She succeeded in getting him away from the card table, but he showed no inclination at all to fall in with her plans.

He listened while she told him that she wished to leave and that her sister had already gone, but when he asked her if she was unwell, she unwisely told him that she was in perfect health, and only feeling out of sorts. His recommendation to this was that she wait until after supper. "Very likely you're only peckish."

Cassandra had the childish urge to stamp her foot. "I am not peckish. This is a tedious party, I am tired, and I wish to go home."

She saw from his expression that he thought her behavior infantile, and it only made her angrier that she could not disagree with him. "My dear Cass, then ask Hannah if she will go with you. I am in the middle of a game and it would be churlish of me to leave unless there is some emergency. If you wish to wait until supper, I shall be happy to escort you back to Tilton House."

Cassandra would sooner have risked the gossip of leaving unattended than ask Matthew's sister to attend her. She knew that part of the reason she was behaving so unreasonably was that she felt she could not tell Matthew the true reasons she wished to leave. She could scarcely confide in her betrothed that she had had two men attempt to make love to her and had witnessed her sister being caught out in adultery.

When she left the card room she was undetermined whether she would flaunt propriety or suffer the humiliation of acquiescing to Matthew's will. She saw Adrian approach her as she once again entered the saloon, and groaned inwardly. The entire evening was taking on all the trappings of a waking nightmare, but she made no attempt to avoid him and even allowed him to lead her to an unoccupied sofa.

"I went too far, didn't I?" he said ruefully.

"Yes, you did."

He didn't speak for a moment, his eyes searching her face. "You're very angry with me, aren't you?"

Cassandra had a sudden, completely uncharacteristic desire to throw herself on his chest and weep until the sobs would no longer come. Instead, she shook her head, and launched into a *sotto voce* account of the events that had occurred since she had left him on the terrace. This was equally out of character, for she lacked neither discretion nor self-containment, but she knew instinctively that she could trust him, and acted upon the impulse. Even as she spoke, she could scarcely believe that she was choosing him as a confidant, but with every word she spoke, the burden was lessened.

Irresistibly flattered by her unexpected trust in him, he listened with a raptness and responded with an understanding that resulted in her changing her mind about her belief that they could never become friends.

Only with Livia did she feel as completely at ease speaking exactly what was in her mind, and even with Livia she would have been more guarded. Certainly the account of her difficult evening that she gave to her sister-in-law on the following morning was considerably more expurgated than the one she had confided to Adrian.

For them to become lovers was unthinkable. But she wanted to believe that she could control both him and her own response to him, and set about convincing herself that now that she recognized and admitted her desire for him, she need only be on guard to keep it in check.

Adrian seemed to accept the limits she placed on their relationship, and for the most part his manner toward her was that of a friend. Only occasionally when they were together was there that in his eyes or in his tone that suggested the lover, and at those times her pulse would beat a little faster. But she refused to acknowledge her feelings, still believing it required only discipline to keep them at bay.

The only thing that disquieted her was the frequency with which Adrian and the memories of the time they spent together invaded her thoughts. Even when she was with Matthew she would occasionally fall into reverie, causing her betrothed to speak to her sharply to regain her attention.

Matthew made no comment at all about her friendship with Adrian, though she had expected him to object in some way. She was relieved at first, and then annoyed, for she was not sure if it was her discretion or his complacence that was the cause. Even the warnings of her family and friends were not repeated, though in the case of Sarah, she was too wrapped in her own concerns for once to interfere in her sister's life.

It was several days before Cassandra saw Sarah again, and a number of attempts to call on her at Fareland House were met with the information that Lady Fareland was from home. When Sarah at last came to Cassandra on a morning when Livia was shopping with friends, she arrived heavily veiled and Cassandra soon learned the cause of her sister's isolation.

There was only one bruise, running aslant across the countess's cheek, but not even the expert application of powder and rouge could perfectly conceal the mark.

Cassandra was horrified. "You must leave Fareland at once. You needn't fear him, for as soon as Harry sees what he has done he will see to it that Fareland never comes near you again."

But Sarah shook her head, dissolved into tears, and refused to embark on so drastic a course. "He said it was less than I deserved, and I am not sure he isn't right. Oh, Cass, it was horrible. At first he only ranted and raved at me and called me unspeakable names." A faint martial gleam recalled her usual spirit for a moment. "He has seduced every maid I've brought into the house, and even my friends have not been safe from his attentions. But he said it was not the same for him as for me."

"Adultery is adultery," Cassandra declared flatly.

Sarah had cast herself across her sister's bed to indulge her tattered emotions, but she sat up and said, "Do not say that awful word." She put her face in her hands and began to weep again. Cassandra sat beside her and took her in her arms. "I have been such a fool, Cass," Sarah continued between sobs. "I have loved him so, but he has been so odious I am quite cast into despair."

Cassandra was not certain which "him" was meant, but as her sister poured out her unhappy, sordid story, it quickly became clear. Robert Moreville was notorious for his conquests, and his name had been linked with a number of women whose reputations were less than pristine, including Hannah McInnes. Apparently Sarah had not regarded his history and had believed his soft words. She had fallen head over heels in love with Moreville and seemed as impervious to insult from him as she was to abuse from her husband.

"I managed to send Robert a letter telling him all

that had happened and how dreadful Fareland was behaving." Sarah paused and could not meet her sister's eyes. "I was so distraught that I even suggested that we elope. His response was horridly unfeeling," she added bitterly, trying not to cry again. "He suggested that I mend my fences with my husband and in future not play him false."

Cassandra commiserated with her sister but was horrified that Sarah seemed to accept the brutality of her husband. "But he only struck me when he discovered that I had written to Robert," she said in his defense. "He saw the letter that Robert sent to me and the references to an elopement and went quite wild with rage." Her tears appeared to be spent at last, and she dabbed at the last of these with the handkerchief that Cassandra had given to her. "Besides, do you suppose I would prefer the disgrace of divorce? I knew when I married Fareland that I wasn't the least bit in love with him, or he with me, but it was a superb match for us both and we did agree to take the worse with the better."

Cassandra could not excuse her brother-in-law or mitigate her opinion of him based on his wife's infidelity, but there was little point in saying so. It was obvious that Sarah had already made up her mind to accept her situation, so Cassandra kept unwanted advice to herself and offered Sarah what comfort she could.

After a time Sarah had recovered her spirits in some measure and stood to leave, declaring that Fareland was due to be home soon and she did not want him wondering where she might be. Cassandra's brow creased. "Can you live with such constraint, Sally?"

Sarah sighed and smiled a little. "I shall have to. It won't last very long, you know. In a few days or a few weeks, Fareland will be taken with some opera dancer or other lightskirt and quite forget me again. Hannah said she had the same sort of difficulty with Freddy in the beginning, but now he does not regard her pursuits any more than she does his."

It was obvious that Sarah had no idea of the part that Freddy had played in her disgrace, and Cassandra decided that telling her would serve no purpose. "I hope you don't mean to take Hannah for your example, Sarah. She is notorious."

"She is no such thing," Sarah said, bristling. "There may have been times when she loved not wisely but too well, but you would not understand. I do. Until I met Robert Moreville, and fell in love with him, there was nothing in my life but loneliness and humiliation. It is commonly known as repenting at leisure," she added dryly. "I hope you fare better with Bourne."

Sarah's confidences raised a number of emotions in Cassandra's breast, not the least of which was concern at the implied warning of the fate of a loveless marriage. She was able to dismiss her fears on the grounds that Matthew was very different in character from both Fareland and McInnes, but, nevertheless, a further doubt was cast on Cassandra's certainty about marrying Matthew.

Matters passed agreeably for Cassandra for a fortnight after Lady Jersey's party. She was frequently in Adrian's company, but she managed to maintain a careful balance between flirtation and friendship without permitting another opportunity to occur where the bounds of propriety were overstepped. It was not until an evening near the end of May, when she and Matthew attended the theater in company with Lord and Lady Fareland, that her agreeable fantasy of being able to enjoy Adrian's company as a friend and without again succumbing to her attraction to him was shattered.

The play depicted on the stage was an indifferent tragedy and Cassandra was bored to the point that drowsiness threatened to overwhelm her. To fight her torpor, she glanced about the neighboring boxes, and in that way discovered that Adrian had joined the party in the box nearly across from theirs. As if feeling her eyes on him, he looked up, saw her, and smiled.

Cassandra turned back toward the stage and saw from the corner of her eye that Sarah was regarding her with a grim expression. But Cassandra, with the knowledge of her sister's *affaire* with Moreville, considered any objection Sarah might have to her friendship with Adrian pure hypocrisy and not worthy of her notice.

At the intermission Cassandra readily agreed to Matthew's suggestion of strolling in the corridor, but Sarah refused a similar offer from her husband and instead sent him to fetch her a glass of lemonade. Her purpose in this was twofold: it would free her from the unwanted company of her husband, which had been pointedly unremitting since her fall from grace; also, she had seen Adrian rise as soon as the curtain had come down and she suspected that he would come to their box. She was not mistaken. He had not seen Cassandra and Matthew in the passageway, and both breeding and propriety forbade his asking for her, so he sat in the chair nearest Sarah and engaged her in agreeable conversation for several minutes, allowing no hint of his disappointment to surface.

Sarah did not object to this, for she liked him well enough and was not averse to the attentions of such an attractive man, even if she knew herself only a substitute. Her intent, though, was to speak to him about Cassandra, and she brought their conversation to the point as soon as the opportunity arose.

"The others will be returning in a moment, my lord," she said instead of responding to a comment he had made about the play. "I have been wishing to speak with you concerning Cassandra. She usually does not want for sense, yet she seems to have the notion that your regard for her is quite without design."

Adrian's smile was slow; this was not entirely unexpected, nor was it unwarranted. "I hold her in a great deal of regard, Lady Fareland."

"But not disinterested regard," she persisted.

"No."

Sarah opened her fan and applied it gently, more

for effect than utility. She regarded him through slitted
eyes. "What is your intent then? Seduction? It will fall
flat, I promise you. Our family is hopelessly respectable and our upbringing was proper to the point of
being prim. Cassandra is too well-versed in the ways
of the world to fall an easy victim."

Not by so much as the flicker of an eyelid did he
betray that he knew of her own lapse from respectabil-
ity. "I quite agree."

Sarah closed her fan. "And yet you pursue her."

Once again he allowed his smile to spread slowly.
"Yes. I do," he said, surprising her with the admission.

Sarah leaned a little toward him, her brow creased
with puzzlement. "But if it is not seduction . . ." She
broke off as Matthew and Cassandra came into the
box.

Cassandra's delight when she saw Adrian was clear
to be read in her face. Sarah looked to Matthew, but
his expression was only a mask of civility. She said
rather pointedly, "Lord Adrian was just about to leave.
The play will be starting again in a few minutes."

As Adrian had been sitting at his ease and had only
risen when Cassandra had come in, it was an obvious
lie, and Cassandra took exception to it. "I would not
wish you to miss a moment of the play, Sally," she
said sweetly. "Lord Adrian and I shall go into the
corridor so that our conversation may not disturb you."
She smiled radiantly at Adrian, who returned an appreciative smile of his own.

Sarah nearly caught her breath in astonishment at
her sister's brazen behavior with her betrothed there
to witness it. "But you will miss the play."

"I find it a dead bore," Cassandra said. "I must
speak with Lord Adrian about Lady Buckinghamshire's
masquerade on Tuesday." Sarah could say nothing to
Cassandra with her husband and Matthew present, but
she glared her displeasure at her sister and received in
return only a bland smile.

"You know, keeping me at arm's length isn't going

to help if you cast discretion to the wind just to vex your sister," he observed as soon as they left the box.

"Sally can be impossibly tiresome."

"And Bourne?"

"What has he to do with it?"

He moved a little closer to her and flicked a forefinger under her chin. "Do you know that one of your most endearing attractions is that despite a fair patina of town polish, you can still be disarmingly naive. If I were your betrothed, I should have something to say about such a sad want of discretion."

"Matthew is not the sort of man to have jealous fancies," she asserted. "He trusts me as I trust him."

"How do you trust him?"

"Implicitly," she said with conviction.

He felt a flicker of annoyance at her unquestioning regard for Bourne's upright character, particularly as she did not hesitate to animadvert upon his own. "Quite delightfully guileless," he said, running the back of his hand along the contour of her face.

She removed his hand gently but firmly. "Are you suggesting that I am overtrustful of Matthew?"

"A little."

"I suppose you will tell me now that he has a mistress."

"It would be quite improper for me to do so," he said primly. "I hope I would not so forget myself."

Cassandra could not keep herself from smiling, though it was a trifle grim. "Which I suppose is your way of saying that he does have a mistress." He quite deliberately did not reply, and allowed Cassandra to understand that that was exactly his intent.

She was a little surprised not only to discover that Matthew, whom she had never suspected of any manner of duplicity, was unfaithful, but also to realize that she was not unduly upset by the knowledge. "I suppose most unmarried men find comfort amongst the demimonde."

"And many married men as well." There was the

suggestion of teasing laughter in his voice. "It is attributable to the weakness of the flesh, I believe."

"I would consider myself a poor wife if my husband needed comfort of any sort away from his home," she averred.

His smile was cynical. "Your attributes as a wife would probably have little to do with it."

"You *would* think so," she said accusingly. "I pity the woman you take to wife."

An unreadable expression came into his eyes. "She would have no need of your pity if . . ."

"If?"

"If I were in love with her." He seemed almost reluctant to say the words, and they were spoken with a curious intensity. The play had begun again and they were quite alone in the passageway. He bent his head and kissed her lightly, much as he had on the night they had met. With no further warning he took her into his arms and his tongue separated her teeth without resistance.

All of Cassandra's care to avoid any encounter that might result in a renewal of his lovemaking was in vain. She would never have thought to be on her guard at the theater, where they were surrounded by hundreds of people. All of her belief that her physical response to him could be disciplined was dissolved. Her heart beat wildly in her breast, her skin burned where he touched her, and she molded her body shamelessly to his. But she gave in to her desire for only a few seconds before she pulled away from him.

Before either could speak, Matthew stepped into the corridor. They were not touching in any way, but Matthew was an astute man and it was clear from his expression that he had a fair idea what had occurred. To her dismay and fury, Cassandra, who was not given to blushing, felt hot color steal into her cheeks.

There was nothing that any one of them could have said without bringing matters to a head and creating a scene and inevitable scandal. Matthew walked unhurriedly to Cassandra's side and placed her arm on his in a possessive gesture. She felt as if her skin were hot, and almost flinched away from Matthew to keep him from touching her and knowing the response that Adrian had awakened in her. She maintained her calm control, however, and even managed to meet Matthew's eyes without another telltale blush.

There was no course left to Adrian but to favor the couple with a brief bow and leave them. Instead of leading Cassandra back into their box, Matthew drew her down the passageway to an alcove that graced the far end of it near the stairs. The nearest box was several yards away and it was unlikely that they would be overheard.

"I have been remiss in my duty toward you, Cassandra," Matthew said with an evenness in his voice that was chilling. "I should have made my feelings known to you sooner. But I know you to be a woman of sense and I had hoped it would not prove necessary. Perhaps if I had, it would not have come to this."

Cassandra felt a flicker of apprehension, not because she feared what he would say to her, but because she knew it was not undeserved. "It has not come to anything at all, Matthew," she said quietly. "Lord Adrian is a friend and nothing more."

He went on as if she hadn't spoken. "Searle has made you the object of his attentions since his return to town. I thought that if I remained unconcerned, it would keep comment at a minimum, but your name has been linked with Searle's and is discussed in every drawing room and club in town. You know I have no use for *on-dit*, but after tonight, I am no longer sanguine that it is no more than talk. I am willing to allow you a degree of latitude as my wife, Cassandra, but I will not tolerate you making yourself the object of every idle gossip in town."

She would not permit herself to be submissive or defensive. "I cannot help what people will say of me, Matthew. *I* know that I have nothing with which to reproach myself, and that is all that matters," she said with frigid dignity, a little dismayed at the ease with which she found herself capable of dissembling. "My dealings with Lord Adrian are open for all the world to see. If you mean to think the worst of me with every man who pays the least attention to me, then we shall certainly not suit and it would be best to end our betrothal as quickly as possible."

He seemed a bit surprised by her counterattack and a little puzzled at how he had so unexpectedly lost ground. "Of course I do not mean to always think the worst of you. But Searle . . ." He broke off and then said as statement rather than question, "He was making love to you."

With his eyes on hers, Cassandra found she could not fob him off with half-truths or outright falsehoods. "Yes, but without any conscious encouragement from me, and I did not permit it to continue. That must have been obvious enough."

"What is obvious to me is that he at least regards you as something more than a friend. And I don't know that all the blame can be his when you have permitted him a degree of intimacy that would be more appropriate to a relative or female friend."

Cassandra opened her mouth to object, but closed it again. Her innate honesty was already troubled and she could no longer lie to herself. She could not control her feelings for Adrian, or his for her, and she knew it would be dangerous for her to continue to be on terms of intimacy with him. "Perhaps you are right," she said, suddenly acquiescent. "I meant only friendship, but he may have mistaken it for more."

"That is patent."

"I shall set him at a greater distance in the future," she promised.

"At a distance!" he said, affronted. "After tonight you should cut him from your acquaintance."

"Don't be absurd, Matthew," she said disdainfully. Intellectually she agreed with him; it was the best and only course for her to take, but she knew she did not wish to take it. She had no time to examine her feelings, but she knew she did not want to cut Adrian completely from her life. "You sound like my father, or worse, my sister. If you need it, you have my assurance that there will not be a repeat of tonight, but I will not permit anyone, not even you, Matthew, to dictate who my friends shall be. Either you trust me or there is no point in our continuing together." Even as she said the words she felt a pang of conscience, which she ruthlessly dismissed.

There was still an angry light in his eyes, but he once again backed down before her firmness and her implied threat to end their betrothal. "I suppose it would cause comment if you gave him the cut direct. But if you continue to mistake my tolerance for complacency, then perhaps we *shall* discover that we do not suit."

Cassandra acknowledged the fairness of this with a faint nod, swallowing her angry humiliation, and permitted him to lead her back to their box. When she sat down again next to her sister, Sarah gave her a faint self-satisfied smile, which said she knew Cassandra had been chastised and which kept Cassandra out of temper for the remainder of the evening.

Adrian's name was not mentioned again by Matthew, and Sarah managed to hold her tongue until the Fareland carriage had set Matthew down at his lodgings. But almost as soon as the carriage door closed behind him, she began to ring a peal over her younger sister's head, informing her in no uncertain terms that she found Cassandra's conduct reprehensible and unbecoming in a gently bred maiden. From this she progressed to expressing the certainty that Cassandra was heading on a course that would leave her totally bereft of reputation. Cassandra had too much breeding and regard for her sister to dredge up Sarah's sins, with her husband present, but she made it quite clear that she had no use for her sister's advice and opinions.

Fareland sat silently during this verbal onslaught, but he finally intervened in what was well on the way to becoming an argument at the schoolroom level.

Sarah at last subsided and Cassandra was glad enough to let the subject drop.

Cassandra was smarting under the reprimand of her betrothed and furious with her elder sister, but her sense of fairness, which was quite scrupulous, forced her to admit that their criticisms, however much she disliked them, were not out of line. She was playing a dangerous game with Adrian, and only she knew just how dangerous it was. There was considerably more than her reputation at stake.

As soon as she was out of her gown and into her nightdress, Cassandra dismissed her maid and sat down at her dressing table to brush out her curls and fashion her thick golden-brown hair into a loose braid. She paused to examine her features in the glass above the table, and to her eyes there appeared a woman who was no longer in the first blush of youth. Yet even self-critically she knew she was attractive. She might not be past her prayers for marriage yet, but if her betrothal to Matthew ended as her previous two had, her age and reputation might well tell against her. It was not very likely that another offer of marriage that she would find acceptable would come her way. Her thoughts were quite sobering. She had no desire at all to remain a spinster, devoting her life to making herself useful to her family.

Once acknowledged, her doubts about her betrothal to Matthew refused to be banished. If Adrian Searle had not chosen this unpropitious moment to enter her life, she supposed she would not now be assailed with uncertainty, for it was less any dissatisfaction with Matthew than her own unbidden and unwanted feelings toward Adrian that had shaken her confidence in her decision.

She put down the brush and leaned forward to peer more closely into the glass. "You want him to make love to you," she said aloud to her reflection. "You might as well admit it." After a moment she picked up the brush again, passing it through her hair with short, savage strokes, though she hardly knew whether her anger was directed at Adrian or herself.

When they had first become betrothed, Ned had made love to her at every opportunity, continually pleading, begging, cajoling, and bullying her to put aside her values and the strictures of her upbringing. Other men, too, had attempted to make love to her, but though Cassandra had found these experiences pleasant enough, no man had engendered in her any desire to surrender her virtue. Then Adrian Searle had gathered her into his arms and a sensation completely unknown to her before, hot and searing and demanding, had filled and very nearly overwhelmed her. It was lust, pure and simple, and she recognized it as such. Adrian was not just physically beautiful—she was sure she could have resisted that attraction easily enough; he had an aura of sexuality that she responded to almost against her will.

She liked Adrian too well to willingly cut his acquaintance, but she feared more than just her desire for him. His last words to her before he had kissed her had thrown her off her guard and permitted the intimacy which she had so skillfully avoided since the night she had melted into his arms at Lady Jersey's party. He had not precisely said that he was falling in love with her, but the intimation had been clear. Even now she saw in her reflection the flush, or rather glow, brought on by the remembrance of his words.

When Ned had first hinted at his love for her, it had been the one thing in the world she most wished to hear. From Adrian, it was the last thing she wanted to know. It was one thing to be attracted to or even to lust after a man of Adrian's stamp; it was another to be in love with him. She had not agreed to curtail her intimacy with Adrian to please Matthew or because of concern that she would be seduced. It was not the response of her body that she feared, but of her heart.

Intellectually she understood quite well that Ned and Adrian were very different men, but they were of a type that was similar: handsome, dashing, rakish, and

self-confident to the point of arrogance. If she allowed
herself to love Adrian as she had once loved Ned, she
had no doubt she would live with the constant apprehension that once again her heart would be trampled.
It was so much simpler, so much less worrying to
marry a man like Matthew, whom she admired,
respected, and held in affection. There were no flights
of grand passion, but no pits of despair either.

Regretfully she saw that the only solution was to do
exactly as Matthew and Sarah would have her do: she
must end all familiarity between her and Adrian, and
further, harden her heart against him so that he would
not have the power to disturb her well-ordered life. It
was her choice to do this, made consciously and without any thought of pleasing Matthew or her family,
but the decision did not give her the peace she had
hoped for, and only sleep put to an end a dispirited-
ness that was akin to despair.

# 5

$A$LBINIA, Countess of Buckinghamshire, had a villa in the King's Road, an inconvenient distance from town without being precisely in the country. Every Season, near the end of May, Whigs and Tories were expected to put aside their differences—or at least hide them behind masks—to attend her masquerade ball. It was not the hopeless squeeze that was usual for such an entertainment, for though it was well-attended and invitations were greatly coveted, the company was limited to the cream of the aristocracy and gentry and government officials. For those who were secure in their positions in society or the government, it was just another social function to attend; for those less sure, an invitation to Lady Buckinghamshire's ball was a mark that success had been achieved and was recognized.

For the Tiltons there had never been any question of whether or not they would receive one of Albinia Buckinghamshire's gilt-edged cards. Nor did the Bourne family expend any anxiety on a fear of being overlooked. Matthew's stepmother was an acknowledged connection of the Duke of Portland, and through his father, Matthew could claim cousinship with half the cabinet. The Bournes, like the Tiltons, had shaped the affairs of the realm for generations and took their positions in society and in government for granted.

Freddy McInnes' position in the Foreign Office was not such that he would have received an invitation, but Hannah, as stepsister to Matthew, could obtain for them what her husband could not. The McInneses attended in the company of Lady Bourne, and they were amongst the first recognizable people that Cassandra, entering the ballroom on Matthew's arm, met.

Despite the nature of the ball, few guests actually sported costumes. Most of the men wore dominoes and masks, and so did many of the women. The dancing had already begun when they entered the ballroom, and the floor was a sea of color, predominantly scarlet, violet, and black as the loose cloaks billowed out with the movement of the dance.

Freddy, looking bored, stood beside his mother-in-law, a regal Queen Anne who beckoned to her stepson as soon as Matthew and Cassandra came into the room. Cassandra neither liked nor disliked Lady Bourne, who was invalidish and usually spent her evenings gossiping amongst the dowagers, and occasionally commanded one or another of her family to her side when that company failed her. Lady Bourne had about her a perpetual air of disapproval that might have discomposed Cassandra if she had allowed it to; as it was, she regarded the summons as a command to be obeyed, though she would have avoided her future mother-in-law, given the choice.

McInnes greeted them with unusual warmth, which was explained when he excused himself and left them almost at once, heading in the direction of the cardrooms, his duty to his mother-in-law performed and his place having been handed over to Cassandra and Matthew. Matthew soon afterward recognized a colleague from the War Office, and with a hasty excuse of business to be discussed, left his stepmother in the care of his betrothed. The dowager complained petulantly that none of her particular friends had yet arrived, and Cassandra resigned herself to dancing attendance on the other woman until one of these could be found.

Cassandra, dressed in soft folds of silk designed to resemble Grecian draperies, her curls tamed and braided into a classical coiffure, stood out with elegant simplicity amongst those in Tudor and Stuart court dress, which were the most popular styles chosen by those who had donned costumes. A fair number of admirers approached Cassandra with the hope of leading her into the dance, but she loyally elected to remain beside Lady Bourne, at least until she could find someone to take her place.

Adrian was not amongst those who sought her out, though she had expected him to be. She had seen him only once since the night that she had decided to place him at a distance, and so brief and public was their encounter that she had had no opportunity to put her intentions toward him into practice. He had informed her that he would be attending that evening in the company of Lord Moreville, and though Cassandra had caught sight of the latter, arrayed in a white domino, she had seen nothing of Adrian.

Cassandra was finally relieved of her duty by the arrival of several friends of the dowager's, but Hannah approached her and further detained her. When Hannah came up to her, Cassandra realized that what she had taken to be gauze draperies of varying length were actually voluminous breeches of the sort said to be worn by ladies of a harem. There was a craze for all things Egyptian, and Hannah was always in the forefront of whatever was fashionable, but Cassandra, who was not readily shocked, marveled at Hannah's daring. For a woman to don breeches, however feminine, and to do so in public, was to court censure of the severest sort. Lady Bourne, a conventional woman, must have disapproved privately, but she made no comment on her daughter's odd appearance, and neither did Cassandra.

The women exchanged the usual greetings and commonplaces. "It is not the easiest thing to make out one's friends tonight," Hannah remarked.

"So many are wearing masks," Cassandra agreed blandly.

"I have not yet seen Lord Adrian."

Cassandra gave her a sweet, false smile. "Perhaps you have not found him out yet."

"Oh, I should know him at once," Hannah insisted with a superior smile. "Perhaps he does not attend."

"Lady Buckinghamshire made Moreville promise to bring him, because she has invited not only the Portuguese ambassador, but many of his staff as well, some of whom have very little English. Lord Adrian is fluent in Portuguese, I have been told."

"It would be wonderful if he were not. But perhaps he has cried off after all," Hannah suggested. "Moreville is here, but alone, as far as I have seen."

Cassandra made a faint shrug of indifference, which she was determined to feel. "Perhaps he has."

"Sarah assures me that Moreville is an amiable man, but I cannot bring myself to like him," Hannah said in a confidential manner. "He is so affected. No doubt Lord Adrian chose not to drive with him in his phaeton. I should not care to be junketing about in the early hours of the morning in an open phaeton."

"I quite agree that a man who wears a dozen fobs and seals and drives only white horses is affected, but his refusal to ride in a closed carriage is not affectation," Cassandra said, coming to Lord Moreville's defense, though she did not like him overmuch herself. "Harry once told me that he becomes violently ill inside a carriage on even the shortest journeys."

"No doubt that is why he has never been to Portugal, though he sets himself up as the ultimate authority on all things Portuguese," Hannah said waspishly. "There is really no one more qualified than Freddy to fill poor Mr. Alistar's position in the Foreign Office, except perhaps for Lord Adrian, and he claims that he is quit of politics since his return from Brazil. I do not see how Moreville can possibly overlook Freddy. Sarah has promised to use what influence she can for him. I only hope it will answer."

Hannah's words increased Cassandra's suspicion, which had been growing over the past few days, that her sister had been reconciled with her feckless lover. Her lips compressed slightly with disapproval. "I would not be sanguine about the degree of my sister's influence.''

Hannah's smile was faintly cynical. ''Oh, but they have patched it up between them,'' she said, confirming Cassandra's fears. ''She's quite in love with him, you know.''

''She is a damned fool,'' Cassandra said bluntly. ''Fareland has been keeping her on tight rein, and if he sees them together it will be bellows to mend for Sarah.''

Hannah was unconcerned for her friend. ''Husbands can be stupidly difficult at times, but Sarah is clever enough to manage Fareland.''

Cassandra was not at all priggish, and given her own attraction to Adrian, she was too honest to place herself above others who were similarly tempted, but she could not but feel disgust at such unblushing amorality. ''I hope you are mistaken,'' she said levelly, letting her distaste show plainly. Then, making the barest excuse, she left Hannah, and presently allowed herself to be led into the dance by an attractive young marquess whose heart she was rumored to have broken the previous Season.

It turned out to be a very pleasant evening for Cassandra, who enjoyed dancing and the agreeable conversation of friends. When she finally did catch sight of Adrian, arrayed in a scarlet domino, he had just joined one of the sets with Hannah. This did not surprise her, but it piqued her. In spite of her decision, she could not help feeling pangs of disappointment and resentment that Adrian had sought out Hannah rather than herself. She was able to laugh at herself for her perversity, but the feelings remained.

Cassandra went in to supper on the arm of her betrothed and they sat at the table with Livia, Lady Bourne, and several other friends. She allowed her gaze to wander about the room while Matthew went off to procure plates of food for her and his mother from the long tables that were laden with lobster patties, oysters, and delicacies of every variety. Adrian was at a table not far from theirs. He was speaking with a dark-visaged man seated to his left, who was a member of the party from the Portuguese embassy, and Lord Moreville was on his right. Harry sat on Moreville's right, and they were engaged in earnest conversation, which, Cassandra thought grimly, at least prevented Sarah from making herself conspicuous by placing herself at her lover's side during supper. The Earl of Fareland and his countess were seated at the opposite end of the room, which Cassandra suspected was by design. Fareland was looking dyspeptic, but that was not an uncommon expression for him to assume, so Cassandra had no idea if his wayward wife had given him cause tonight to be sour.

The McInneses were supposed to have sat with the Bournes, but were placed at the same table as Adrian and Harry. Seated beside the Portuguese ambassador was Hannah, speaking in her usual animated manner and gesturing frequently toward her husband, who showed more interest in his glass and his plate than in advancing his career.

Cassandra, determined not to take any particular notice of Adrian, had no notion how often his gaze rested on her during supper, but Moreville, who had noted his interest, said, "She's even lovelier than her sister, Lady Fareland, but I wouldn't have much hope there if I were you. There are several who will tell you that they learned to their sorrow that she has a heart of ice."

Adrian's smile was faint. "Ice can be melted if enough heat is applied," he said succinctly, winning a bark of laughter from the older man. As he got up from the table, he saw that Hannah was regarding him unsmilingly and supposed that she had heard the exchange. Adrian was always ready to oblige any willing female with a taste for flirtation, but he had no real interest in Hannah, who had of late hinted that she held him in a regard that was not reciprocated. His interest was already fixed on Cassandra, and the comparison between Cassandra's cool elegance that resisted and chal-

lenged him and Hannah's open pursuit of him enhanced
his esteem for Cassandra as it lowered his regard for
Hannah.

Adrian was saved from conceit about his attractiveness to women by a healthy cynicism. Sometimes it
was simply too easy. He was no despoiler of inno-
cents, nor did he intentionally break hearts, but there
was a certain sort of woman of his own caste, worldly
wise and knowledgeable of the rules of polite dalliance, with whom he was all but guaranteed success. If
he wanted such a woman, she was almost certain to be
his, and without illusion he acknowledged that her
conquest of him was as much a trophy to her as his
conquest of her was to him.

Hannah was one of these women, and when he had
first met Cassandra he had assumed her to also be of
that sisterhood, but within a fortnight he was regarding Hannah as obvious and too coming, and his original design to seduce Cassandra was mitigated by a
respect which forced him to reexamine his intent, though
his desire for her had grown rather than abated. If he
was to have Cassandra—and he was determined on
this—and it was not to be seduction, then there was
only one alternative, and for the first time in his life he
was unsure of the response of the woman he had
chosen to single out for his attentions. It was also the
first time that it had truly mattered to him.

He still made no particular haste to seek out
Cassandra. He knew that he had upset her at the
theater and likely called down the wrath of her betrothed on her as well. He was too adept at playing
the game to approach her too soon, before his lack of
attention became noticeable to her and hopefully redirected any anger she felt toward him into concern at
his neglect.

But Cassandra surprised him as she so often did. In
the first place, she showed not the smallest sign of
being vexed by his unattentiveness, greeting him in an
offhand but pleasant manner and continuing her conversation with Maria Sefton until its natural conclusion

permitted her to turn her attention to him. Not did she ring a peal over him. She was neither petulant nor cold, only perhaps a little distant and more formal than usual.

"I thought I should be in your black books," he said leadingly.

"Oh, you were for a day or so," she acknowledged without self-consciousness. "If you had been foolish enough to call on me the next morning, I would have informed you in no uncertain terms that I never wanted to set eyes on you again."

"I suppose I should be sorry for what happened that night," he said with disarming candor, "but I cannot be."

"I can," she said emphatically. "It has been wrong in me to encourage your friendship when I know perfectly well that there is an attraction between us that prevents it from being unexceptionable."

"That sounds rather like a dismissal," he said flatly. He had expected anger, but not rejection.

"It might be best," she said, surprising herself, for she had not intended to say so. "I am to be married in a short time and it would be unjust to both Matthew and to you to encourage you any further."

He smiled, but for once it was not echoed in his eyes. "Perhaps I am not the one you should dismiss from your life," he suggested. She looked startled by his words and he said, his voice darkening, "Cass, I want you. I don't believe you feel so little for me."

"You should not say so," she said, sounding shocked, but at the same time almost amused. "Oh, damn you! You have discomposed me when I swore you should not. Just go away. I won't let myself be disgraced for your sake. If you had any sense of honor you would respect my betrothal and not try to induce me to be false to Matthew."

"How cowhearted I should be!"

"And I should be henwitted if I succumbed to your blandishments. I won't, you know, so you might as well give it up."

He dropped his already low-pitched voice even lower in register. "If I had found you as cold as your sobriquet implies, I should have done so long ago. A true ice maiden might be content married to cold fish like Bourne, but you are not such a one."

"There are those that would not agree with you," she said with a self-mocking laugh.

Before he could reply, they were interrupted by the man with whom Adrian had been sitting at supper. He spoke to Adrian in Portuguese and Adrian, though he cursed him silently for the intrusion, answered in the same tongue. He then turned to Cassandra. "My friend Dom Luis da Vieira wishes to be presented to you. He says that you are the loveliest woman in the room and therefore the only one worth cultivating."

Dom Luis made her a courtly bow and Cassandra found her hand taken into his possession for a lingering kiss, accompanied by a look so intently worshipful that she was a little disconcerted. But a glance at Adrian showed that he was enjoying her discomfort, so she quickly recovered her countenance and smiled upon the Portuguese nobleman, readily consenting to his request, made in halting English, to lead her into the dance.

As she spoke no Portuguese and Dom Luis' command of English was less than masterful, it was a relief to discover that the set that was forming was for a country dance that would separate them for much of the time, but her relief was tempered by annoyance when Adrian also joined the set, again with Hannah, giving her an infuriating smile when he caught her eye.

It was in the early hours of the morning, with not many hours to pass before dawn, that the Tiltons at last took their leave of their hostess. Many of the others, including the Farelands and the McInneses and even Matthew, accompanying his mother, had already returned to town, but Harry, engaged in discussion with Moreville, Canning, and Castlereagh for the better part of the evening, had given little thought to the hour and it was only when Mr. Canning declared that he had early appointments that morning that the quartet emerged from their hosts' study, where they had spent far more time than in the ballroom.

Harry and Robert Moreville lingered in the front hall, their discourse on the situation in Portugal continuing while Cassandra, Livia, and Adrian, who was to return to town with Moreville, waited with varying degrees of impatience. Livia was quite used to her husband's political passions and, unperturbed, engaged Albinia Buckinghamshire in conversation. Adrian did what he could to amuse Cassandra, but weariness had evaporated her earlier humor and her responses to him were short and almost rude.

Both the viscount and the earl were oblivious of the discomfort they were causing to the others and might have gone on until dawn if Adrian had not taken the matter in hand, suggesting that he give his place in Moreville's phaeton to Tilton so that their discussion might continue, and offering to ride in the Tilton carriage as escort to the ladies. Harry applauded this arrangement, Livia was pleased as well, and Cassandra offered no opinion at all, allowing Adrian to hand her into the carriage without either comment or thanks.

The moon was full and the road well lit as Moreville set his horses along the King's Road at a smart trot, the Tilton carriage following immediately and a bit more sedately behind. It was not a long drive to town, but to Cassandra, who did not wish to encourage any familiarity with Adrian and so took no part in his conversation with Livia, it seemed as if they crawled along the road and she wished herself in the phaeton, which she imagined to be well ahead of them.

"Has Harry had slugs put in the traces?" she said aloud, her tone peevish.

Adrian broke off what he was saying to Livia and the latter turned to Cassandra and said mildly, "You would not wish for haste in the dark. I know it is full moon, but I think the brightness of it only makes more of the shadows, and every care should be taken."

"We must make a tempting target for highwaymen," Cassandra responded dourly.

"Oh, Cass, don't say so." Livia's voice expressed incipient alarm. "You know I hate traveling out of the city after dark, and I have been trying very hard not to let myself think of such things."

Cassandra suddenly sat a little more upright and very still. "Listen!" she commanded. "Was that a shot?"

The others were obediently silent, but the only sound to be heard was that of the carriage and the horses.

"Cassandra, if you are quizzing me, it is really too bad of you," Livia said anxiously.

"Late hours often give rise to fancies," Adrian said with just a hint of teasing condescension in his voice, but enough to set up Cassandra's back. "My mother used to call them the three-o'clock horrors."

"I am not accustomed to succumbing to horrors," she snapped, and was suddenly cast sideways from her seat against the door. Livia had felt the first jolt and reached instinctively for the strap beside her. Adrian, reaching for Cassandra as she fell, was pushed into Livia, and the door against which Cassandra had fallen flew open. If Adrian had not been lying half across Livia holding on to one of Cassandra's arms, she would certainly have been thrown from the carriage. As it was, her head and shoulders went out of the open door and only Adrian's quick action to pull her to him saved her from serious, perhaps fatal injury as the carriage careened into bushes and low-slung branches along the edge of the road and finally came to rest at a crazy tilt, two wheels into the ditch, and held from being completely on its side only by the thick growth beside the ditch.

There was a great deal of commotion. High-pitched shouts, clear with distress, and the terrified cries of the horses filled the night air. Cassandra had been pulled from the floor, and half-sat on, half-lay against Adrian, but there was nothing amorous about his touch as he gently eased himself out of the seat and her into it. He knelt on the tilted floor and demanded to know if she were injured in any way. There was a strange intensity in his voice, but Cassandra was too shaken to take note of it, and in any case, assured that she had suffered no physical injury, he turned his attention to Livia, who also informed him that she had taken no harm.

The carriage was suddenly jolted and tilted a little further in the ditch. "Dear God," Livia ejaculated, trying to maintain her celebrated aplomb, but her white face and staring eyes, visible even in the near-dark of the carriage, gave her away. "What has happened? Where is Harry?"

There was another jolt. "The horses are plunging in their traces," Adrian said, and pushed open the opposite door, which faced nearly skyward, scrambling out of the carriage and jumping down to the road with Livia calling on him to be careful. In a few moments the jolting stopped, but Livia and Cassandra exchanged glances that acknowledged each other's fright.

"If you did hear a shot," Livia said, unable to prevent herself from voicing her worst fear, "perhaps Moreville and Harry were held up by highwaymen and we fell in the ditch to keep from striking their disabled carriage."

"I am sure it is no such thing," Cassandra said bracingly, her nerves calming as all movement ceased and the alarming sounds from outside the carriage abated. "No doubt we mistook a bend in the road in the dark and slid into the ditch." Both imaginings proved to be in part correct.

It seemed to both ladies a long wait before Adrian returned to them. He informed them that they would have to get out of the carriage before it could be righted, and refused to answer any of their anxious questions until he had lifted both Cassandra and Livia safely to the ground. Lord Moreville's phaeton was lying completely on its side, not in the ditch, but across the road. Livia caught her breath in alarm and dismay when she saw the ruined phaeton. "Oh, my dear Lord," she cried, her voice trembling. "Where is Harry?"

She would have darted away to find her husband, but Adrian took firm hold of her and said very calmly, "Harry is well, only shaken. He is attending to Moreville as best he can. He needs your help, but I want to explain to you what has happened so you are not unduly alarmed."

Cassandra and Livia both chafed at the delay but obediently listened as Adrian told them that the phaeton had indeed been waylaid by a highwayman. Moreville, when ordered to stand and deliver, had whipped his horses to greater speed and for his defiance had been shot by the bravo. "When he slumped forward," Adrian continued, "the reins fell out of Tilton's reach and the frightened horses ran headlong until one of the wheels caught in a rut in the road and came off."

"They might have been killed," Cassandra said with awe at the tragedy they might now be facing. A sudden thought came to her. Perhaps this was what he was preparing them for. "Moreville is not dead, is he?" she asked bluntly.

"No, but he is in a bad way, I fear. His wound is in his shoulder, but Tilton could not manage to save both himself and Moreville when the carriage overturned, and Moreville has another injury to his head, which is far more serious."

Livia would not wait to hear any further, and insisted that Adrian take them at once to her husband and the injured earl. Both the Tilton coachman and guard had also escaped injury, and the latter was struggling to control the pair from the phaeton, both of which were obviously terrified, heads held high and eyes rolled back to show the whites. The coachman was doing what he could to free only slightly less frightened animals from the broken traces of the Tiltons' town carriage.

Cassandra's eyes witnessed the chaos about her as they followed Adrian to a grassy verge where Lord Moreville lay, but the full extent of the disaster they had suffered registered in her mind only when it was relieved of her fears for her brother's safety. There was no immediate opportunity to express this relief, or for recriminations; assuring his wife and sister that he was well except for a few bruises, Harry left them to do what they could for the injured Lord Moreville, who appeared to be drifting in and out of consciousness, while he ran to assist Adrian and his servants with the horses.

Neither Livia nor Cassandra could do much more than Harry had done for Moreville, which was to stop the blood oozing from his shoulder and to make him as comfortable as possible, which was the more difficult task. At one point the earl attempted to sit up, was almost immediately overcome with a sort of convulsion, and then lapsed into a more peaceful unconsciousness.

"What if he should die, Livy?" Cassandra said, putting into words the fear of them both.

"He isn't going to die," Harry said, returning to them. "He lost a bit of blood, had the devil of a shock and a good sound bump on the head, but once we can fetch a doctor to him he'll be right enough."

Cassandra thought her brother's tone a little too hearty, but she accepted his judgement because she wanted very much to believe it herself. The horses were being led off into a grassy clearing at the opposite side of the road, and appeared passive enough once they had been freed of their tattered bonds. The coachman remained in charge of the horses while the guard, Adrian, and Harry managed to right both carriages. It was immediately apparent that both were completely undriveable. The phaeton, one wheel gone and the shaft shattered, was nearly in pieces; the town carriage looked whole enough but proved to have a broken axle. At that hour not another carriage passed them, and along this particular stretch of road there were no cottages or inns where help could be sought.

The three men conferred in the middle of the road for several minutes while Cassandra watched them, resenting not being a part of whatever decision they might make, but aware that it would be unfair to Livia to leave her alone with their charge. It was as well that it was Harry who once again came to them while Adrian and the guard crossed the road to the horses. She would forgive her brother slights that she would have found insufferable from Adrian.

Harry explained that the guard, who had ridden postilion and was used to being astride a carriage horse, would take one of the Tilton horses and ride to find assistance as quickly as possible. "I am sorry I cannot send you and Cass home," he said to his wife. "We might have fashioned something out of the broken traces to give you at least two of the horses, but I am afraid the carriage will have to be repaired before it can be moved."

Both ladies indicated that their comfort did not signify. Harry sat down on the grass beside his wife and once again, in soft words, assured her that all was well with him. Cassandra felt *de trop* and she would have returned to sit in the now-upright carriage, but the moon had set, and though she would have been reluctant to admit it, the calamities of their ill-fated journey had taken a toll on her usually steady nerves and she was hesitant about wandering along the dark road alone.

In the end, though, she did conquer her misgivings. Livia sat with her head against her husband's shoulder as they spoke in soft murmurs, scarcely aware that Cassandra had left them. When she had crossed the ditch, which was fairly wide, the first time, she had had Adrian's assistance. On her own there was nothing for it but to gather up her draperies, which fit her more closely than a conventional skirt would have done, and to leap across it as best she could. She gained the road without mishap and paused to rearrange her robes, which she had had to raise almost knee-high to free her legs for the leap.

She heard a soft laugh and looked up to see Adrian approaching her. "If you have been there all along," she said waspishly, "you might have helped me across the ditch.

He laughed again, deep in his throat. "But then I should have been denied an excellent view of your well-turned ankles, and a goodly portion of calf as well."

"You are a detestable man," she informed him, but without reproach. "You can at least walk me back to the carriage."

"I can," he agreed, offering his arm, "but you can't sit in it if that is what you had in mind. It isn't as broken up as Moreville's phaeton, but with the axle broken, any weight inside might cause one of the wheels to come off as well."

Cassandra had not forgotten her earlier rebuff of him, nor her avowal to set him at a distance, but in the circumstances she was grateful for his company and she fell back into the easy intimacy with him that she had enjoyed before. They walked slowly along the road and discussed what had happened as best they knew. In spite of his injuries, Cassandra blamed Lord Moreville for the entire mishap. "It is just like him to be arrogant enough to think he can outmaneuver a highwayman pointing a pistol at him," she said censoriously. "He might have been killed, or Harry, or even one of us when their accident caused ours. It need not even have happened," she added, whipping her anger to a fine froth. "If he was not driving at such a pace, our carriage would not have fallen so far behind and I doubt any highwayman would be brave enough to stop two carriages together."

"It has been known to happen," he said. "*I* am surprised that any brigand would have stopped Moreville at all."

"Why? It was an expensive vehicle and likely to be owned by a rich man."

"Yes," he said slowly, for he was just putting his suspicions into coherent order as he spoke, "but at this hour two men dressed in silk dominoes are likely to be returning from an evening of pleasure, carrying

little about them of value. It would also be a safe
wager that everyone about here knew of Lady Buckinghamshire's masquerade ball. It is an annual event,
after all."

"Does that signify?"

"My dear Cass," he replied, "if you were a robber,
would you choose an open carriage containing two
men who likely have no more than pin money on them
and a few trinkets such as rings and seals, or would
you wait for a well-appointed closed carriage that might
prove a much greater prize?" He looked significantly
at the diamond-and-pearl bracelet she wore, a comple-
ment to the diamonds that glittered in her ears. Livia,
because she was not in costume, was even more richly
adorned.

She acknowledged that his point was taken, but
added, "Perhaps because it was so late, he thought that
no other carriage would come along."

They had come to the carriage, and stood beside it
on the side facing the ditch. He shrugged himself out
of the domino he still wore. "Perhaps. It is merely
observation. A basic tenet of court intrigue is that that
which is unusual may well be dangerous." He opened
the door and tossed his domino inside, causing the
carriage to rock wildly on its springs. He had clearly
not exaggerated its uselessness even as a place to wait
while help arrived.

"Perhaps it was just a very stupid highwayman,"
Cassandra suggested wearily. Her earlier tiredness had
been forgotten in the excitement of the accident, but
now it returned in full measure, and if she had been
alone she might well have sat down in the road.

"But a damned good shot."

"No doubt he fired wildly and Moreville had the
bad luck to catch the bullet." She shivered, for it was
far colder now than when they had left Tilton House
so many hours previously. "I wish Moreville no harm,
but I am so grateful it was not Harry who was injured."

He offered to retrieve the domino for her to put on,
but she shook her head. "Then I should be too warm,

and I am so tired that it would undoubtedly put me to sleep in spite of everything."

Made aware of her fatigue, he pointed out another grassy patch where they might sit, a little beyond the disabled carriage. "If you do not mind staining your dress."

She laughed. "I don't often have cause to dress up as a Greek courtesan," she said, referring to the way the folds of silk clung to her figure as if they had been dampened, which they had not.

"They were renowned as the most beautiful and most learned women of their age."

"But at what cost?" she said primly.

He assisted her across the ditch this time and onto the grassy bank, which was so sloped that sitting was accomplished only with precarious balance, but Cassandra was grateful enough just to be sitting at all. They continued to talk in the easy way of friends about the evening just past, mutual acquaintances, and the likelihood that either the guard would soon return with help or someone returning to town from the ball would come upon them and offer assistance.

Her muscles were tired from dancing and sore from being bounced about the carriage, and one of her legs began to cramp. She moved it to stretch it a little and nearly slid into the ditch. Adrian caught her by the waist and pulled her against him, not releasing her immediately when she had regained her balance. She turned a little to look at him, surprised that he would think this an appropriate time for dalliance. It was not yet dawn, but the sky had lightened perceptibly and there was sufficient light for her to read the covetousness in his eyes. But he recollected himself almost immediately, and his expression changed and his smile was apologetic. "I'm sorry, Cass," he said, releasing her. "I didn't intend that. I hope I am not such a clodpole as to try to make love to you here."

"I wish you would not try to make love to me at all," she said with less-than-perfect truth. "But," her conscience prompted her to admit, "it felt good to be held for a moment. Comforting. It must be the shock."

He immediately put his arm about her again, but was careful to do so in an avuncular way, though it was not what he was feeling. She leaned against him and rested her head against his shoulder as Livia had done with Harry. It felt very good indeed, and this was sobering enough to make her sit upright again after only a minute or so.

"What is it, Cass?"

"I should not be here with you."

He sighed, unable to conceal his exasperation. "Do you know fair charmer, that as endearing as your occasional capriciousness can be, at times it is quite tiresome."

"It isn't just that we are alone together, it is the way that I feel when we are."

He had not expected such honesty. "And how is that?" he asked, perhaps a shade eagerly.

She did not flinch from his steady gaze, but neither did she answer directly. "Whatever my inclination, I could never betray Matthew. I am to be his wife."

"Do you think, if the inclination is so strong, that you ought to wed Bourne?"

"It is not so strong that I cannot resist it," she retorted.

"You needn't." His tone was a caress. "Marry me, Cass," he said impulsively.

She stared at him with amazement for a full half-minute before she said, "You can't be serious."

A faint self-mocking smile hovered on his lips. "I own myself a little surprised."

"But I am already betrothed," she said, knowing the words were stupid, but not knowing what else to say.

"Give Bourne his *congé,* Cass," he said with a brutal disregard for that man's feelings. "Believe me, you will not suit."

"And *we* shall?" she asked, incredulous. "It is absurd. I like you very well, my lord, I will even acknowledge that there is an attraction between us, but that is not enough to make me wish to cry off from my betrothal. Even if I were not betrothed to Matthew, I could never marry you." The vehemence of her response was as much to convince herself as it was to convince him.

He was not deceived; he recognized her words as bravado. His response to this was to kiss her lightly on the lips. She sat very still, at first not responding, but gradually, in spite of herself, the kiss deepened. No part of their bodies touched except for their lips and tongues. Cassandra felt her flesh tingle with the anticipation of his touch, and when she could bear it no longer, she embraced him. With his body pressed against hers, sheer molten desire wrapped about them like a fiery cloak.

It was he who withdrew from the embrace, making a small sound in his throat that might have been triumph. "If you marry Bourne, feeling as you do for me," he said quietly, "then you *are* playing him false."

Cassandra was more shaken by her emotions and his unexpected proposal than she had been by the accident. "It is mere attraction," she insisted. "We would both be fools to give in to it. Once it had dissipated, we should probably be bored with each other inside of a year."

"That's nonsense. I admit to the attraction, but for me at least, it is far more."

She refused to hear him. If she could have risen gracefully and negotiated the ditch without difficulty, she would have left him. "I have seen too often how differences in character destroy a marriage. Sarah and Charles were perfectly suited, or so we thought. Look where it has brought them. They cordially dislike one another; he makes love to half her friends and she makes a cake of herself chasing after Moreville, her heart on her sleeve, while it is plain for anyone to see that he does not return her regard in equal measure."

"I give you my word I would never disgrace you or force you to seek elsewhere for comfort."

"And you, my lord? Will you promise an equal fidelity?" she asked scathingly.

"Yes," he said without hesitation, though he had given it no previous thought.

But Cassandra had heard such words before. "Once a man's hopes are attained, his oaths are kept at leisure."

"Some men," he agreed. "Your reputation for coldness is unjust. It is fear, I think. Someone in your past laid a mortal wound to your heart. Was it Tarkington? Don't paint me with his brush."

"You are from the same mold," she said, confirming his assumption. "You are beautiful men with great charm and address who make easy prey of my sex. Ned made many promises of fidelity, but he couldn't keep them. It was not in his nature."

"And you assume it is not in mine?" His voice was deceptively gentle, but she sensed his growing anger.

"It is my misfortune that I am attracted to men who are the perfect heroes of fantasy, but who would make abominable husbands."

"What of your paragon Bourne?" he said, unable to keep the acid from his tone.

"My affection for Matthew has grown out of familiarity and respect. There is no grand passion, I admit, but I want no such thing."

"Slow and steady takes the course," he said dryly.

"Exactly," she said in a clipped way, and then altered her tone considerably, to turn the matter off as lightly as she could. His offer was so unexpected that she could not believe that he really meant it, and she did not want him to see how much he had discomposed her. "I am very sorry if I have disappointed you in any way, but I am half-inclined to think it is only an aftermath of this wretched night. After you have had a bit of sleep, you will probably be very grateful for the escape you have had from parson's mousetrap."

He was silent for a moment. "Perhaps," he said after a time, simultaneously relieving and disappointing her.

Even as he spoke, there was the sound of approaching horses, and then shouts. Adrian stood and helped Cassandra to her feet. Within the hour she and Livia were again traveling along the road to London, and Lord Moreville had been attended by a proper physician and was placed in a closed carriage for the return journey, hardly in a position to object. When they reached Tilton House it was full morning and Cassandra refused an offer of breakfast, so exhausted, both emotionally and physically, that she did not even spare a thought for Adrian or his startling proposal.

# 6

WHEN Matthew called the following morning
to take Cassandra driving as they had planned, he was
greeted with the intelligence that she had met with an
accident on the road and was still abed. His chief
concern, of course, was that Cassandra and her family
had escaped injury, and when he returned later in the
afternoon to assure himself on this score, Cassandra
received him in her sitting room dressed in a pretty
floral-patterned round gown, her bronze curls tied up
loosely and allowed to cascade to her shoulders. The
informality of her appearance was intentional, as she
was to remain at home for the day, but she had no
notion of what a charming picture she presented, awakening possessiveness in her betrothed.

Though Cassandra had told him of Harry's lucky
escape, she had managed to avoid mentioning Adrian
by name to Matthew, not, she told herself, because
she had anything to trouble her conscience, but because she wished to prevent any unpleasantness if
Matthew should take exception to his escorting her
and Livia home from the masquerade ball. The deception, however mild, was in vain.

"Where was Searle?" he asked with just a hint of
intensity to put her on her guard. "I understood that
he had come in company with Moreville."

"He gave his place in the phaeton to Harry so that
Harry and Robert Moreville could continue an earlier
conversation," she said truthfully.

"And Searle? How did he make his way home?"

The temptation to lie was powerful, but it would be

quite easy for him to discover the truth from another source, if he chose. Repressing a sigh, she replied, "He was with Livy and me in the town carriage."

"By whose suggestion?"

Cassandra compressed her lips. She did not care for either his questions or his tone, but there was a faint twinge of guilt that she had again allowed Adrian to make love to her, however briefly, in defiance of her own resolve and her implied promises to Matthew. "His own," she responded, and it required control to keep her tone from being short. "Actually, I had cause to be grateful that he was with us. When our carriage was drawn up short and slid into the ditch, I fell against the door, which flew open, and I would certainly have been injured if Lord Adrian had not caught hold of me and pulled me back into the carriage."

"How opportune," said Matthew, his inflection enigmatic. "And how odd, Cass, that you neglected to mention his timely rescue when you first told me of the accident. I should think your own risk would be of signal concern to you."

"I suffered no hurt of any sort," Cassandra replied with an air of indifference, "and in light of all that occurred, my experience was of no consequence."

The matter was allowed to drop, but Cassandra had no doubt of Matthew's displeasure that she had once again been in company with Adrian. She knew that he was at least in some part justified for his suspicious, but she could not help resenting his attempts to control who her friends would be, which she felt stemmed from possessiveness rather than love.

Though Sarah, Livia, Matthew, and even Ned Tarkington had at various times commented and made clear their disapproval of her friendship with Adrian, her brother, a temperate man with a personal philosophy of meddling as little as possible in the lives of his family and friends, had given Cassandra no hint that he had even noted her friendship with Adrian. The evening following their accident, Cassandra found herself alone with Harry while they waited for Livia to join them for dinner. She had not given a great deal of credence to Adrian's comments about the accident, but was curious enough to wonder if her brother had found anything odd in the circumstances. Her questions were put obliquely, for she did not wish to create suspicion. His responses told her he had taken the events of that night at face value, but he was too astute to assume her questions merely casual.

"Why, Cass? Did *you* see anything to trouble you?"

"No," she replied with truth.

"But something has given you concern. I am certain of it."

Cassandra gave a little sigh for the failure of her carefulness. She made her tone as dismissive as possible. "It is nothing, really. Only a comment that Adrian made suggesting that he thought it unusual for a highwayman to stop a small open carriage on a night when he might have known there would be many rich prizes traveling that road from Lady Buckinghamshire's to town. He did not make anything particular of it, he merely mentioned it."

Harry was thoughtful for a few minutes. "It is *unusual* but not unheard-of," he said after a time. "In any case, it did happen and that is the end of it." With only a slight pause he said, "Are you in the habit of addressing Searle by his given name, Cass?"

Cassandra was startled. She was always careful to address Adrian intimately only when they were alone, and had not even noted her slip. "No," she said hastily, and then with more honesty added, "Well, at times."

"You shall probably send me to the rightabout, telling me this is no business of mine," Harry said with a faint smile, "but Sally had mentioned to me that she is a little concerned with your growing intimacy with Searle. I must say that, personally, I rather like him. He is intelligent and I know that Strangford commended his ability to the Foreign Office on more than one occasion. But if you are going to marry Bourne, it won't do to get yourself talked about with Searle."

"My reputation couldn't stand it, could it?" she asked, somewhere between agreement and annoyance.

"No," her brother replied baldly, "it could not."

It was pique more than anything which made her speak, for she had not intended to tell anyone of Adrian's proposal. "Suppose I told you that Adrian also wishes to marry me?" she said on impulse, sorry for it even as she said the words.

Harry was plainly surprised. "Has he spoken to you?" Having gone so far, she admitted that he had. "As a man of honor he should not have done so," Harry said severely. "You are already promised in marriage."

"Would you think better of him if he tried to give me a slip on the shoulder?" she asked acidly.

"I would have thought better of him if he had been man enough to contain his feelings so that an attraction between you had never been allowed to grow. What do you intend to do?"

"I think he did only mean to seduce me in the beginning," she said with forthrightness. "I am still not even certain that he really meant his offer; I chose not to take it very seriously at the time. I refused him, of course," she added before her brother could ask the question. This last was a flat statement, but accompanied by a twinge of emotion that she resolutely refused to acknowledge.

"I am glad of it. Bourne will make you an excellent husband."

It was what she believed herself, but hearing it said, she could not help bristling a little. "Oh, yes. He is a pattern card of all virtues."

She had tried to restrain her sarcasm a little, but Harry would not let it pass. "What are you about, Cass?" She assured him it was nothing, only tiredness and perhaps the aftermath of the shock of the accident. He appeared to accept this, but added. "If nothing else, marriage to Bourne will secure your future. I know you do not need his fortune, but that is better than marrying a man who does need yours."

"I have never heard that Lord Adrian is hanging out for a rich wife," she said, unable to resist coming to his defense. "I admit I don't know the source of his income, but he lives well, as an equal with us and all of our friends."

"That is partly what concerns me, Cass. I don't know the source of it either. I have heard some stories of investments in America, but it is exactly that sort of vague explanation that usually serves to cover a less-palatable accounting."

"Such as?"

"Gaming would be my guess." He held up his hand to keep her from interrupting him. "I know you will say that he is not known as a gamester. That is true and his 'fortune' may be the result of just extraordinary luck. But what better way to secure a fortune by marriage than to appear not to need it? There would be no need to suspect his motives."

"I begin to understand why I am the only Tilton in the known history of our family who has no taste for politics," she said sardonically. "You *should* approve of Adrian as a brother-in-law; you would deal famously. You both have minds that seek suspicion in every circumstance."

"There is also the matter of his reputation," Harry said, pressing onward. Having taken it so far, he meant to do whatever he could to prevent her from folly.

"Is this more concern from dear Sarah?" she asked sweetly.

"It is my own concern. I am not really condemning him, merely warning you. He is a very pretty fellow, you know, and you are scarcely the first young woman to lose her heart to him. I won't go into detail, in fact I don't know that much of it," he admitted with candor. "But it was pretty much common knowledge that his father more than once called in old favors to get him out of entanglements, though it never came to open scandal."

"Then it was never more than common gossip," she said scathingly. "No doubt of the very sort that I have been subject to just because men choose to find *me* attractive. In fairness, his friends should warn him away from me, for in my case I have earned a title, Ice Maiden, to account for my sins."

Harry sighed and Cassandra could not really be offended with him, for she knew that unlike her sister, Sarah, his motive was not interference in her life, but a sincere concern for her welfare. "I won't deny that I have a dread of any scandal, but I care more for your happiness than I care for that. If you are determined to have Searle, I will do what I can to stem the gossip that will occur when you jilt Bourne."

"But I have told you that I have refused Lord Adrian."

"I know what you told me," he said with a half-smile.

Livia joined them in another minute or so and their conversation was brought to an end. Harry's objections to her association with Adrian meant more to her than those of anyone else. She loved and respected her brother above any other person she knew, and his opinion affirmed for her that she was right not to take heed of Adrian's proposal, in spite of the unwanted emotions he could arouse in her.

She decided that she would follow a middle course, neither seeking Adrian's company nor overtly shunning him. But he proved virtually impossible to avoid. For the next fortnight every party, assembly, dinner, and ball she attended was certain to find him amidst the company. She half-expected him to continue to press his suit, but there was no hint of dalliance in his manner and he made no mention at all, either directly or by allusion, to his offer of marriage which she had rejected. In fact, as often as not he spent no more than a few minutes of his time with her, and their conversation was so unexceptional that Matthew might have stood at her side and had no cause for any renewal of his suspicions.

Since the night of the accident, she had not allowed

herself to think on his proposal at any length, or her response to it, and in the succeeding days she assumed that her estimation that his words had been impulsive and subsequently regretted was correct. Under the circumstance, she could not wish for it to be otherwise, but in her quiet moments she was aware of a small empty feeling. Cassandra wondered if Adrian's behavior was calculated to pique her, for whether or not it was his intent, it was the result of his seeming indifference. In spite of her determination to turn her mind to other things, he was in her thoughts so often that she had frequently to force her mind to other channels for fear that she was in danger of becoming obsessed.

Cassandra's suspicions were not entirely off the mark. Adrian quite deliberately did not single her out, knowing that it would serve him better to give her time to ruminate on his offer than to continue to pursue her when she had rejected him so summarily. But there was another cause to his carefulness to appear no more than friendly. He had been as astonished as she when he had blurted out his proposal.

Yet, though his offer had been impulsive, his wish to marry Cassandra had existed before that night. His original intention toward her when they first met was flirtation. But when he had felt her response to his kiss, and admitted that he himself had been shaken, he was forced to acknowledge that he was not above seduction. It was as their friendship grew that he recognized that his strong feeling for her was something more than physical desire. He wanted her, that was certain, but he wanted all of her, not just her body, and he wanted her to want him in the same way.

Given her unhappy experience with Tarkington and the fact that she was already promised to another, he recognized that his offer was precipitate, to say the least. But his retreat did not mean that he was retiring from the lists. He was now exercising the caution and careful strategy he should have shown from the beginning.

His first self-imposed order was to prove to Cassandra that her insistence that she and Sir Matthew were well-suited was utter nonsense. Quite apart from the fact that he and Bourne were rivals for Cassandra's affection, he did not much like the man and would have deplored her choice of Bourne even if there were no self-interest involved.

Bourne was certainly not a stupid man, and Adrian was careful not to underrate him, but neither had the baronet the facility of mind that his rival possessed, and Adrian used this to his advantage whenever possible. Engaging Matthew on topics that were on the surface innocuous, with a few well-chosen, carefully disguised leads Adrian could usually manage to bait the other into making statements that showed him to be pompous, inflexible, or pedantic, and, always, Adrian took care that Cassandra was present to observe her betrothed at his worst.

Cassandra was not ignorant of what was happening, but her feelings about it were very mixed. On the one hand, she was exasperated with Adrian for his attempts to expose Matthew's least endearing characteristics, as though she were foolish enough to be blind to the faults of her betrothed, but on the other hand, she was certainly no less annoyed with Matthew for so easily succumbing to Adrian's ploys.

Normally Cassandra was not tempted by the exclusive, if tepid, delights of Almack's select assemblies. She had dutifully graced the rooms of this shrine of the Marriage Mart for her first two Seasons, but since then she only occasionally put in an appearance, such as she did about a fortnight after the accident, and then she did so only at Livia's suggestion because the latter planned to meet friends there.

Cassandra had her own motive for agreeing to accompany her sister-in-law. Matthew had no use for Almack's, declaring that it was like a damned cattle sale, and the entertainment, consisting principally of dancing with blushing, conversationally inept young girls or gaming for chicken stakes, was not likely to tempt the more sophisticated tastes of Adrian Searle. As she dressed that evening in a sea-green silk gown with an overdress of lace tissue, she found she was actually humming to herself, happy at the prospect of one evening which would be free of all wariness or irritation.

Determined to enjoy herself, Cassandra did not find the task very difficult. She engaged in agreeable conversation with a number of her friends and was petitioned by admirers to join them in the dance with a flattering frequency given the competition of so many lovely and ingenuous young girls. In fact, she mentioned to Livia, when they met in the refreshment room, that she had quite revised her opinion of the club. It was not until quite late in the evening that an incident occurred to banish her pleasure in the evening.

Ned Tarkington had always had a fondness for Almack's, no doubt, Cassandra had once declared, because of the display of so many beautiful young women, each wrapped and carefully packaged like an expensive box of chocolates for a dowager with a sweet tooth. She was not at all surprised to see him almost as soon as she arrived. He had only presumed to advise her on that one occasion, and after a short period of coolness between them, they returned to the casual friendship they had maintained in spite of the fact that he had broken her heart and she had publicly humiliated him by jilting him less than a month before their wedding was to have taken place.

Ned was a superb dancer and Cassandra always enjoyed standing up with him, particularly for the intricate steps of the cotillion. It had been remarked on many occasions that when they were on the floor together there was no other couple to match them, and Cassandra enjoyed the exhilaration that comes from performing well. When the dance was done, both were a little flushed with the exercise, and she allowed him to lead her to a quiet, cooler corner near the musicians, where a curtained alcove concealed the door that led to a chamber frequented by the musicians

before and after they had begun playing. If she had
had any cause to be on her guard, she might have
remembered that in this very spot Ned had brazenly
made love to her all but in the sight of the patronesses,
which, if they had known of it, would have meant
complete social ruin for them both. Stolen kisses were
not permitted within the sacred precincts of Almack's.

He had no doubt had practice using it as a trysting
place during the intervening years, she later decided,
for he managed to maneuver her actually into the
alcove and behind the curtain, out of sight of the
company before she realized that his intent was something more than a respite from the warmth of the
room. She tried to put him off without making a scene
between them, but he chose to regard her resistance as
modesty, and in the end she found herself with her
back to the wall, firmly locked in his embrace. She did
not find it difficult at all to prevent herself from responding to his kiss; in fact, she was so furious with
him that the intimacy nearly disgusted her.

She freed her arms sufficiently to place them on his
chest, and pushed him firmly away. He was not offended; he even laughed a little. "You needn't play
the shy maiden with me, Cass. You forget that we
once shared embraces that were far from shy." His
words earned him a stinging blow to the face. His tone
changed abruptly. "You are grown missish, Cass. It
doesn't become you."

"You are not changed at all," she said, her voice
tight with rage. "How could you suppose that I would
welcome your advances? I would sooner be mauled by
a beggar."

"You are become suddenly particular." He sneered.
"I'd wager Searle does not find you so."

"How dare you say so!"

"Cut line, Cass. Everyone is saying that Bourne has
been handed his horns before a single vow has been
exchanged."

Her eyes blazed with such rage that he prudently
took a step backward. But he needn't have been con-

cerned. Cassandra's anger was well beyond merely wishing to box his ears. "I would despise you for this, Ned, but you are unworthy of my contempt," she said with a coldness that was more searing than any heat. "I am ashamed to remember that I once loved you."

She swept past him, but paused to compose herself at the edge of the raised platform where the musicians played. A hand touched her arm, and she started, fearing that they had been seen by one of the patronesses. It would be too ironic and too cruel for her ruin to come at the hands of Ned.

But it was only her sister, though Sarah's censorious expression confirmed her fear of discovery, at least in part. "You are a complete idiot, Cass," her sister said in a loud whisper, speaking almost into her ear to be heard over the music. "If you are set on disgracing us all by your conduct, at least have the sense not to do it here, of all places. You needn't tell me you were hiding in a corner to fix a tear in your hem, because I won't believe you."

Cassandra did not reply at once, and in the time that lapsed, Ned stepped out of the alcove, ignoring the sisters as he passed them. Angry spots of color showed high on his cheeks, and it was possible he did not even notice them. Cassandra's smile was sardonic. "If you are judging my conduct by your own, I can imagine what you will make of that. Since you are scarcely above reproach, Sally, you should be careful where you cast stones."

"Is that a threat?" the older woman demanded.

"No," Cassandra said with a serene smile calculated to infuriate. "I merely mention it." Cassandra did not remain to argue with her sister, but turned and left. In spite of everyone being seemingly inclined to accuse her of courting scandal, Cassandra had no taste for public display—though when she next saw her sister in private, she intended to have a few words with her that Sarah was not likely to find very pleasant.

It was all the more exasperating to Cassandra, because in the time since the accident she had been an unwilling confidante to her sister, who was distracted with fear for her lover's welfare and visited Tilton House daily to learn what she could of the progress of his recovery, since she could not obtain information any other way without exciting comment. Sarah had certainly not heeded Cassandra's advice to give up her lover, even knowing that discovery by her husband that the affair continued would certainly be disastrous.

When Cassandra next saw Adrian, on a morning visit to Lady Spenser, he found her more encouraging than usual, and when the arrival of several other visitors made a good excuse for him to rise and cross the room to sit by Cassandra, he was greeted by a decidedly welcoming smile. "I only hope they have already heard every detail of the accident," he said of the new arrivals. "I am almost tempted to put forth the theory that it was really French agents who caused the accident, just to give the talk a new turn."

She looked up at him sharply. "*Is* that what you think?"

"No, of course, not," he said with a smile. "Why would I?"

"You said you found it suspicious that Moreville's phaeton was stopped by a highwayman."

"Did I? I don't recall. I fear I said a great many stupid things that night. It was the shock, no doubt."

A devil danced in his eyes, and she knew he was quizzing her. "Yes, you did," she replied, and his broadening smile acknowledged that they understood each other.

"Do you go with the Tiltons to Caver Castle at the end of the month?"

Cassandra was a little surprised by the question, because it was only at breakfast that morning that Livia had received the invitation and informed her that she had been included as well, though Cassandra was barely acquainted with the Caverstones. "Does this mean that Caver is to be graced by your presence as well?"

"I could scarcely refuse the invitation of so old and dear a friend as Roger Caverstone."

"I suppose you shared a nursery with him," she said dryly.

"No, I've known him only since we were at Eton." He paused and then added, "Actually, Caverstone shared a study with my brother and I was only allowed there on sufferance, but Caverstone remembers me kindly, apparently, for I have received an invitation. The Caverstones are famous for their house parties, and since this one is to celebrate Lady Caverstone's thirtieth birthday, it should last a full fortnight. If you go, I suggest you bring all the money you can afford to lose at cards, and a hard head for champagne."

Cassandra laughed. "I was not sure I would go with Harry and Livy, but with such temptations, how could I refuse?"

"I have another invitation I hope you will not refuse." Her expression invited him to continue. "One of my friends from the Portuguese embassy is leaving for Brazil at the end of the week and has given me his Spanish mare as a parting gift. She is a sweet goer, but not up to my weight, I fear. Could I persuade you to try her paces with me in Green Park? If we go early in the morning, we may let the horses out without giving offense to anyone."

He did not indicate that there would be anyone else in the party, and even with her groom to accompany her, Cassandra was risking further censure to ride alone with him. But the temptation was a powerful one. She loved to ride above any other exercise, and Spanish horses were famous for their excellent breeding. A debate raged within her, but it was a short one. "Yes, I would like that above all things." They agreed to meet on the coming Thursday and Cassandra said nothing of her engagement to anyone, not even Livia, to avoid any possible argument or recriminations.

Cassandra had deliberately set the hour for their ride early. Neither Harry nor Livia was a particularly early riser, and she had the breakfast room to herself, assuring Hattley, the Tilton butler, that she required nothing more than coffee. She took her coffee into a saloon on the ground floor at the front of the house, and while she did not precisely watch for him at the window, when Adrian arrived, riding a raking bay and leading a dark brown mare, smaller in stature, but perfect in conformation, she stepped into the hall almost as soon as he had been shown into the house. Her groom was already at the door waiting for them, and they started for Green Park at a sedate walk.

At first their conversation was confined to Cassandra's comments and questions about the mare she was riding, and his responses, but as the groom fell behind to a discreet distance, they spoke the things that were really in their thoughts.

"I ought to have paid my respects to Lady Tilton before we left the house," he remarked, guessing that she had taken pains to avoid such a meeting.

"It's wasn't necessary," Cassandra assured him.

"Or possible?

"What do you mean?"

He smiled briefly. "Does your brother or his wife know how you are engaged this morning?"

Annoyed, she looked away. "I don't recall that I mentioned our engagement to ride in Green Park to Harry or Livy, but I certainly wouldn't have kept it from either of them if they had inquired into my plans."

"And Matthew?"

"What about Matthew?" she said tartly.

"Would you have mentioned our engagement if he had inquired into your plans?"

"Unless you intend to lure me into the woods and ravish me, I see nothing to conceal in what we are doing."

"Nor do I, but yet you are evasive," he insisted.

"You imagine it, my lord," she replied frigidly.

He laughed. "If I am 'my lord,' then I have scored a hit."

She cast him a sidelong glance through her lashes

and then smiled. "If you had any notion how I am badgered because of you, you would not wonder at a little dissembling."

"Why should you be badgered because of me?"

"Harry thinks you are a fortune hunter; Livy fears that I shall jeopardize my betrothal and make scandal; Sarah is delighted that I am to marry the stepbrother of her dearest friend and would disown me if Matthew cried off; and Matthew believes it is his right and duty to be the arbiter of all my acquaintance." She had begun by speaking lightly, but before she was through with this speech, there was a distinct note of bitterness in her voice.

"I had no idea! By all means, you must cut me dead the very next time we meet."

"I should," she said severely. "And it is time that I told you that it won't work. I am quite aware of what you are about."

"Are you?" he said, regarding her with fascination as they passed through the gates of the park.

"Yes. I am not blind to the fact that Matthew possesses faults; were he a paragon, I should probably find him an intolerable bore. I don't need you to point out his less-admirable qualities to me. Doing so reflects more poorly on you than on him."

"You mistake me, you know," he said, uncontrite. "I assure you that Bourne doesn't need my help at all to make an ass of himself."

"If you did have any regard for me, you would behave with more discretion," she said, ignoring his provocative remark.

"Fustian. I behave toward you with considerably more discretion than my inclination leads me. What it is, is that you are beginning to realize that in Bourne you have a sow's ear when you supposed it was a silk purse, and you would have discovered that at length even if we had never met. You ought to thank me, I think, for helping you to see it now, before you had taken an irrevocable step."

The disarming smile crept back into his eyes, and

she could not prevent herself from responding to it. Her answering smile was no more than a flicker, but he said bracingly, "That's better. I was beginning to fear that pomposity was catching."

"You are the most arrogant man I have ever met," she said, exasperated, but without heat. In spite of his deliberately provoking outspokenness, she could not really be offended with him. He frequently said things that set up her back, but it was more the kernal of truth his words contained than his impertinence that was the cause of it.

To change this dangerous subject, she suggested that they let their horses out for a gallop along the principal lane, offering to race him to a set point at the other side of the park. He agreed, and Cassandra, calling to her groom to keep up with them as best he could, put heel to her mount and they were off at a pace that would have caused the fainthearted to suffer spasms.

Cassandra beat him, but by so little that she could not accuse him of holding back to flatter her. "Menina is wonderful," she said, patting the victorious mare on the neck in praise. "Please say you will sell her to me. You may name your price and I shall pay it without question."

His slow smile was suggestive, but he did not say anything to put her to the blush. "She is yours if you want her. In fact, I knew she would not do for me and I only accepted her with the intent of giving her to you if you liked her."

"Like her? I love her," Cassandra replied. Mindful of Harry's contention that the impression Adrian gave of having no need of a rich wife was false, she could not resist a leading question. "But can you afford such generosity? If you were to offer her for sale at Tatt's, she would fetch a handsome sum."

He understood her at once, appreciating her concern but disliking her continued lack of trust in him. "Are you thinking that your brother's suspicions are true? I doubt my personal fortune is the equal of his, which I have on good authority is sufficient to put Golden Ball's nose out of joint, but I can well afford a few fripperies, and even make love to an heiress or two with a clear conscience. It began with a rather modest investment in a gold mine in Brazil, went on to a bit of judicious speculation in a shipping company, and is now safely ensconced in the five-percents. Shall I give you the name of my man of business for a reference?"

She knew she had courted the edge of his tongue and was mortified. "I wasn't suggesting—"

"Yes, you were," he said more easily. "The only way you can hope to mollify me is to accept Menina."

"You know it would be improper for me to accept such a gift from you," she said, but with genuine regret. "Please let me pay you for her."

Instead of continuing to press her to accept the mare as a gift, he surprised her by merely shrugging and saying, "If you wish. What is important to me is that you have her."

He would not immediately discuss a price because he claimed to have given it no thought. They had left the wide lane that ran the length of the park and were walking their horses beneath a canopy of sunlit leaves on one of the many small paths that crisscrossed the park. They heard the sounds of other riders but paid no particular attention to them until they came close enough to be recognizable. The sight of two of the riders caused Cassandra to catch her breath in a little gasp.

"We can turn into a side lane and avoid them," Adrian suggested as he too made out the features of the approaching riders.

Cassandra, who had at first looked completely dismayed, raised her chin and said, "No. It is not we who have any cause to blush at a meeting."

Since the day that Adrian had hinted to Cassandra that Matthew had a mistress, Cassandra had made it a point to discover if this were true, and if so, who she might be. Matthew's light-o'-love proved to be a Mrs. Maybrith, an attractive widow of impeccable breeding who did not move in such exalted circles as the Tiltons and the Bournes. Cassandra, though, was assured that the liaison had ended before her betrothal to Matthew, so she had never hinted of her knowledge to him. But she had not allowed the matter to rest until she had had the woman pointed out to her, so now she had no difficulty at all recognizing Mrs. Maybrith as she rode beside Matthew.

The other couple riding with them proved to be Hannah McInnes and a man unknown to Cassandra. Hannah was at the forefront of the party and spurred her horse to ride a little ahead to greet them. "Good morning, Cass. I didn't know you cared for early-morning rides. You must join Matthew and me some morning. We do this quite regularly." She then fixed her smiled on Adrian. "My lord, it is an even greater surprise to meet you. I recall you once told me you thought it barbaric to get up with the chickens for no better purpose than to go jogging about the park."

His returning smile was no more than civil. "No doubt I thought so at the time."

"Perhaps it is the company that tempts you," Hannah said archly.

"Perhaps," Adrian responded with an uncharacteristic want of gallantry.

Matthew did not betray any obvious discomfort at being discovered by Cassandra in the company of his mistress, but his greeting to them was brusque and it was Hannah alone who spoke with them for several minutes. Both parties rode on after this, with Matthew meeting Cassandra's steady gaze for only a brief moment before they parted.

In spite of herself, Cassandra could not resist casting a glance over her shoulder at the others when they had passed, and saw that Mrs. Maybrith did the same. That did bring color high into Cassandra's cheeks, and when she turned back and saw Adrian regarding her gravely, it deepened.

"Why did you subject yourself to that?" he asked quietly.

"I thought you wanted me to be aware that Matthew is a hypocrite."

"Not if the cost is to be your pain."

"There isn't any pain." Cassandra was not sure what she felt. As before, she knew it was not her heart that was troubled, but she could not be sanguine about such open infidelity even in a man she was not deeply in love with. She did not feel injured, but she felt betrayed. With Matthew she might not have a grand passion, but she thought she had found something more and sure and lasting, an understanding of minds rooted in affection. For the first time, her fundamental faith in him as the man who would make her the ideal husband was shaken.

"You are plainly upset," he said, not allowing her to dismiss the matter.

"I don't know what I am feeling," she admitted. "I would as lief talk of something else."

But, unwilling to forgo an advantage over his rival, he would not oblige her. "Can you really believe that he would make you happy?"

"What is happiness?" she said crossly. "The absence of sorrow? Seeing Matthew openly consort with that woman has certainly disconcerted me, but it has not cast me into despair."

"I thought your principal objection to *me* was that you doubted my fidelity," he said quietly.

"Perhaps what I need to accept," she said, not looking at him, but very aware of his eyes on her, "is that the ideal for which I am searching does not exist. I could lower my standards, of course, but I think I would rather abandon the idea of marriage altogether."

"It would be a shocking waste if you did."

"It would be a worse waste to spend the rest of my life in bitterness and tears," she replied. "I have the means to be independent. Marriage is a choice for me, not a necessity."

They continued to ride in silence for a little time, and then he said, almost as if to himself, "I am certainly set in my place. Even the polite contempt in which spinsterhood is held is preferable to marriage to me."

"You know you did not really mean your offer," she reminded him. "You said yourself that night that you didn't intend it."

"I meant I did not intend it at that moment," he said. "It was hardly an ideal time to be making proposals."

"You have never mentioned it since," she said briskly, to keep any emotion from showing in her voice.

His lips twitched into a quick smile. "As you pointed out to me, you are already promised. I spoke my feelings too quickly. I decided that it would be best if I left you in peace for a bit to learn for yourself what you really want."

"You mean you did what you could to cause Matthew to show at a disadvantage."

He laughed. "We have already had that argument."

"This entire discussion is redundant."

"Including your answer to me?"

She did not ask him what he meant, because she knew. Her heart began to beat a little faster despite her will that she remain calm and unaffected. As they were on horseback with her groom only a discreet distance behind, at least Adrian could not disorder her senses by taking her in his arms. "Please, Adrian," she said, looking away from him again. "I wish you would not . . ." She broke off as he stopped and caught her reins near the bit, forcing her to stop as well.

"Cass, you tell me I mustn't speak to you of marriage because you are already betrothed, but if I do not, you will end up married to that damned court card. I love you, Cass. I once told you I was not vain, and I hope it is not vanity to say that I think you care for me. Marry me, Cass. I won't make you extravagant promises or claim that I can't live without you, but I do pledge to love you with all that is in me to give. I may not expire for love of you, but if you won't have me, there will be a part of my heart that will surely die."

His words were more seductive than his kisses. A silent battle waged in her heart; pragmatism won. It was not that she regarded her decision to marry Matthew as irrevocable, or that she feared the inevitable scandal that would erupt when the world learned that she had ended one betrothal to embark on another— her fourth. Her feelings for both men were ambivalent, and she knew that a decision that would so affect the remainder of her life had to be made calmly and with sense, not impulsively with emotion. She forced herself to look up at him. "I am sorry if I give you pain, but I cannot."

"Why? Because you love Bourne?" There was no sarcasm in his words.

She shook her head, not in denial, but to refuse to respond directly to the question. "I just cannot. Please accept that."

"Not without reason."

She made a little self-mocking laugh. "When I know, perhaps I may tell you."

Adrian was a self-possessed man, certainly not given to vulgar displays of temper, but, twice rejected by Cassandra, and for the sake of a rival he could not even respect, his legendary sangfroid deserted him. "Then you mean to marry that slow-top, Bourne?"

"He is no such thing, and you know it," she said reprovingly.

"He's a damned turnip sucker."

"At least he is a respectable, honorable man, not a ramshackle loose fish who goes about making love to women who are not free to respond," she retorted.

"Not free to, perhaps, but who do," he said with a faint sneer.

"You are despicable," she said heatedly. "I wish you would just go away for good and leave me at peace." She pulled at the reins to free them from his grasp and accidentally jabbed at her horse's mouth.

This display of poor horsemanship, however unintentional, did nothing to soothe her temper.

In another humor, he might not have taken her at her word, but her vehement dismissal stung him to the quick. "Is that what you really wish me to do?" His voice was so soft it was just understandable.

"Yes," she replied without equivocating. But it was her anger that spoke, for she had no idea at all if that was what she wanted.

"Very well. Send me whatever you think fair for the mare." Without even a word of parting, he turned his horse and went back down the path the way they had come. Cassandra sat perfectly still for some time. The little mare pawed the ground and shifted her weight with impatience, but Cassandra did not heed her. After a discreet interval her groom approached her and asked if she wished to return to Tilton House. Cassandra looked at him blankly, as if trying to recall his name. In another moment she recovered her usual composure, and they too turned and retraced their steps.

# 7

$C$ASSANDRA was surprised to find Matthew waiting for her when she arrived home. It was past the usual hour of breakfast and he was sitting in the morning room with Livia. When Cassandra entered the room Livia's eyes frankly questioned her, and Matthew's expression was severe to the point of austerity.

Cassandra had no idea what he might have said to Livia, but she would not allow herself to feel intimidated or defensive. She came into the room with a smile, saying amiably, "I did not look for you to call this morning, Matthew."

He said in a voice that was cool and level, but nothing more, "I have something I wish to discuss with you, Cassandra."

Livia stood a little apart, her eyes resting first on one and then the other. "I was crushing some dried herbs in the stillroom when Matthew called," she said to Cassandra with a fixed smile. "I seem to have lost the recipe of the mixed spices that you gave to me. If you remember it, I hope you will come and help me when you are done."

Cassandra knew it was not spices that they would discuss when she joined her sister-in-law in the stillroom. "Yes, of course," she said a little absently, and seated herself in a straight-backed chair.

Matthew did not sit again when she did, but crossed the room to look out the window at the garden. Cassandra decided not to rush her fences and sat quietly with her hands folded in her lap. She might have taken him to task about Mrs. Maybrith, but she preferred to hear what he would offer first. What he did say astonished her. "You have no respect for your oaths, I take it."

"My oaths?" She was momentarily puzzled.

He turned to face her. "It was understood between us that you would not again risk disgrace and humiliation for us both by continuing to engage in a public flirtation with Searle."

She could scarcely believe that he was daring to accuse her when she had just discovered him in the company of his acknowledged inamorata. The absurdity of it made her utter a mirthless laugh. "And you, Matthew? What of Mrs. Maybrith? Please don't waste time telling me that she is an old friend. I have made a point of discovering her relationship to you."

He was obviously taken aback by her counteraccusation, but continued to hold his ground. "Very well, I won't make pointless denials, though I assure you you are mistaken. And even if you were not, it is a very different matter for you to make yourself conspicuous in Searle's company."

"It is?"

He went on as if she hadn't spoken. "What is at issue is that I do not cast my private concerns in your face," he said. "How the devil am I supposed to look the other way when not only I continually observe your preference for that man, but my friends and family take note of it as well?"

"I see," she said as if just coming to an understanding. "If one conducts one's *affaires* privately, in back alleys and amongst people that one would not even introduce in one's own circle of friends, then it is acceptable. You must instruct me in such things, Matthew. Until now I have always conducted myself in a straightforward manner for all the world to see. No wonder I have been the subject of gossip for small minds."

"Your levity is ill-timed, Cassandra," he said angrily. "I make no claim to virtue beyond the ordinary, but I do nothing of which I am either publicly or privately ashamed."

"Whose sense of propriety did I offend, Matthew?" she asked in dulcet accents. "Your doxy's? Or perhaps it was your sister, that paragon of wifely virtues, who was outraged. Unless you are blind or deaf, you must know that she has been pursuing Adrian shamelessly since his return to town."

"I don't interest myself in my sister's affairs."

"But you have no compunction involving your sister in yours," she said with a faint sneering smile. "Most *gentlemen* of my acquaintance would not introduce their sisters to their lightskirts."

"You do an injustice to a woman you do not even know," he said, his voice tight with rage.

"Ah. Now, that is interesting," she said, regarding him as if he were an unusual specimen. "A man so honorable that he defends his mistress's character to his intended wife."

"Mrs. Maybrith is not my mistress. She is a friend of Hannah's."

"Birds of a feather, no doubt," she said with a smile that was intended to be infuriating. "I fear we are at *point non plus*, Matthew," she said, rising. "You do not believe my protestations about Lord Adrian and I do not believe yours about Mrs. Maybrith." She walked over to him, pulling off the sapphire-and-diamond betrothal ring he had given her. "Is this what you wish from me?"

He looked at her, at the ring, and back at her again. "No. What I wish is that the woman to whom I am betrothed will not cause me to blush for her conduct or cast any shadow upon the name I will give her."

Cassandra, too, looked at the ring she held. There was a strong urge in her to press it upon him, but once again her sense reigned over her emotions. She put it back on her finger. "I would have hoped you would be more concerned for a shadow cast upon your heart," she said quietly.

"My heart?" he said, not understanding.

Cassandra sighed heavily. "It is of no consequence. You have had your say about Adrian and I mine about Mrs. Maybrith. If you have anything more to say to me, it must keep until tomorrow. I don't wish to quarrel with you, but I am completely out of temper, and if you stay, I shall probably end by casting your ring in your face." She turned without waiting for his reply, but as if in afterthought, she turned back toward him for a moment and added, "If there is more you wish to say to me, you may call after luncheon. I have other engagements until then."

She saw a flash of anger in his eyes and supposed she would pay for that shaft, but didn't care. She left him to make his own way out of the house and returned to her bedchamber to wash and change out of her habit before joining her sister-in-law in the stillroom.

When Cassandra went into the stillroom, Livia greeted her with a welcoming smile and offered her an apron to protect her dress. Few London houses were equipped with stillrooms, but Livia, who had an enthusiastic enjoyment of housewivery, had turned a small seldom-used rear sitting room into a miniature version of her large, well-equipped stillroom at Tillings, the Tiltons' principal seat in Hampshire. The items with which the room was stocked were imported from the country, of course, but they were sufficient to satisfy the viscountess and added considerably to her contentment.

As Cassandra had suspected, Livia wished to speak to her of more than herbs, though at first they did just that. Conversation lagged a little as they worked, and after a time, Livia's clear, unlined brow creased, and her tone, when she spoke, was unusually grave. "I know you shall say it is really none of my concern, but it is, you know, for I am most fond of you, Cass. I should hate to see you hurt, and so, of course, would Harry. I don't know what occurred between you and Matthew this morning, but I have never seen him in such a black mood before, and I cannot help but note that of late there seems to be a . . . civility in your manner toward each other. It should not be so between a man and a woman who are to be married in several weeks."

Cassandra had almost forgotten the wedding was so soon. The prospect did not fill her with pleasurable expectation as she was sure it should have. She sighed. "He was upset because he saw me riding in the park with Adrian, but—"

"Oh, Cass, you did not!"

"I did nothing at all," Cassandra replied a little indignantly. "I rode with Adrian with my groom accompanying us in all propriety. What I was about to say was that while we were there we were met by Matthew, and he was with Mrs. Maybrith."

"Who?"

"You would not know her. She is a friend of Hannah's apparently, but more to the point, she is Matthew's mistress. He claims she is not, but I think the very nature of his attack against me this morning confirms that she is. He did not at all like being discovered in her company, so he upbraided me for being with Adrian. It is, after all, quite unexceptionable for any young woman to ride in Green Park with a gentleman if she is properly accompanied, which I was."

Livia put down the sprig of mint she was holding and regarded her sister-in-law for a silent moment. "Do you still wish to marry Matthew?" she asked.

It was not what Cassandra was expecting and she was a little surprised by it. She wanted to respond with an unqualified "yes," but found she could not. She picked up a towel and wiped a few flakes of dried lavender from her fingers to give herself a moment of thought. "Yes," she said at last. "I think I do. I am not as certain as I was a month ago, I admit, but I still think that Matthew will make an excellent husband."

"Then what are you about with Lord Adrian?"

Cassandra scarcely knew how to answer the question. "I dislike having it decided for me who my friends shall be, by Matthew or anyone else," she replied, knowing it was only a part of the truth. "Not only he but also Sarah and Harry and even you have questioned or criticized my friendship with Adrian since the beginning. I like Adrian and enjoy his company, and I don't at all see why it is of concern to anyone else."

"Are you in love with Lord Adrian?" Livia said, asking yet another question which threw Cassandra off balance.

"I don't know," she said honestly.

"But you may be?"

"I don't want to be," Cassandra said firmly. "I want to marry Matthew and set up my household and have his children and live the orderly, comfortable life with him that I had planned." Without any warning, even to herself, that she was about to do so, she began to cry.

Livia at once came around the table at which they were working, and kneeling beside Cassandra's chair, put her arms around her sister-in-law, saying nothing, but providing strength and support. It was a brief storm. Cassandra fetched a handkerchief from a pocket in her skirt and quickly dried her tears. "I don't know why I am being so absurd," she said, her voice still breaking a little. "I am still out of temper with Matthew, I suppose." She paused and then said almost diffidently. "Should I be sunk utterly beneath reproach if I *were* to end my betrothal to Matthew?"

Livia smoothed back a curl that had come loose from its pin and fallen forward onto Cassandra's face. "You have just said that you want to marry Matthew. You do not mean to cry off, do you, Cass?"

"It has occurred to me that I seem to possess singularly poor judgment in the choosing of a mate," she said with wry bitterness. She saw a look of dismay come into Livia's eyes and said bracingly, "Of course I am not going to cry off. I am just indulging in a fit of premarital nerves."

Livia's smile was a little wan. "I know," she said. "I felt the same way myself at times as the wedding neared, and I was quite in love with Harry, you know. Mama felt the cure was to throw myself into the preparations for the wedding so that I did not have time to indulge in megrims, but you and Matthew have decided on such a quiet ceremony that there is little to prepare. Perhaps we should leave for Cheltenham as soon as we return from Caver. We planned to go by mid-July anyway, so it will be no more than a few days early. The change is sure to keep you in spirits until we leave for Bourne Hall in August."

She stood up. "It is not that I have anything at all against Lord Adrian. I quite like him and I know that Harry does too, but Harry is very unhappy that you have permitted him to dangle after you in such a way that it has caused a great deal of talk. If it is just flirtation, then it is foolish, but if you love him . . ." She stopped and Cassandra looked up at her.

"I told Adrian again this morning that I would not end my betrothal to Matthew and marry him," Cassandra said, her voice not giving away her feelings. "From his reaction, I would say that he is finally convinced of it, so it is moot. I will marry Matthew in August and finally lay to rest my reputation as a jilt." She took Livia's hands in hers. "I won't disgrace you and Harry, I promise you that. You are as much my sister as Harry is my brother, and I love you both too much to hurt you in any way."

"I am more concerned about the hurt that you do to yourself," Livia said, returning the pressure of Cassandra's grip.

"There is nothing in the least to be concerned about," Cassandra assured her. "I have my life well in hand and I am entirely pleased with the choices I have made."

That morning, after he had returned to his lodgings, Adrian was in an equally disquieted mood. He had really believed that Cassandra had feelings for him beyond friendship, but his confidence in this belief was beginning to wane. He knew she was not in love with Bourne—she readily admitted it—but Adrian had to acknowledge that that did not mean that she was in love with him. Perhaps she was what her reputation claimed her to be, a breaker of hearts without one of her own to lose.

He had used every weapon in his romantic arsenal to capture her heart, but had failed so completely that short of carrying her off to Scotland against her will—which was nonsense reserved for lurid romances—he did not know what else he might do to win her. He was not precisely ready to abandon hope, but he was definitely in the hips, his pride hurt as well as his heart.

He had intended to go to Caver at the beginning of the coming week, accepting the invitation largely because Cassandra would be there. He had even employed an agent to find him a house to rent in Cheltenham because the Tiltons had plans to remove there early in July. Now he had all but decided against both and was gloomily considering a precipitate return to Brazil or some other remote spot, which would be preferable to remaining in England and having to watch Cassandra go about on the arm of Bourne as his wife.

Adrian was slouched in a chair in the reading room at Brooks's, turning over these things in his mind, when Ned Tarkington came into the room. Tarkington had come in search of a friend and at first paid Adrian no particular notice. But seeing that he was early or his friend late, he glanced about the room with more care, and when he saw Adrian, he approached him.

Adrian did not see Tarkington until he sat himself in the next chair, and he responded so blankly to Ned's greeting that Ned felt obliged to say, "We have met a number of times through mutual friends and acquaintances."

Adrian politely straightened his posture. "Yes, I recall," he said with no discernible welcome in his manner. He regarded the intruder balefully. In his present humor he had not the least wish to speak with Cassandra's former betrothed, whose sins and defects of character were often ladled into his own dish.

But Ned Tarkington was not so easily put off. He

sat at his ease and even signaled a footman to bring them some Madeira.

Adrian sighed. "May I be of service to you in some way?" he asked with cool civility.

Ned Tarkington had never really accepted that he no longer held any place in Cassandra's heart, and in Adrian he recognized his first serious rival for her affections. He knew she was not in love with Bourne, and discounted him along with other, less successful suitors. His own amorous advances to Cassandra at Almack's had really been more to assure himself of his mastery over her than because he had felt any burning desire to make love to her. When she had so signally failed to respond, he had not thought that she had repelled him on his own account, but supposed immediately that it was because Adrian had supplanted him in her regard. "I hope we may come to an understanding of sorts. There is a small matter I think it would be well for us to discuss," he said, giving Adrian a winning smile that was meant to disarm.

"Indeed?" Adrian's response was unencouraging. He could not imagine what business Tarkington could have with him and doubted it would be a matter he would find agreeable.

"You will no doubt think what I am about to say impertinent, but you must understand that I stand as something of a brother to Cassandra Tilton."

"Do you?" Adrian's brows rose a little. "I would have supposed she had a perfectly adequate brother in Lord Tilton."

"Cassandra and I were betrothed in her first Season, you know, and would now be comfortably married if it were not for a sad misunderstanding." He paused, and Adrian, assuming something was required of him, nodded, acknowledging his awareness of this. "I only speak now because I wish with all my heart to see her happily settled at last. You see, I quite blame myself that she is virtually on the shelf and deemed such a care-for-nobody that she has gained for herself the title of Ice Maiden."

Adrian had heard from Cassandra an account of their "sad misunderstanding" and somehow managed not to smile at the grossness of the understatement. "How could you be at fault? Didn't christen her with the epithet yourself, did you?" he asked, perfectly deadpan.

Ned was annoyed by this deliberate obtuseness, and his tone was a little snappish. "Of course not. Though after our parting we were neither of us heartwhole, it was much harder on Cass."

"Since she is to have Bourne now," Adrian pointed out dryly, "it was not a lasting *malaise*."

Ned's smile was a bit forced. "I only wish I might believe her heart is engaged, which is why I have been bold enough to speak with you. This may well be Cassandra's last chance for happiness. She is four-and-twenty, you know, and only her beauty prevents her from being condemned as an ape leader. It would be a terrible thing if anything occurred to cause any misunderstanding between her and Sir Matthew."

"A misunderstanding such as you yourself had with Miss Tilton?" Adrian asked, his tone deceptively pleasant.

Tarkington regarded him speculatively for a moment before answering, unaware of how much Adrian knew of his past history with Cassandra. "Let us have the tree without any bark on it, if you like. I know from my experience with her that despite her reputation, Cassandra is not at heart a cold woman."

Adrian regarded him for a long moment. "Then let us hope her husband has skill enough to warm that organ," he said at his blandest. He could not suppose that Tarkington's attempt to warn him off was with the interests of Matthew Bourne in mind, and shrewdly guessed that the other man still had an interest of his own in Cassandra. He found it interesting that Tarkington clearly thought more of him as a rival for Cassandra's affection than Bourne. He placed his empty wineglass on a table within reach of his chair and sat back at his ease to see how far the other would go.

Ned made no effect to conceal his scorn. "I doubt Bourne would be able to rouse a fire in Venus. But you might."

"Rouse a fire in Venus? My dear Tarkington, are you castaway?"

"No, of course not," Ned said impatiently. "My concern is that I know from my own experience that once aroused, Cassandra's nature is as passionate as any man might wish. I would hate to see her gain a far more infamous reputation through one more skillful than Bourne at inducing warmer sentiments in her."

"You think I mean to seduce her," Adrian said plainly.

Ned's brow creased as if he did not care for such plain speaking, but he said, "Don't you?"

"I fail to see what concern it is of yours, whatever my intent."

"I have told you—"

"You have told me a great deal of impertinent nonsense," Adrian said, sitting straight in his chair and leaning forward a bit as if he meant to rise.

Ned bristled. "You are willfully misunderstanding me," he accused.

"Oh, I understand you better than you think."

Seduced by Adrian's amiability into supposing him harmless, Ned blanched a little at the clear menace in his voice. "I have no wish to offend you." He gave an uncertain laugh. "You sound as if you are on the verge of asking me to name my friends."

Adrian's smile was plainly contemptuous. "I would only meet another man of honor."

Tarkington's complexion went white and then red, and Adrian sat back in his chair again, waiting for the challenge he expected to be issued. But it didn't come. They were approached at that moment by Gerald Dunston, and after exchanging with the marquess the barest greetings demanded by civility, Ned made the first excuse that came into his head and left the room.

The icy anger died out of Adrian's eyes, to be replaced by an expression of delighted surprise at the unexpected sight of his brother. Concern for his wife had sent Dunston back to Somerset within three days of their arrival in town, and Adrian had supposed that he would not see his brother again until his wife was safely delivered.

The marquess sat in the chair vacated by Ned and said to his brother, "What were you and Tarkington quarreling about? I didn't think you were more than acquainted."

"We aren't."

His brother shrugged. "You had a look about you as if you were about to plant him a facer. I suppose I might have misread you, but I do know you rather well," he added apologetically.

Adrian smiled. "The thought occurred to me," he admitted. "But Tarkington is rather a coxcomb, not worthy of my fists or my steel."

"Was it a dueling matter?" Dunston said, surprised.

"I thought it might be, but he hadn't the bottom for it. He was casting aspersions on a lady's honor. Or at least I think he was," Adrian said with complete honesty, for the other's obliqueness had left some room for doubt.

Dunston was himself too much a man of honor to press him for further details, so instead he changed the subject by informing him of the purpose of his unexpected visit to town. "Annabelle says that I am making a complete pest of myself and thinks I need diversion. With her mother, elder sister, and two aunts all hovering about her, I suppose it is true that I am more underfoot than a help to her, but the truth is, I just don't know what to do with myself. I've never been a father before," he added artlessly.

"Nor have I," said his brother gravely, but with a smile in his eyes. "Do you want me to help you cast yourself into the gaiety of the Season? But I have already failed at that, since I could not hold you here when we first came up to town, and in any case the Season is all but at an end."

"No. I want you to come back with me to Dunwhittie."

Adrian laughed. "Then we should both be underfoot."

"Not at all. With you at Dunwhittie I would have some refuge from the petticoats that surround me on all sides. You can give me company on my rounds of the estate and we can ride and fish, and, most important, you are the one person in the world who can tell me to my face that I am behaving like a damned fool when I go into a taking about Annabelle."

Adrian could scarcely refuse such a plea, and in any case, after Cassandra's rejection of him yet again, it suited his humor to leave town for a time. To lick my wounds, he thought with a trace of wry self-amusement, and agreed to return to Somerset with his brother on the following day. Dunston then politely, but belatedly, expressed the hope that he was not taking his brother away from any pressing engagements.

"No," Adrian assured him. "Caverstone is having a number of people at Caver for an extended party to celebrate his wife's thirtieth birthday, but I had just decided against going, so it is of no consequence."

Dunston was biting thoughtfully at his lower lip and did not speak for a moment. "I imagine the Tiltons will be there if it is the usual set that is invited." He paused and then said, as if coming to a decision, "I've heard that you've been getting yourself talked about again. Up to your old tricks, Adrian? I can't say I blame you for taking up the gauntlet with the Ice Maiden, but cutting out the man she is promised to marry is taking it a bit far."

"If I were to nobly stand aside and allow her to throw herself away on that court card, I would be a damned chucklehead," Adrian said bluntly, causing his brother to smile a little.

"Have I misjudged you, young'un?" he asked. "I've heard it's odds on that you'll give her a slip on the shoulder before the ink is dry on her marriage lines."

"Is it?" said Adrian, seemingly impressed. "It was fifteen to one less than a sennight ago."

Dunston, unlike Ned Tarkington, did recognize the dangerous glint in his brother's eyes and said, "Like that, is it? Well, I suppose I wish you happy, but it's going to raise the devil of a dust."

"Don't pick out a bride gift yet," Adrian said with a wry smile. "She won't have me."

"Oh. But I thought you meant . . ."

"It is certainly what I meant, but I am paid out for my vanity—or arrogance, as she would term it. She made it clear to me not two hours ago that I have nothing to hope for."

"I am not surprised at it," said the marquess, his expression pained. "What odd hours you choose for your lovemaking. Are you quite certain that it is final?" he added more gently. "You must consider her position, after all. She is already betrothed, and given her . . . ah, previous experiences, it can't be an easy decision for her to make."

"Even if she loves me?"

"Particularly if she loves you. Love, in its earliest stages at least, is a very confusing emotion even when there is no impediment at all. Surely you know that." Adrian nodded, and his brother went on. "I oughtn't to encourage you, I know, but I'd like to see you settled and happy in the way that Annie and I are happy, though I confess that I wish your fancy had fallen on an easier choice."

"So do I," Adrian said with a quick smile. "Perhaps I should just take her at her word and let it be."

"Can you?"

"I don't know. Perhaps I shall discover that at Dunwhittie."

# 8

*A*T first Cassandra was not particularly concerned that Adrian seemed to be avoiding her as assiduously as he had put himself in her way before. If nothing else, his absence did a great deal to ease the tension between her and Matthew. Matthew even went to the length of apologizing for his behavior the morning they had accidentally met in the park, begging her pardon with unaccustomed grace. For the first time since they had exchanged their first unpleasant words at their betrothal ball, Cassandra found herself entirely in charity with him again.

Perhaps realizing that he had been remiss with his lovemaking, Matthew began to display an ardor that was unprecedented for him. They were frequently unchaperoned for short periods of time, as was common for betrothed couples who would soon be celebrating their nuptials, and he took advantage of one of these occasions when they were returning in a closed carriage from a visit to one of Matthew's aunts, who lived near Hounslow.

Cassandra had found the afternoon a trifle tedious, though not unpleasant, and lethargy made her quiet. Matthew also had little to say as their carriage traveled toward London, and what conversation there was was desultory. Cassandra was a little astonished, then, when, quite without prelude, he gathered her into his embrace and bestowed upon her a kiss that was far from his usual almost brotherly salute.

She was willing enough to respond to him; after all, in less than two months she would be his wife, but she found to her dismay that she could not. She knew that she risked his displeasure and possibly more if she rejected his advances, but her lack of feeling made her acutely uncomfortable. She put a hand against his chest and gently pushed him away from her. "I am sorry, Matthew, but I cannot."

"It is I who beg your pardon," he said, releasing her at once. "I did not intend to forget myself in such a way. You are very right to call me to order."

This very proper apology should have done him credit in Cassandra's eyes, but she was aware of a flicker of exasperation. Adrian did not apologize for his advances, and challenged her to deny her own desire for him. She did not wish to compare Matthew with Adrian, but such thoughts were frequent though quite unbidden. Neither the embrace nor the kisses of her betrothed could arouse in her the delicious sensations that Adrian could inspire with a casual touch, and in spite of their better understanding, Cassandra could not again capture the certainty she had had in her future with Matthew.

Adrian's continued absence compounded her inner turmoil. She missed him and, in spite of herself, feared that her final refusal of his offer had given him such a disgust of her that he was deliberately avoiding her. It would be for the best, of course, but whenever she contemplated the possibility that it was true, she fell into a flat despair. She felt no better when she heard through a mutual friend that Adrian had actually left London. She could not tell if she was the cause of his sudden departure, but he had told no one where he was bound and had left the very day after their ride in Green Park, so it was easy to assume the worst.

Outwardly, of course, none of the agitation of her mind showed in her behavior. She was, as ever, a self-possessed young woman. Not even Livia, sensitive to mood changes in her loved ones, seemed to notice that there was anything especially troubling to Cassandra. In fact, Harry, thinking to commend her, mentioned to her that he was glad she had had the sense to realize that her feelings for Adrian had been mere infatuation before she had done any lasting harm to her relationship with Matthew.

On the day that she had last spoken to Adrian, Cassandra had made up her mind that she would not join her brother and his wife on their visit to Caver Castle. She did not want to spend what was to be nearly a sennight's stay at Caver in such close society with both Adrian and Matthew.

Livia was disappointed and said so. "I was so looking forward to having you there, Cass. There is more of politics than pleasure in this visit, and without friends to while away the time it may be a bit tedious at times."

"How can you say you would miss my company?" Cassandra said, incredulous. "I doubt there will be a person there with whom you are not acquainted."

"Oh, I shall *know* everyone, friends and colleagues of Harry's, and their wives, but that is not the same thing as having a *particular* friend with you."

Cassandra was pleased and a little flattered that Livia placed so much value on their friendship, and began to think she would go after all, particularly as she reasoned that if Adrian were avoiding her, she might suppose that he would not come to Caver after all. She even did what she could to convince herself that it would be an excellent opportunity to spend time with Matthew mending her fences before the wedding.

She informed her sister-in-law of her change of heart after breakfast two days before the Tiltons were planning to leave for Sussex. "I am glad of it," Livia said happily. "I only hope you are not disappointed about the time you hope to have with Matthew. Half the cabinet will be there, you know, and I'd wager my new ruby earrings that the men will spend more time closeted together behind closed doors than engaging in the pleasure parties planned by Lady Caverstone for her guests." She tied off and snipped the thread on a petticoat flounce she was mending. "Actually, for us it will be quite a family party. I can scarcely credit it, but Harry told me this morning that Sarah and Fareland will be there. Fareland has never been political, and I was surprised at it, but Harry said that Sally quite pestered him to secure them an invitation."

Cassandra had no difficulty at all deciphering her sister's motive for wishing to go to Caver Castle, and Livia's information brought a grim set to her lips, but since she had never told Livia about her sister and Lord Moreville, she said nothing now, only offering up a silent prayer that Sarah would do nothing foolish or scandalous while they were at Caver. To Livia she said, "It is worse than that. Matthew told me that *he* has managed to persuade Caverstone to include Hannah and Freddy McInnes in the party. I suppose Hannah thinks being included in such exalted company will help Freddy's career, but since it is likely that he will be foxed for three-fourths of the time in company with the very men he is supposed to make an impression on, it is likely to prove the reverse."

"I can't think why everyone is so mad to go to Caver," Livia said, tilting her head a little like an inquisitive sparrow. "I would as lief let Harry go by himself and meet him at Cheltenham in a week's time, but he would be quite hurt if I even suggested it, so I shall not. In any case, now that I shall have you with me, I expect it won't be so boring after all."

Cassandra didn't say it, but her thought was that the one thing their visit was not likely to be was boring.

Adrian was not at Caver when they arrived. Cassandra had not realized that she had, in spite of everything, hoped he would be there until she felt disappointed that he was not. She would not allow herself to ask Lady Caverstone if he was expected, but for the first two days at Caver she found herself looking about every room she entered hopefully, as if she expected to see his tall, well-formed frame. She was not consciously aware of doing so until Hannah McInnes asked her plainly whom she was looking for. Cassandra felt mortified for behaving in such an obvious way and took herself to task for her foolishness. Her hope of increasing her intimacy with her betrothed was unsuccessful as well, and this did nothing to help her banish Adrian from her thoughts.

It was exactly as Livia had predicted. Most of the men spent the time in earnest conversation with each other. There were men like Fareland and two or three others who held no position in the government, and they could be counted on to escort the ladies into the village of Caverstone or on walks in the home wood or rides about the estate, but of her brother, Harry, Matthew, and many of the others, there was little to be seen beyond time spent together at meals.

Cassandra found that she did not object to this. She did not know quite why it was so, but since their arrival, it seemed to her that nearly everything that Matthew said or did served to irritate her. And it was as well that Lord Moreville was also most often to be found with Mr. Perceval or Harry or some other colleague. Whenever Moreville came into a room that also contained Lord and Lady Fareland, there was a palpable tension in the air, or at least it seemed so to Cassandra, who knew how volatile the situation was.

Charles Fareland, who at the best of times was not an amiable man, was self-contained to the point of being taciturn, and Cassandra could only marvel at her sister for arranging for an invitation to Caver, where Moreville was certain to be amongst the company. In fairness to Sarah, she behaved with perfect propriety at all times and showed not the least public partiality for Lord Moreville, but Fareland was no fool and he had to know that his wife was hoping for clandestine meetings with her lover.

Sarah even commented on her husband's watchfulness of her behavior. "There are times when I feel quite smothered," she confided to Cassandra as they strolled about the garden, colorful with a proliferation of blooms. "Last night I was lying in bed, but not yet asleep, and I heard him open the door that connects our rooms and look in to see if I was in my bed."

"What did you expect?" Cassandra said without sympathy. "Charles knows that you and Moreville have been lovers. Did you think he would take your word for it that it was ended, when you press him to attend a party that can have no interest for you beyond the company of Lord Moreville?"

"You are here, and so are Harry and Livy," Sarah said defensively. "I don't think it is so wonderful that we should be invited as well."

"I do," Cassandra said directly. "And depend upon it, so does Fareland."

"He is forever watching me," Sarah complained. "There are times when it makes my flesh crawl, as if someone were walking over my grave. He hates me, you know. At times I think he wished I were dead." She shivered, and Cassandra found her own hair was standing on end.

"Don't be absurd," Cassandra said briskly. "I have never seen a man less likely to murder his wife than Fareland. Even if she *does* deserve it. He is too fond of his creature comforts to risk Newgate or the gibbet."

"I don't know why I talk to you," Sarah said, petulant that her melodramatic fantasies were exposed as nonsense by her sister's matter-of-fact response. "You can have no idea of my sufferings. I've never loved Fareland, but I found it no worse than tiresome to be married to him until I met Robert. Now that I realize what it is to be in love, it is unbearable to be tied to Charles."

"I was still in the school room at the time, but I don't recall that you were constrained to marry Fareland."

"It was a superb match. Everyone said so. Fareland is rich and titled and he was very attentive, at least in the beginning." She was silent for a few minutes and then sighed. "I believed it when I was told that an arranged match was as likely to be happy as a love match. Now I know that is nonsense."

"And yet you encourage me to marry Matthew when you know I am not in love with him."

Sarah looked at her with surprise. "But you needed no one's encouragement when you accepted Matthew's offer. It was what *you* wanted."

It was Cassandra's turn for surprise, for she could not refute what her sister had said. More to the point, she could plainly see how differently she had come to feel toward Matthew since the night of their betrothal ball.

Two men came out onto the broad flagstone terrace. With the sun in her eyes, Cassandra did not recognize either man at first, but as she passed into the shade of a rose arbor she saw that one was her host and the other Adrian Searle. No matter how hard Cassandra tried to control her feelings, her heart began to hammer in her breast. Sarah had sat on a stone bench facing away from the terrace and did not see the men, but Cassandra, watching them through a screen of green leaves and pink blooms, saw Caverstone gesticulate in their direction and then return inside the house, while Adrian headed along the path toward the rose garden.

Cassandra sat on the bench beside her sister, barely listening to Sarah's continuing animadversions on her husband and her wretched marriage. She had no doubt he was coming to seek her out, and in spite of her hope that he would come, she wished now that she might escape the meeting. It would be the first time they would meet since that morning in Green Park, when she had again refused his offer, and she had no idea what he would say to her, or for that matter, she to him.

Sarah saw him as he approached them. "Good heavens, Cass. Do you know who is here? Lord Adrian." She cast a suspicious glance at her sister. "Did you know he was coming? It is really too bad of you to make me feel like Jezebel if you knew *your* lover would be coming here too."

"He is not my lover," Cassandra said firmly but quietly, for he was near enough to overhear normal speech.

He smiled at her as soon as he saw her, with that teasing spark of amusement in his eyes that she could not help responding to. He was the most beautiful creature she had ever beheld in her life, and she felt an urge to cast herself in his arms that was all but overwhelming.

Their greetings were attended by no such impropriety. "I have come from Dunwhittie with the best of tidings," he said at once. "My brother's wife, Annabelle, is delivered of twins, a boy and a girl. Gerald was in a far greater taking than Annabelle, who, I am happy to report, had an easy delivery."

Both ladies exclaimed joyfully at this news and demanded the particulars of mother and babies, which Adrian obligingly gave to them. Cassandra had the wry thought that *this* was certainly not what she had expected to discuss with him when they finally met again, and found herself just a little disappointed that his departure from town and absence from the house party had apparently had nothing to do with her at all.

"This means an end to your hope for the succession," Sarah said, quizzing him.

"I never had any. Gerald enjoyed racketing about town, but he was bound to marry and produce an heir eventually. If this is any sample of how Annabelle means to go on, he shall probably have a whole quiverful of heirs before they are done."

"He is fortunate to have a brother who regards him without rivalry," Cassandra commended.

"Oh, I didn't say that," replied Adrian with a laugh. "I envy his marksmanship with a pistol and the way he sits his horse over the most abominable country. Like any brothers, we each of us have our talents which the other envies."

"I hope Dunston does not envy you your ability to capture so easily the heart of nearly every woman you smile upon," Sarah said with a glance toward her sister that earned for her an angry glare.

But Adrian replied lightly, robbing her words of the

power to embarrass him, "I only wish it were that easy. You seem well able to resist my smiles."

"But *I* am married and must."

"My dear Lady Fareland," he said, as if astonished, "you must guard against such revolutionary ideals."

"And you, my lord, must guard against such hardened cynicism." She got up and shook out her skirts. "Have you told everyone your news?"

"Only Caverstone, who met me when I arrived."

"Then probably no one in the house knows of it at all. Men do not pay proper regard to such things. If you permit, I'll return to the house and tell everyone your news. I know they will be as delighted as we are."

Adrian readily agreed, but Cassandra, who still felt a little constrained with him, had no intention of allowing her sister to succeed with such an obvious ploy to leave them alone, and insisted on returning to the house as well. The path was not wide enough for three abreast, so Sarah, somewhat reluctantly, accepted Adrian's arm, and Cassandra, by her own wish, walked a little behind them.

But when they reached the house, Sarah hurried inside, and Adrian, by placing a hand on her arm, held Cassandra beside him for a moment. "Do I find you well, Cass?"

"Perfectly," she replied. "You have been missed by your friends."

"By at least one friend, I hope," he said softly.

She withdrew her arm from the pressure of his hand. "Oh, by us all," she said with apparent indifference, and went into the house.

The house was almost unnaturally quiet, with only the occasional sound of a servant going about his duties to break the silence. The library was quite empty when Cassandra entered, and she was grateful for it. She sank into one of the comfortable leather chairs near a window and permitted herself a full half-hour of unchecked rumination about her relationship with

Matthew and her feelings for Adrian and what it meant to her present peace and the prospects of her future.

She was not really surprised or dismayed when the library door opened and Adrian came into the room. "Hiding from me, Cass?" he asked as he sat in a chair beside hers.

"If I were, I appear to have failed," she said dryly.

"It won't do, you know," he said. "I missed you quite out of proportion to the time I was away."

"You didn't even think enough of your leaving to tell anyone of it."

"After what you said to me in Green Park, I didn't think *you* would care where I'd gone, as long as I had. Are you really indifferent to me now, Cass?" he asked quietly and with unaccustomed diffidence. "Did you miss me at all?"

She opened her lips to deny it, but could not with his eyes upon her. She smiled ruefully; he would have his answer. "Yes. Damn you."

His faint smile had only a hint of triumph, betrayed none of the relief he felt at not having his worst fears realized. It quickly faded and was replaced by an intent expression that she knew well. "Is your answer still the same to me?"

"I don't know," Cassandra replied, startled into honesty by the abruptness of his approach. She got up and walked over to one of the tall sash windows overlooking the shaved lawn. She turned her back on this vista and sat on the wide, low still facing him, but with a greater distance between them. "I had a very pleasant settled life before you came into it. Now I don't even seem to know my own mind from day to day. It would have been better for us both if you hadn't come here."

"I had to," he said simply, "though I didn't mean to at first. When you sent my mare back to the mews I decided to give you exactly what you wished for: I would leave you in peace to marry your cold fish. Then Gerald came to town that same day to ask me to come to Dunwhittie, and I thought it was for the best.

But separation wasn't an answer for me, Cass. I don't think it was for you either."

She bowed her head and stared unseeingly at the pattern in the Turkey carpet. "No, I suppose it wasn't," she admitted.

He got up and went over to her. "You can't marry Bourne, Cass. You know you couldn't do it feeling the way you do about me."

"But *that* is the difficulty," she said with a note of real anguish. "I don't know what I feel about you."

"I do. When you are in my arms you tell me with your body what your lips refuse to say."

She raised her head. He was standing dangerously close to her. "That I am attracted to you? How could I deny it after what has passed between us? But what has that to do with love?"

"Good God," he said as if the words were torn from him. "What the devil do I have to do to prove to you—?"

But what he wished to prove remained unsaid. The door opened and Harry came into the room, his expression betraying nothing as he beheld them. They did not spring apart like guilty lovers, but there would have been no point in pretending that they had been discussing commonplaces. "Ah, there you are, Cass," Harry said with unstudied amiability. "A footman told me he thought he saw you come in here. Livy sent me to fetch you. She was concerned when she went to your room to borrow your pearls and found you had not even been up yet to dress for dinner."

"I was searching for a book to read after I retire tonight," Cassandra said, knowing she did not deceive her brother. "Please tell Livy that she may certainly have my pearls and I shall be up to dress shortly."

Harry's smile was pleasant but there was a note of implacability in his voice. "It is really quite late, you know. It would be best if you came up at once, and then you can tell Livia yourself and not keep us all waiting for you at dinner."

It was several years since Harry had stood as a

guardian to her, but she responded to his authority out of her regard for him and obediently rose and left the room. Harry followed her to her bedchamber. When he had closed the door she turned and said, "Was that really necessary, Harry? I am not in need of a duenna."

"No. You are not," he agreed. "You are of age and your own mistress. You owe me no explanations. I confess to thinking more of myself than of you at the moment. If you won't heed the danger to your reputation and the advice of those that care for you and have only your best interests at heart, that is entirely your own affair and I only hope you may not regret it. But I do ask you this. Please behave circumspectly at least while we are here. I think you know that this is more than just a party of pleasure for some of us. The work we are about is too important to be disrupted by petty scandal."

Hot color flamed in Cassandra's cheeks. "I hope I am not so lost to propriety, whatever you may think, Harry."

He patted her arm affectionately. "Don't poker up, there's a good girl. I only meant that if you mean to hand Matthew his *congé*, wait until we get back to town. No matter how much you try to keep something like that quiet, in the intimacy of a party such as this, everyone will know something is amiss within the hour."

"I have no desire to wash my dirty linen in public," she said with asperity.

"But you mean to send Bourne about his business, don't you, Cass?"

"It is possible," she admitted reluctantly.

He sighed, a sound somewhere between exasperation and resignation. "You're to be married to Bourne at the beginning of August," he reminded her. "I think you'd better know your mind damn soon." He paused and his features lightened. "Well, enough said about that. I'd better not keep you from your dressing or you will be late for dinner."

When Matthew entered the saloon on the ground floor where the company was assembled before going in to dinner, he saw Adrian almost at once. Cassandra, who was waiting to see what his reaction would be, fancied she saw a change in his expression, but if so, it was no more than a flash, and when he came up to her he made no comment about Adrian's presence and his manner toward her was not constrained. His tolerance, though, did not survive the span of a day.

On the next day most of the men who had previously absented themselves from much of the festivities joined the ladies for their morning ride. The only members of the party missing were Lord Moreville, Mr. Canning, Mr. Perceval, and Lord Adrian Searle, who had gone into their host's study immediately after breakfast and given instructions that they were not to be disturbed. Cassandra was a little surprised by Adrian's inclusion, for she knew that he proclaimed frequently and publicly that he had had his fill of politics.

Hannah, riding beside her for part of the way, enlightened her. "Freddy thinks they are going to make a decision about appointing someone to Mr. Alistar's vacant post before we return to London. I had hoped that Matthew would be included in that discussion, but he tells me that it is strictly an internal matter of the Foreign Office and that any interference from the outside would not be to Freddy's favor. But at least Adrian has been included, though he is no longer officially attached to the Foreign Office since he resigned his post." Cassandra, digesting Hannah's use of Adrian's given name, and her easy assumption that Adrian would further her interests, did not respond, and Hannah continued, "There is probably no one in the government who has more firsthand knowledge of the Portuguese than Adrian, and his recommendation of Freddy will go quite well, I should think."

Well-mounted on her hobbyhorse, Hannah continued in this vein for several more minutes, but Cassandra heard very little of what she said. She would have been very surprised to learn that Adrian had recommended Freddy McInnes, of whom he plainly had so little opinion that he did not even waste his energy on contempt for the man. But Hannah obviously thought it quite certain that he would lend his weight to help her husband. Because Hannah had teased him into some sort of promise? Or perhaps as an atonement for having made love to Freddy's wife? It was an unprofitable train of thought, but Cassandra fostered it, searching for anything that would make her wish once and for all to put Adrian out of her life.

She was not experiencing any notable success in this endeavor when Matthew separated himself from Mrs. Perceval and Livia and joined Cassandra and his stepsister. Hannah wasted no time acquainting him with the subject of her monologue, and his response was a quick, contemptuous snort. "I should be surprised indeed, Hannah, if your hopes are realized, at least insofar as Adrian Searle is concerned. He may not be entirely without self-interest in the matter."

Cassandra knew perfectly well she ought to pass up such obvious bait, but could not let it pass. "You do Lord Adrian an injustice, Matthew. I have never known him to be a mean-spirited man. I have no idea at all what his opinion is in this matter, but I would certainly acquit him of acting only in self-interest, whatever he may or may not say or do."

"It would appear that Lord Adrian has found a champion in you, Cass," Matthew replied with an unmistakable edge to his voice.

"As would any man who I felt was being unjustly condemned," she said coolly, and then turned to Hannah in a pointed way and brought the subject to an end by asking her a question about a mutual acquaintance. Matthew continued to ride beside them for a short time in a silence that was far from companionable, and then finally rode off to find more congenial company.

Cassandra was well aware that she was very close to burning her bridges with Matthew, even though she had not yet admitted to herself that she had made up her mind to end her third betrothal. It was not a dread of the consequences of this that held her back, but an uncertainty about her feelings for Adrian. She wanted him. Desperately. But she was still not ready to call her longing for him love. Once she had jilted Matthew, she would have to give Adrian an answer that he could not refute, and she simply was not ready to do that.

By the time the company assembled that night for dinner, she had successfully avoided exchanging anything more than commonplaces with Adrian, though matters concerning him that were far from commonplace were constantly in her thoughts. Whatever decision had come from the discussion that morning of the vacancy in the Foreign Office, it remained unknown, at least to Cassandra, and apparently to Hannah as well, for she was obviously in a state of anxious expectation for the remainder of the day. By dinner, Cassandra assumed that no one had approached Freddy, and Hannah was in a frenetic humor, flirting outrageously with all of the men and laughing at nearly everything that was said to her, usually a bit too loudly.

Cassandra expected her to eventually fasten her attention on Adrian, and she was not disappointed. Adrian was one of the first men to join the ladies in the withdrawing room after dinner, and Hannah singled him out the moment he came into the room. Cassandra, standing by the pianoforte sorting through music for something to play, was well fixed to watch them covertly, and she did not resist the temptation to do so. Hannah linked her arm in Adrian's and would have led him toward a sofa, but Adrian stood firm. After a minute or two of conversation, Hannah reddened visibly and dropped her hand away from his arm. For a moment Cassandra, astonished into staring openly, thought that Hannah would create a scene in some manner, for the rage was plain to see in her expression. But she simply walked away from him.

Cassandra looked about her to see if anyone else had observed, but the others were engaged in their own conversations and did not look to have noticed that scandal had nearly erupted in their midst. When

Adrian came over to her a few minutes later, she said without preamble, "You have been putting La McInnes out of countenance. Is that sensible?"

" 'Heaven has no rage'?"

"I was thinking more in terms of unpleasantness when we are all in such close society, but yes, that too." She could not help feeling a little surge of happiness at his implication that he had scorned Hannah. "Hannah has a rapier tongue and she is indiscriminate in her use of it."

He shrugged with unstudied indifference. "She has no poison about me in which to dip her barbs, and in any case, I don't refine too much upon it. She has the hide of a rhinoceros."

Cassandra, glancing up and seeing Hannah's fulminating gaze on them, was not so sanguine. "What did you say to her?" she said, turning back to her perusal of the music.

"I believe I suggested that she would be wise to look to her husband, who is in a fair way to drinking himself under the table as usual," he said, a touch of sardonicism in his voice. "She has been pestering me for the past month to use what influence I have to secure Alistar's post for McInnes, but I told her plainly that the king himself probably couldn't manage it with Moreville, Perceval, and even Portland, I have heard, against it. Could you play this, do you think?" he added, handing her a piece of music he had unearthed from the bottom of the pile.

She took the printed music and saw that it was a piece by Mozart. "It is for four hands," she said, handing it back to him.

"Yes. I know. Can you play it?"

She had had no idea that he played, and it concerned her a little to realize she had all but given her heart to a man she knew so little about. The piece did not look easy to sight-read, but she accepted the challenge and discovered that he played so splendidly that he was even able to cover her occasional mistakes.

When they were done, she turned and regarded him frankly.

"Have my shirt points wilted, Miss Tilton?" he asked, quizzing her.

"I was thinking how little I know you. You play exceptionally well, my lord."

"The result of a tutor who bound me to my studies and beat me soundly if I did not practice several hours a day," he said, and added in a softer tone, "We might remedy our lack of knowledge of each other."

Cassandra did not ask him how this might be accomplished, for she knew well enough what he suggested. She did not respond, instead turning to an admirer who was begging for more music. With a pretty modesty she declared that she was no match for Adrian's skill and begged that he would play more without her. For Adrian to refuse or to follow her as she rose from the instrument would have been churlish, so he gracefully acquiesced and Cassandra made her escape. It was not long afterward that, pleading the headache, she went up to her room.

Cassandra had no headache, nor was she at all tired. After undressing and dismissing her maid, she picked up a book to read, but made little progress, even though it was a novel by her favorite author. She knew that Harry was right. She had to make a decision about her betrothal to Matthew and resolve her feelings for Adrian without delay. It was not her nature to be indecisive, but the entire peace and contentment of her life hinged on her making the right choice now, and she feared it.

She had been so sure of her betrothal to Matthew. So sure that the life she would have with him would bring her exactly what she most wanted. She had had love and passion with Ned and had been equally certain that she did not wish to base a marriage on pure emotion. Then Adrian had come to her betrothal ball, and she had never really known her own mind since.

It was a warm night, even away from the metropolis, and Cassandra sat curled into a chair clad in only a pale blue silk nightdress. When she heard the scratching at her door, she assumed it was Livia come to see if she still had the headache, and so she rose and opened the door without putting on her dressing gown.

It was Adrian. He was still fully dressed and had obviously not yet gone to his room. This was so unexpected that she regarded him blankly until he moved past her, closed the door, and turned the key in the lock, pocketing it.

She hardly knew whether to be angry or laugh. "Adrian, you can't—" she began, but was silenced as she found herself enfolded in his arms. The kiss was long and lingering and she did nothing at all to resist it. He released her only to scoop her into his arms and carry her across the room to the bed.

"Adrian, stop this," she said as firmly as she could. "Put me down at once. You can't suppose I mean to allow you to ravish me?"

He paid her not the least heed. When he reached the bed he laid her on it tenderly and knelt with one knee on the bed beside her. "I won't ravish you," he said, speaking for the first time.

In the dark shadows created by the bed hangings and the unsteady light of the candles, his eyes were very dark and seemed to glitter as his pupils caught the light. Looming over her, he reminded her of a dark bird of prey. The vision that this conjured up of herself as a field mouse to his hawk was too much for her gravity, and tension was released in soft laughter.

He got into bed beside her but did not immediately touch her. He propped himself up on one elbow and looked down at her. In spite of his outward display of assurance, it was not until this moment that the last of his anxiety at what her response would be began to fade. But he wanted more than passive acquiescence. "Well, at least you are not screaming the house down," he said, smiling. "Tell me you are not in the least in love with me and I promise to give you the peace you claim to crave and never importune you again."

He spoke with such quiet confidence that it was

obvious what he expected her answer to be. "I . . . I sometimes think I am obsessed by you," she said unsteadily, still not willing to commit herself.

"It wasn't out of sight, out of mind, was it?" he pressed.

"I've said I missed you."

"Ah, my beautiful girl, it was so much more than that for me," he said softly, and his lips found hers. There was none of the usual passion in this kiss, but something far more enticing: an exquisite gentleness that spoke of his longing for her far better than fevered kisses would have done.

She felt the length of his body against hers, and the beat of his heart seemed to mingle with the pounding of her own. He untied the ribbons that bound the bodice of her nightdress and pushed back the soft material, exposing her breasts, which hardened in the cool air. He caught his breath at the sight of her bared white flesh, as though he were beholding the nakedness of a woman for the first time.

If it was mere seductive artistry, Cassandra acknowledged that it was successful. Every touch seduced her will to resist him little by little. As his lips found her taut nipples, little fingers of pleasure played upon her spine, gathered in her thighs, and spread upward with an exquisiteness that she longed to have overwhelm her. His hand parted her thighs with no resistance at all.

We're going to make love, she thought, and the realization of the inevitability of it gave her back her will to resist. He did not accept this rejection meekly, but gathered her to him again, reclaiming her lips and defying her to resist him. With her own desire fighting her, it was almost impossible, but she managed it. She pushed away from him more forcefully and sat up. "You said you wouldn't ravish me," she reminded him, her voice unsteady.

"I hoped it wouldn't be necessary," he countered, but without menace, so she did not fear him. "Come to me, Cass," he said, his voice dark with desire.

"I can't," she said, hoping her voice didn't sound as unsettled to him as it did to her.

He sighed heavily, and looked away from her, but after a minute he sat up also. "You aren't going to marry Bourne," he said with no trace of doubt.

Cassandra could not contradict him. "No. I am not."

"Because of me?"

"Yes."

"Will you marry me, Cass?" he asked without any trace of arrogance.

Her heart fairly screamed the word "yes," but she said, "I want to spend my life with a man who makes me feel comfortable, not one who keeps my pulses racing."

"I should endeavor to do both," he parried. "A rapid pulse is not so bad a thing if properly tempered by a contented domesticity."

She smiled doubtfully. "And you would promise me that?"

"I would promise you that," he said with quiet simplicity. "It is what I most exactly wish for myself." Cassandra desperately wanted to be convinced, but the memory of similar words spoken to her by Ned prevented her from saying the one word that would assure her happiness and his. He saw her hesitation and understood her fears, all the more so now that he knew what manner of man Tarkington was. He gently embraced her again, but without passion. "I know you are afraid that I will betray you and hurt you, but I swear to you on all that my honor is worth to me, I want no other woman but you. Lying with another woman might give me release, but never satisfaction."

Cassandra tried to harden her heart against his words, but for the first time since she had schooled it against loving Ned, she had lost her control of that organ. Tears sprang into her eyes, but they owed nothing to sorrow. He recognized them for what they were and pulled her tight against him again, kissing her as he had at first, with exquisite gentleness.

Now that he was sure of her, he accepted her refusal

to immediately consummate their acknowledged love for each other meekly. The only off note occurred when Cassandra refused to inform Matthew and her family immediately of her decision. He took immediate exception to this, feeling that it made her promise to him less absolute.

"You are not being fair to either of us by not letting Bourne know how matters stand at once," he insisted with a touch of asperity. He was not conscious of any particular urge to pay Matthew out for the times he had asserted his rightful possessiveness of Cassandra, but he meant for there to be no future opportunities for such a display.

"We shall be back in town by Friday, and I shall tell him then," Cassandra said, refusing to be convinced. She got up from the bed, fearing a different sort of persuasion, which she might find harder to resist. "I think it would be wrong of me not to tell Harry and Livia first what I mean to do, and I don't want to do that until we are home. I wouldn't want to do anything that would be upsetting for them."

"Such as plighting your troth to me," Adrian said caustically.

"Now you are not being fair," she chided, putting on her dressing gown for good measure. "You know Harry has fears that you have designs on my portion, and they both dread the inevitable scandal. It will be nothing short of a nine-day wonder when it is announced that I am ending my betrothal to Matthew and am to marry you instead."

"If you marry Bourne, you may save yourself a good deal of trouble," he offered, getting up.

"It would serve you right if I did change my mind." She went over to him and put her arms around his neck. "Nothing will prevent the gossip, but if we do nothing to put anyone out of frame while we are here, it will at least avoid any premature whispering that will be conjecture of the worst sort. What are a few more days?"

Her lips were very close to his, inviting him to kiss

them. But he in his turn would not allow himself to be seduced. "It is a few days of our life which can never be recaptured and which might have been spent together."

"Very pretty," she commended, "but I am not persuaded. Do this to please me, Adrian?"

He didn't like it but he could not refuse, and so he left her untouched when he wanted more than anything to make her his incontrovertibly, and in the morning, when he saw her at breakfast, he greeted her with the casual civility of an acquaintance.

# 9

$I$T was Hannah McInnes who first suggested an expedition to the ruins of Lissell Abbey, which was some twenty miles from Caver, a moldering but picturesque pile which she declared would be exactly the place for a picnic. This was the day of Lady Caverstone's birthday, but no particular entertainments had been scheduled until the evening, when a party to which many of the Caverstones' neighbors had been invited was planned. The earnest discussions which had so occupied the men of the party at the outset appeared to have been satisfactorily concluded, or at least settled for the moment, and the scheme was lauded by all.

There were nearly thirty guests at Caver Castle, but Lord Caverstone's excellent stable was equal to mounting them, and all but a few of the ladies elected to ride. Lady Caver left to inform her cook that a cold luncheon packed into baskets would be required, and her guests returned to their various chambers to dress appropriately for the outing.

Adrian was about to mount the stairs when he felt a hand on his arm and turned to face Matthew Bourne. "I would like to have a word with you, Searle."

Adrian regarded him for a moment, supposing that this interview would be similar to the one he had had with Ned, but even more directly to the purpose of warning him away from Cassandra. It was not unexpected, and perhaps long overdue, but now, secure of Cassandra, he had little patience for it and regretted agreeing to Cassandra's wish to wait until they returned to town to inform Bourne how matters now stood. "Of course, if you wish it," he said with a brief nod, resigning himself to the unavoidable.

He waited for Matthew to begin, but Matthew said, "I think it would be best if we were more private. The small saloon just before the library will do." Adrian agreed reluctantly and followed him to that room.

"I think it is time that we speak plainly to one another," Matthew said, without waiting for Adrian to sit down or bothering to do so himself. "As you know, it is little more than a month before I shall be married to Cassandra Tilton. I certainly wish to be understanding of her preferences and friendships, but by allowing you to single her out for your attentions she has left herself open to censure. I cannot believe that as a man of honor you would wish to harm her in any way. If a word in your ear could prevent any future unpleasantness, I would be very remiss not to utter it."

Adrian listened to this pompous speech, keeping fragile control on his temper. He regarded his rival through hooded eyes. "My good fellow," he said with a drawl expressive of extreme ennui, "you have just put a great many of them in both ears. I am obtuse, no doubt, but what precisely am I to infer from your volubility?"

Matthew was annoyed by this want of wit, unaware that that was the intent of it. "I wish you to sever your connection with Miss Tilton."

"Do you speak for Cass?" Adrian asked, deliberately using her given name because he knew it would further disturb the baronet.

"She is a young, gently bred woman," Matthew replied. "She is not always to know what is best for her. A husband's guidance must at times supersede her immediate wishes."

Adrian nearly laughed in his face, but managed to say with a commendably straight face, "If you think that Cass will be easily led, you don't know her well enough to marry her. Perhaps you should sever *your* connection with her. It is better advice than you have given me."

Spots of color came into Matthew's face. "You are damned impudent."

"Am I? I think you'd better speak with Cass before you make decisions for her." It was not Adrian's intention to hint of his understanding with Cassandra, but the words were out and he could not regret them. "You might discover that your guidance is no longer required."

The color in Bourne's face deepened to an angry flush. "What the devil does that mean? You had better explain yourself, my lord."

Pushing away the pricking of his conscience, Adrian said with a smile that was quite intentionally lascivious, "Oh, I don't think that's necessary, do you?"

From his expression, Adrian half-expected Matthew to call him out in a jealous rage, but like Ned Tarkington, the baronet had more concern for his skin than his honor, and Matthew merely said coldly, "Perhaps not." Without another word, he turned on his heel and left the room.

When he had gone, Adrian cursed himself soundly. He recalled only too well the contempt he had felt for Ned Tarkington when that man had hinted that he and Cassandra had been lovers, and now guilty of the same crime, he turned that contempt in full measure upon himself. He knew he ought to have restrained his too-ready tongue, whatever the provocation, and could only hope he hadn't endangered the very happiness he had worked so hard to bring about.

Mrs. Cooper, Lady Caverstone's housekeeper, was persuaded to make up three large hampers of food, and a little over an hour after Hannah had suggested it, the entire party was mounted and ready to start off, with the exception of Lady Agatha Sellet, who declared she would liefer starve than pursue her lunch across the countryside on the back of a smelly horse. Since everyone was well-acquainted with Lady Agatha's dislike of horses and willfully contrary nature, her comments placed no damper on the party and she was left to her own devices while the others prepared for a day of rustic pleasures at Lissell Abbey.

Cassandra knew it would not be easy to behave toward Matthew as if all were still well between them, but she supposed she could be actress enough to carry it off, however much she might dislike the necessity of dissembling. Left to her own feelings in the matter, she would have pleased Adrian by telling Matthew at once, but the practical side of her nature, which refused to allow her to have her head, knew that she had made the wise decision.

She was genuinely sorry to have once again mistaken her feelings, for she had no wish to give Matthew pain even if it was to his pride rather than his heart. She meant to tell him the very day they returned to town, and though it would not be a pleasant interview and she did not look forward to it, yet her spirits soared whenever she thought of the aftermath, which would give her her freedom to marry Adrian.

As they rode toward Lissell Abbey, Cassandra was careful always to ride with several of the others so that Adrian could not single her out, which she feared he might do, since he had only grudgingly accepted her decision to wait before telling Matthew and her family. But Matthew was not put off by her strategy and skillfully maneuvered her into riding beside him alone. Cassandra was not pleased with this, in part because she knew that Adrian would take her to task for it, but mostly because at this point she certainly wished for no intimacy of any sort with Matthew.

Her disinclination to be *tête-à-tête* with Matthew increased as he made no effort at even polite conversation and responded to her efforts with a clipped coldness. She would have been a fool not to realize that he was extremely vexed about something, so she subsided, supposing he would inform her of the cause when he saw fit. Her conscience alone prevented her

THE ICE MAIDEN                 163

from riding off and allowing him to stew alone as he
pleased.

He slowed his pace until the others had outstripped
them and were out of earshot. He then said abruptly,
"I have something I must say to you, Cassandra, and I
don't care to wait until we return to the house. Since
the very night of our betrothal ball you have shown a
marked regard for Lord Adrian Searle that has consist-
ently skirted the bounds of propriety. We have never
pretended that ours was a love match, but certainly
our promises to each other should command mutual
respect. I shall not stand the fool while you and your
lover laugh up your sleeves at me."

Cassandra pulled up her horse and turned to stare at
him in angry astonishment. "My lover? How dare you,
Matthew?"

"There is nothing to be served by lying. Searle does
not even honor you enough to protect your name. He
made it quite clear to me in what relationship he
stands to you." This was not strictly true, but it was
what he had chosen to read into Adrian's words, and
Cassandra's expression, which was of shocked dismay,
removed the last of his doubt.

"*He* told you that? When?"

"This morning before we left. Why should it surprise you that he holds you in no respect when you
have abandoned your honor to him?"

Cassandra stared at him expressionlessly for a moment, her emotions a combination of fury, which made
her distrustful of what she might say to him, and guilt
because she knew that he was not so very far from the
truth. Not daring to answer him, she turned and applied her heels to her horse. Matthew continued beside her. "I shall permit you to cry off," he informed
her. "If you do not, I shall certainly do so, allowing it
to be known that I had little choice. I see no reason
why my honor should be impugned when it is I who
have been hardly used."

"I don't know what Adrian has told you," she said,
barely controlling a tremor in her voice as rage threat-

ened to express itself in furious tears, "but you are mistaken. Adrian Searle is not my lover. Though you expected me to accept your protestations about Mrs. Maybrith, I won't condemn you for a hypocrite. Nor shall I beg you to reconsider ending our betrothal. I had come to the conclusion myself that we should not suit, and I intended to tell you as soon as we returned to town."

"No, Cassandra, we should most certainly not suit." He drew rein again. "Pray offer my apologies to our hostess and Lord and Lady Tilton."

"You are returning to the house?"

"I am returning to London. I have already directed my man to pack and have my carriage made ready."

Cassandra had spoken over her shoulder, but now she pulled up her horse and turned toward him again. "If you leave in such a way, it will cause a deal of talk."

"No doubt you will say all that is necessary. You have a talent for deception; I don't doubt it will come to your aid." With these words he turned and kicked his horse into a canter and left Cassandra in the middle of the road.

Cassandra sat where she was for a few moments, staring after his retreating figure. She could not really condemn Matthew. She knew she had been less than fair to him, even if she had not deceived him intentionally. Robbed of one object for her anger, she turned to a more convenient source. She found it hard to believe that Adrian would tell Matthew that they were lovers even if it had been true in the fullest sense, but she didn't doubt that he had said something to Matthew to put him in such a state, and she could only conclude that he had done so to force her hand.

Only one or two people commented on Matthew's absence, and Cassandra, with a mind to the fact that she would have to explain his return to London as well, put it about that while they had fallen a little behind the others, a groom had ridden up to them with a message for Matthew to return to the house. If no one questioned her too closely—and no one was likely to, except possibly Hannah McInnes—she hoped to manage with a vague story of his being sent for by the bailiff of Bourne Hall to resolve some pressing problem on the estate. The only thing which would land her in the suds was if any servants were questioned about the nonexistent message, and this was even less likely. In any case, the excuse needed to serve only until they were all returned to London. Then, when the news was published that she was not to marry Matthew after all, everyone would guess the truth, but it wouldn't matter any longer.

When the party reached the abbey, the day was fairly advanced due to their easy progress and it was decided that they would partake of the luncheon before exploring the ruins. Adrian did not join the Tiltons as he had at Mrs. Lytten's *al fresco* party, and Cassandra ate sparingly, her anger making up for her lack of appetite. It didn't help her humor that she knew she had to tell Livia of her quarrel with Matthew, and the result of it, before they returned to the house. She could scarcely pretend that nothing was amiss when Matthew had so abruptly returned to town. The others might or might not accept whatever excuse she concocted, but Livia would never believe anything short of the truth.

The Farelands had sat with them for luncheon, and Cassandra did not want to speak in front of Sarah, who would probably condemn her, and so she said nothing, the task of dissembling she had earlier imagined to be of no great difficulty much more onerous now. When luncheon was finally finished the company began to gather to begin the exploration of the ruin, with the guidance of their host, who informed them that while most of what remained of the abbey was sound, there were areas, due to rubble and occasionally falling debris, that were not. Others, grouped in twos and threes, chose simply to enjoy the surrounding grounds, which were quite lovely, though in a wild sort of way.

Lord Moreville, in the company of Hannah, was one of the latter, and Sarah, who watched them go off in a way that Cassandra found pathetic, was persuaded reluctantly by her husband to join the larger expedition. As she and Livia packed a few remaining items into one of the hampers, Cassandra seized the opportunity for a word with her sister-in-law. She did not embroider the truth in the least, but told Livia plainly that she had already made up her mind to end her betrothal to Matthew and marry Adrian. She was considerably more vague about the reason that Matthew had accosted her and ended their connection himself. But Livia was too discerning to let it pass, and reluctantly Cassandra admitted that he had accused her and Adrian of being lovers.

"Is it true?" Livia asked after a silent moment.

Cassandra used the excuse of wrapping up a bit of bread to avoid meeting her eyes. "Not precisely."

"But near enough, I expect," Livia said flatly. "Then it is just as well that you are to marry him, isn't it?"

But at the moment Cassandra was furious enough with Adrian to want to make herself a widow before she was a bride. Cassandra looked up and saw the subject of their discussion approaching them. She put the bread in the basket and stood up. "Are you very upset with me, Livy?"

Livia reached up and took her hand. "How could I be? I only want you to be happy, Cass."

"I am happy with Adrian," Cassandra assured her with a confident smile. "Happier than I can ever recall feeling before. To please me," she added, "will you promise not to tell Harry that I am to marry Adrian until I have the opportunity to do so myself? He disapproves of Adrian in some ways and I want to assure him that I am making the right choice."

Livia agreed, though reluctantly, for it was not in her nature to keep anything from her husband. "I think Harry will take it better than you think," she said. "He, too, only wants your happiness. I only wish that you had met Lord Adrian before you had plighted your troth to Matthew—it would certainly have saved a deal of fuss," she added with some asperity, "but you should know that I would not lend my voice to those that would condemn you." This was quite generous, considering that some of the mud generated by the inevitable gossip was certain to spatter her and Harry as well. She let go of Cassandra's hand and greeted Adrian as naturally as if Cassandra had said nothing to her at all.

"The abbey is really rather a bore except for the cloister, which is pretty intact and worth seeing," Adrian said after informing them that he was quite familiar with the ruin. He addressed Cassandra and Livia equally. "We can go there directly and avoid the dull parts if you'd care to see it."

Livia, with only a quick speaking glance at Cassandra to give herself away, declined, claiming no interest in ruins. "I know Caroline Andry is of a similar mind, so we may enjoy a comfortable coze together while the rest of you get nettles caught into your clothes and bruises from falling over rocks."

Cassandra was glad of her refusal to join them and permitted Adrian to take her arm and lead her across the grass. "Matthew is gone," she said almost at once.

"I noticed he had returned to the house. Perhaps that is all to the good. He may be wishful of fixing his interest with Lady Agatha."

As Lady Agatha was respectably married and no less than sixty, Cassandra did not regard this feeble attempt at levity. "He is gone back to London," she said baldly.

"Is he? I hadn't hoped for such luck. What reason did he give?"

"I think you can guess it," she snapped.

"I might," he concurred, his faint hope that Matthew would not inform Cassandra of their earlier interview dashed. "I suppose it had to do with me, if you say it like that."

They entered the opening into the cloister, which was still the shape and breadth of the door which had once been there but was now rotted to dust and bits of iron. As soon as they were inside, she stopped and stepped in front of him so abruptly that he stepped back. There was the sound of voices and laughter drifting toward them, but far enough away that there was no doubt of their privacy. "You wish me to believe that you are not cut from the same cloth as Ned, but even he would not behave as reprehensibly as you have done. How dare you tell Matthew that we are lovers?"

She expected the sort of teasing, coaxing half-denials with which Ned always met her accusations of misconduct, but the smile had faded from his eyes. "I did not do so precisely, but I allowed him to infer it," he said, feeling the sting of her rebuke more than she could know. "I should never have done so, I know. In my defense I can only say that I did not mean to do so, but allowed my dislike of the man to get the better of my sense. And honor." He might have told her that she was mistaken about Ned having more character than to behave in a similar way, but he would not look to lessen his guilt by condemning Tarkington.

His calm admission took some of the wind out of her sails, but she was far from ready to excuse him. "And so you dishonor me."

"There is no dishonor in loving each other if you are to be my wife." He raised his arms as if to embrace her, but she stepped back to avoid it and he dropped his arms again to his sides. "I truly did not mean to injure you in any way. I would never do so. But I can't be sorry that Bourne knows or that he has had the good sense to retire from the field."

"I am not some prize in a tourney, my lord," she said coldly. "We can scarcely announce our betrothal on the heels of Matthew's departure, so in the meantime I shall have to submit to a great deal of whispering and conjecture while pretending that I notice none of it, and it will be far worse when we return to London and the news is spread abroad."

His expression which was one of unaccustomed somberness, gradually lightened as she spoke. "Then you still mean to marry me?"

Cassandra looked surprised. "After today I may have to," she said tartly. "You would be well-served if I did send you packing."

His response to this was to laugh. "I would be," he agreed, "but how I thank God that I am not. It has taken me nearly three months to convince you that we are clearly made for each other. The prospect of another three spent in similar entreaty is a bit daunting."

"It would be unjust of me to put you to such trouble," she said caustically.

"Yes. It would," he agreed, and took her into his arms. They might have gone on in this highly pleasurable manner indefinitely but Cassandra reluctantly called on him to note that the voices they had heard on entering the cloister were distinctly nearer and they were likely in danger of discovery. "What of it? I suppose I may kiss the woman I am to marry if I please."

"As far as everyone knows, it is still Matthew I am to marry."

"It would be best, I think, if we were to marry as quickly as possible," he said. "Since you dread the gossip, that will be one way to silence it. Once you are my wife, with the protection of my name, there will be nothing for anyone to say."

"No, they will be silent, but watch my figure for interesting changes," she said dryly.

He laughed. "So shall I."

They walked through the cloister in the direction of the main part of the abbey. "We might as well snap our fingers in the face of the world and make a grand occasion of it," he suggested. "We could be married from St. George's and hold our wedding breakfast in the ballroom at Tilton House so that we can invite all our particular friends to the celebration."

She regarded him severely. "In the circumstances, I think a quiet wedding would be in better taste."

"How poor-spirited," he exclaimed. "In that case I

see no point to waiting. I'll see to a special license as soon as we are in town."

"I suppose it would be best, but there is no need for unseemly haste," she admonished. "I shall have Harry give notice to the papers at once that I have ended my betrothal to Matthew, and then, in a few months when the talk has died down and it is old news, we may be married quietly, and perhaps we can scrape through with a minimum of scandal."

"I can see I have been sadly mistaken in your character," he commented. "I thought you enjoyed setting the world on its ear, and now you appear to set propriety above all." But he was not to be put off. His tone became more serious and he added, "I don't intend to wait to please your notions of propriety. The fete at Carlton House the night before Prinney leaves for Brighton will mark the unofficial end of the Season. We can leave for Dunwhittie the following day and be married by the end of the week. My brother has houses in Wales, Scotland, and the Lake District, as well as in Somerset, and we might even look about for a house of our own in the fall, so we may be well-amused. By the time we take our places in the world next Season as a married couple, it will certainly be old news."

Cassandra acquiesced so meekly that he regarded her suspiciously, which made her laugh. "I mean to make you a pattern-card wife," she said with unaccustomed primness.

"You are more likely to lead me a pretty dance," he informed her ascerbically.

Cassandra was saved from having to answer this slur upon her character as they finally met up with Lord Caverstone and the party he was guiding about the ruins. No one gave them much notice when Adrian and Cassandra joined the group. Cassandra, however, noticed that Hannah and Robert Moreville had also met up with the others, and the latter was now walking beside Sarah. From the glowering look on her brother-in-law's face, Cassandra feared there might

well be another scandal in the family, and wondered
how she might separate her sister from her folly without setting Sarah's back up and perhaps creating the
very scene she wished to avoid.

Adrian, following his beloved's gaze from one to the
other of that domestic triangle, managed to read her
thoughts with fair accuracy. Privately cursing the fair
countess for being so pigeon-headed, he deposited
Cassandra with Fareland to distract that gentleman
from the vision of his wife gazing longingly on her
lover, and by the simple subterfuge of telling Moreville
that he had something to say to him concerning a
matter they had discussed the previous day, he deftly
removed him from Lady Fareland's side. Sarah, casting
Adrian a baleful glare for his interference, went over
to Hannah and fell into step beside her.

Cassandra, grateful for Adrian's maneuvering, hoped
that it had gone undetected by everyone else, for it
would only add to the gossip if Sarah's family recognized her *affaire*. When she saw Adrian and Moreville,
deep in conversation, head slowly in the opposite direction toward the front of the abbey, she breathed a
sigh of relief and gave up trying to converse with her
brother-in-law, whose replies were monosyllabic and
curt to the point of rudeness. The group passed out of
the great hall of the abbey and into the cloister, and
though Cassandra had no particular desire to view it
again, she drifted along with the others because she
did not care to wander about the main part of the
abbey unescorted, particularly since Lord Caverstone
had warned them that there were areas that were
unsafe for exploring.

As they walked along the still partially covered path,
Lord Caverstone regaled them with an informal history of the abbey, which Cassandra found most interesting, and it was not until she had left the cloister and
was once again outside the abbey that she realized that
Fareland was no longer with them. Trepidation and
exasperation warring for supremacy in her breast, she
looked about, discovered that Sarah, though she was

no longer with Hannah, at least had not tried to rejoin her lover, and decided not to allow herself to be concerned. Several of the others had elected to remain in the abbey for a bit, so it might be no more than that, and in any case, Adrian was probably still with Moreville, and he would know what to do to prevent open confrontation between the two men.

The picnic luncheon had been eaten, the ruins explored, and conversation on the delights of rusticity exhausted. It was clearly time to return to the house to repair from so much exercise and fresh air before dressing for dinner and the party to honor their hostess's birthday. Hampers and blankets were gathered and packed into the cart. Most of the company had mounted and a few had even started down the lane in the wake of the carriages that had gotten off first, when it was noted that two of their number were absent. As one of these was Lady Barbara Hampton and the other Robert Moreville, knowing smiles were exchanged amongst a few. Lady Barbara was a dashing widow who managed to maintain her reputation principally because she was the daughter of a duke and one of the richest women in the realm in her own right, and Moreville's conquests of the fair sex were legendary, though it was not like either to be so openly indiscreet. One or two rather ribald remarks followed Lord Caverstone as he dismounted and headed toward the ruins to find the truant pair.

Sarah, sandwiched between Livia and Cassandra, said in a pointed whisper, "I think they are being disgusting. I am sure it is no such thing as they are suggesting."

"You mean you hope it is not," Cassandra said. "I hope they are found making love in the cloister. Perhaps then you would realize what a fool you are for that man."

"That is sage advice coming from you," Sarah rejoined with a nasty edge in her tone. "I notice Matthew left us before we even arrived, and I for one thought little of your claim that he was fetched back to the house by a message."

While Sarah was still speaking, Lady Barbara appeared, running toward them from the direction of a nearby stream, a bit breathless and exclaiming that they could not leave without her. "I suppose we may expect Moreville to appear out of the bushes at the other side of the abbey," said Freddy McInnes in a stage whisper, embarrassing those about him who heard the remark but not raising a blush on the countenance of Lady Barbara.

"Oh, is Moreville still in the abbey?" she said, a question so obviously artless that no one doubted its sincerity.

"We thought he might be with you," Lord Caverstone said, his tone as inoffensive as he could make it.

Lady Barbara's color did rise a bit then as she took the meaning of his remark, paired with the one made by McInnes. "I haven't set eyes on Moreville since before we first went into the cloister and he went off somewhere with Lord Adrian."

"Then perhaps we should ask Lord Adrian where he is to be found," Hannah said brusquely, impatient for the delay.

"As a matter of fact, we parted in the great hall," Adrian replied. "He wanted to go back through the cloister, so we went off in opposite directions. I have no idea where he went from there."

It was too late to call back the carriages and ask the occupants of these if they knew the whereabouts of Lord Moreville, but the mounted guests all disclaimed having set eyes on the missing earl since at varying times before the majority of guests had left the interior of the abbey.

"Well, he must be somewhere," Lady Barbara said as she remounted her horse with the assistance of a groom. "Who else is not here?"

"We thought he was having a last word with you," Freddy said with a leering smile that left no doubt of his meaning. "There's no one else. Everyone is here now 'cept Moreville."

Caverstone sighed. "Lady Barbara is right. He must be somewhere. He can't have gone back to the house by himself, for his horse is still here. I hope he hasn't had a misadventure in the abbey. We discourage people from going near the living quarters because the passageways are treacherous. We'd best go look for him."

At these words, the men from the party dismounted, and after a few exchanged directions, half of these went into the abbey and half spread out over the grounds. The ladies, remaining mounted, exchanged desultory conversation. It was not very long before the men who had gone into the abbey returned, and their grim faces made it clear that the missing Moreville had suffered some misadventure.

"What is it, Roger?" called out Lady Caverstone to her husband, who led the small band back into the open. "Is Moreville injured?"

"I'm afraid so," Caverstone said, his voice clipped and controlled. Adrian, Mr. Canning, and Lord Knowles, who were amongst those who had searched the grounds, returned at that point and they and all the other men, except for Lord Caverstone, Mr. Canning, and Harry, agreed to return to Caver with the ladies and send assistance to those who remained with Lord Moreville.

Many protested at this, exclaiming a desire to help Moreville, but Caverstone was insistent that he and the two men remaining with him were adequate to meet Moreville's needs and that any more would only make unnecessary fuss and get in the way. Several of the others thought this rather high-handed, but no one defied him, and the reduced company turned their horses and began the return to Caver. Adrian and two or three of the others set their horses off at a brisk canter. After assuring herself that Sarah, though she was white-faced and her eyes had a desperate look, was not going to cause any unpleasantness, Cassandra applied her heels to her horse and went after them, causing Livia, left alone with Sarah, who was clearly only just maintaining her control, to uncharacteristically heap silent maledictions on her departing sister-in-law's head.

Cassandra was well-mounted and soon caught the others up, arriving at Caver almost beside Adrian. She slid down from her saddle without waiting for assistance and went up to Adrian as he was drawing up his stirrups and asked him outright what new accident had befallen Lord Moreville.

Adrian gazed at her without expression for a moment and then said in a flat, abrupt way, "Moreville is dead."

Cassandra was almost startled into repeating the word aloud, but checked herself. "How can it be?" she said, clearly stunned.

"I have no idea," Adrian responded curtly. He patted his horse's neck and then simply walked away from Cassandra, leaving her prey to wild imaginings.

She had no further opportunity to speak with him, for he took a fresh mount and accompanied those who returned to the abbey. She could scarcely contain herself for the wait until he or Harry returned and would bring further news of the accident. There was one advantage, however, to the turmoil the accident had caused: no one attached much notice to Matthew's departure. Even Cassandra herself forgot about him to the point that when Hannah asked if Matthew had been apprised of what had occurred, she nearly replied that she supposed he had, as if he were still at Caver.

The most difficult part of the waiting was keeping control of her sister, who, in her anxiety for her lover, threatened to cast herself headlong into ruin. Cassandra's efforts were not helped by the wry smugness of Lord Fareland, who clearly felt that Moreville, whatever his injury might be, had gotten no more than he deserved. She was quite glad when he finally took himself off with one of the other guests to pass the time with a hand of piquet.

Cassandra insisted that Sarah remain with her, fearing that a retiring to her room to indulge her grief might be commented upon, but when nearly an hour had passed with no word and Sarah looked increasingly as if she might collapse or be sick or both, Cassandra relented and took her up to her own room so that they would not be disturbed by Fareland should he take it in to his head to seek out his wife in her own chamber.

Cassandra was no adherent of the efficacy of laudanum, but in the circumstances she had her maid procure some and sat with Sarah, who had been quietly weeping since they had come into the room, until she finally fell into a restless sleep. Adjuring her abigail not to leave Lady Fareland without fetching her first, she returned downstairs to see if any news had arrived from the abbey.

The litter that was borne back to the house as the day began to wane told its own story. The figure upon it was shrouded from head to toe, and a few of the ladies who had been on the watch exclaimed the dreadful news to the others before the returning men could even enter the house.

Since Lord Moreville had apparently been alone at the time of the accident, little was known of what actually happened, but the assumption was that he had attempted—for an unknown reason—to go through the portion of the abbey which housed the monks' cells and the extensive kitchens, all of which were in an advanced state of decay. The warnings of their host, unheeded, had been horribly fulfilled, and Moreville, falling in the rubble and striking his head on a sharp rock, had paid the greatest price for his contumacy.

It was a very plausible explanation, and in the first shock that was felt by everyone, it was accepted without question. Only one or two commented on the irony of Lord Moreville's having scraped through his previous injury at the hands of the highwayman, only to meet his end at a private party amidst friends. If anyone thought it a little too ironic, no one voiced the thought aloud.

Cassandra knew by Harry's grim countenance and his clipped and reticent manner of speech that he was upset beyond what was called for in the circumstances, and assumed that there had to be more to Moreville's death than was made known. Her mind was too facile not to make the connection between the first and second accidents, and Harry's manner, so reminiscent of the day after her betrothal ball, when Mr. Alistar was found murdered, caused her imagination to draw fantastical conclusions. But she knew better than to tease her brother with questions he would probably refuse to answer.

But she felt no such restriction with Adrian, and after a quick visit to her bedchamber to assure herself that Sarah still slept in blissful ignorance of the horror that awaited her, she managed a private moment with him by waiting for him to come up to dress for dinner and summoning him into a small sitting room as he passed. "Was it really an accident?" she asked the moment the door was closed.

"No, of course not," he said abruptly.

She blanched. "He was murdered!"

"I told you the truth about Moreville because I trust your discretion," he said, speaking with more coolness than he had ever used to her before. "It won't be secret long if you bandy that word about."

"I thought I might speak freely with you," she said, stung by his criticism.

"In a matter such as this, I doubt anyone dare speak freely," he said cryptically, and then asked, "Has Lady Fareland been told yet?"

Cassandra did not know why Moreville's death should have upset him to such a degree, but she had no doubt that this was the cause of his unusual brusqueness, and she refrained from further questions for the moment. "No," she replied. "I gave her some laudanum because I feared she would make a scene when we returned, and now I have been putting off awakening her because she may well fall into hysterics when she learns that he is dead. I think I shall have to confide her *affaire* with Moreville to Livia, though I am certain she guesses already. If anyone can keep Sally calm, it will be Livy."

"Then by all means tell her. There is enough commotion as it is, without a domestic scandal to make it worse."

Cassandra agreed, and in the same quick way he had asked her about Sarah, as if he were a general and she an aide-de-camp reporting the result of a reconnaissance, he demanded to know what was being said of Matthew's unexpected departure. Cassandra's patient forbearance was wearing a bit thin, but she answered easily, "Very little, actually. I was prepared to elaborate on my original excuse that he was called urgently to Bourne Hall, but no one has asked me about it and I would be a fool to volunteer information that I would have to make up from whole cloth in the first place."

He gave her a grim smile, very far removed from his usual dazzling expression that had the power to deprive her of breath. "Matthew's undertakings have very little to interest anyone, in light of what has occurred. It couldn't have happened at a better time, from our point of view."

Cassandra had not particularly liked Robert Moreville, but she thought this remark insensitive, and said so. "I thought I might speak freely with you," he said, mocking her, and Cassandra stared at him for a moment in hurt surprise.

"Are you angry with me from some cause?" she asked, more perplexed than angered by his manner.

He gave vent to a short sigh. "No. It isn't you. I'm sorry." He smiled suddenly in his more usual way. "I slept poorly last night, and this has been an eventful day. But at least now you have seen me at my worst and know what to expect at the breakfast table of an occasional morning. Do you wish to cry off?"

Cassandra smiled, knowing he was now quizzing her. "Not just yet," she responded in kind. "But you know with me it is never a certain thing."

He ran the back of his fingers along her cheek and kissed her lightly. "I know. That is why I intend to wed you as soon as may be. I won't give you the chance to change your mind. What have you told Harry about Bourne's leaving?"

"Nothing. I told Livia the truth, all of it, but I made her promise not to tell Harry that we were to be married until I could do so myself. I doubt that in the circumstances Harry will even notice that Matthew has gone."

"You will tell him as soon as we return." It was not quite a question and just short of a command.

"Yes," she said, laughing. "There is nothing in this world that could make me cry off. I love you, Adrian." He took her in his arms and they were lost to time for a full quarter-hour until Cassandra recalled that she had better speak with Sarah before she went down for dinner, or risk her discovering the truth from another source.

Actually, Sarah, who was awake when Cassandra came into the room, took the news far better than Cassandra had hoped. It was true that her complexion was as white as the sheet she lay upon and that she declared herself too ill to even contemplate dinner, but there were none of the hysterical tears that Cassandra had feared. The following day Cassandra, with the agreement of Livia, in whom she had confided what she knew of Sarah's relationship with Moreville, decided that it would be better if Sarah remained in her room pretending to a touch of influenza rather than join the others, despite how it would look. Sarah's countenance was such a ghastly shade of gray and her eyes so red and sunken that her appearance was certain to cause more talk than her absence. Sarah showed a tendency to fall into the vapors only when Fareland was mentioned or there was the prospect that he would visit her, and though it was not an easy task, Cassandra managed to keep him away.

Tacitly, the party which was to have continued through the end of the week began to break up the following day. Curiosity and concern were overwhelmed by fear of becoming involved in what might yet prove to be a nasty scandal. Despite a refusal to openly acknowledge Lord Moreville's death as anything more than an accident, Lord Caverstone, as magistrate for his district, felt obliged to query each of his guests on his whereabouts from the last time that Moreville had been seen alive and well until it was realized that he was missing. After this there was no containing the speculation that the earl's death was not an accident, but no one was able to glean the slightest information from those who might know the truth of the matter, and so the guests returned to town to concoct their own theories over dinner with friends.

The Tiltons were among the last to leave on Friday morning, three days after the accident. Adrian had left the previous day with most of the other guests, and Cassandra, though she had had little more than public contact with him in the interim, felt the loss of his support more than she cared to admit.

# 10

*T*H E journey from Caver to London was not long, but wearisome, for it had begun to rain soon after they started out and the roads rapidly deteriorated, causing them an uncomfortable ride. Cassandra convinced herself to put off speaking with her brother until the following day. The Farelands had returned home the previous day and Cassandra sent a note to her sister offering to call if she wished for company, but her missive was returned to her with a brief message from the Fareland butler that Lady Fareland was out for the evening.

On the following morning Cassandra knew she could no longer cry craven, and after breakfast, before Harry could join his secretary in his study, she linked her arm through his and asked if they could walk out in the garden for a few minutes before he turned to matters of business.

"Of course, if you like," he replied without hesitation, though Cassandra knew from conversation on the journey home that he had many pressing matters awaiting him.

"I have news that may not please you, Harry, but I hope you will be happy for me," she said as they walked out onto the gravel path.

He sighed. "I suppose it is Searle."

Cassandra, though she had not meant to appeal to his emotions, nodded and said, "I love him very much, Harry."

"Yes," Harry said quietly. "I suspected it was that way with you after Sir Matthew left so abruptly." He sighed again, a heavy sound. "I had hoped it would not be so."

"You are wrong about him, Harry. I really have no doubt that his love for me is genuine. He does claim that the source of his income is judicious investment, but there is no reason at all to doubt him. Many men have parlayed a small amount into a fortune in such a way. I cut my eyeteeth years ago. I can't believe I could be so taken in."

Harry put his hand over hers, a gesture of sympathy that she found both vexing and a little alarming. "I can't say what Searle's true feelings are for you, Cass, but if what I am coming to fear is true, it will be impossible for you to marry him. I am very sorry," he added, and there was no doubting his sincerity.

There was something so ominous in his tone that Cassandra felt as if her heart had been clutched. She stopped, feeling as if her legs would give way if her brother removed the support of his arm. "Well, what is it, Harry?" she said as steadily as she could manage. "If you are going to assassinate his character, I have a right to see what weapons you mean to use."

Harry gave a short, mirthless laugh. "A very apt choice of words, Cassandra, though you do not realize it. I think it might be best if we sat down over there," he said, nodding toward an iron bench near a grouping of shrubs which overlooked the rest of the garden.

"Moreville's death was no accident," Harry said, causing his sister to stare at him.

"I know," she replied, "but what has that to do with Adrian?"

The viscount's eyes narrowed. "How did you know that it wasn't an accident?"

The question was spoken with such abruptness that Cassandra wished she had held her tongue. Adrian had warned her to be discreet; no doubt he should not have told her himself. But she could think of no lie to account for her knowledge, and she knew that Harry would not let her bluff her way out of an answer. "It is being suggested by more than one person," she said, and added, "But it was Adrian who told me that it was true in fact."

Harry's eyes opened a little. "Did he? Did he say how he knew this?"

"No. But he was with you and the others when you returned with the body, so I assumed it must have been in some way obvious and known to each of you."

"It was obvious," Harry answered, "but only to those of us who actually found Moreville. We moved the body to conceal the manner of his death before the others arrived from the house so that we might have time to discover the truth without embroiling us all in a sweeping scandal. When Searle returned with Hart and Knowles, it appeared to be nothing more than what we claimed it to be, a death by misadventure."

Cassandra sat quiet for a long moment before speaking. "How did Moreville die?"

"He was struck, and struck repeatedly, on the head by a jagged stone. We found it next to the body, the blood and hair on it leaving no doubt that it was the weapon used. It was not in such a position that he could have fallen on it, and in any case, it was clear that the wound was caused by several blows."

"No one could take anyone unawares in the abbey," she said with determined skepticism. "There is so much litter about that it is impossible to move about silently. I can't believe that Moreville simply stood there and allowed himself to be killed."

"No," Harry said with a grim smile, "it is unlikely, particularly after his meeting with the highwayman, which, as you yourself suggested, was also somewhat suspicious in nature."

"Then perhaps it was an accident," she said bracingly. "You may see too much significance in it because of that dreadful accident."

Harry shook his head. "*I* believe that Moreville fell, or was pushed off balance, or even tripped—in fact, the knees of his breeches were dirty and torn—and while he was down, or perhaps struggling to his feet, his assailant struck him. Standing over a kneeling man,

I don't think it would require much in the way of finesse or even force. And the weapon was easy to hand."

"But who would wish to kill Robert Moreville except perhaps for a husband who . . .?" Cassandra broke off abruptly, remembering that Fareland had disappeared as they were leaving the abbey. But a greater shock was in store for her, and put all thought of her brother-in-law from her mind.

Harry, not hearing the latter, answered the first. "I do not yet understand why he would wish to murder Moreville, but I think you should know that the circumstantial evidence, at least, is telling against Adrian Searle."

"Adrian!" Cassandra was so aghast that she raised her voice and was hushed by her brother.

"No one admits to seeing Moreville again after he approached Searle and they wandered off together while in conversation. Several people did note, however, that they had turned in the great hall in the direction of the living quarters, which was where the body was found."

"What does Adrian say?" she asked, tight-lipped.

"That he left Moreville in the great hall and proceeded through the abbey rather than coming out through the cloister, though that was the quickest way to return to the grounds."

"But this is absurd," Cassandra said with a short, desperate laugh. "Next you will say that he was in two places at once and held up Moreville's phaeton on the King's Road."

"He may have had an accomplice," Harry said with perfect seriousness. "There is also the matter of Mr. Alistar."

"Alistar! Dear God, Harry!"

"As I've said," Harry said with unimpaired control, "I don't yet understand the motive, but I know that in every case, the common denominator is Adrian Searle. He left our house that night at the same time as Alistar and Petersham, going off with them even though it was in an opposite direction to his lodgings. He claims, of course, that he was visiting a friend, and parted company with Alistar at Curzon Street. Petersham left them before that, so all that we know is that Searle was the last-known person to see him alive. He declines to mention the name of the person he visited, for reasons of honor," Harry added with an arid smile. "In the case of the incident on the King's Road, you will recall that it was he who came with Moreville, and it was his suggestion that I trade places with him in the phaeton."

He was clearly not finished with his case against Adrian, but Cassandra had heard enough. "I cannot believe what I am hearing, Harry," she said, but her brother held up his hand and begged her to hear him out.

"The connection between Alistar, Moreville, and Searle is all too obvious," he continued. "There was a great deal of confusion in the last days before the Braganzas fled to Brazil, and a good many rumors of collaboration of both high-ranking Portuguese ministers and even some of the English. Antonio Araujo, minister of foreign affairs, was certainly suspected, and he and Searle were known to be on very easy terms. Strangford thought enough of it to comment on it in his dispatches, though, in fairness, he did so without in any way impugning Searle's character."

"Which is more than you are doing," she said indignantly. "What earthly reason could Adrian have for collaborating with the French?" It was so preposterous that she was almost relieved. A more plausible motive would have shaken her.

"The most common reason of all. Money."

"No!" The word was an explosion, and she stood up. "I can't believe such a thing."

"I can."

Brother and sister turned to see Sarah standing a few feet from them on the path leading to the bench. With their backs to the house and engrossed in their discussion, they had not heard her approach.

"Oh, my poor Robert." Her voice was a soft wail. "Murdered!" she cried, and then in fine dramatic tradition crumpled like a bit of tissue and fell into a dead faint across the path before either could reach her.

By tacit agreement, the Tiltons decided it was best to leave their sister unconscious for the moment, and Harry carried Sarah into the house directly to Cassandra's own bedchamber without trying to revive her. Livia was out on a morning call and they had the good fortune to meet no servants in the halls on the way upstairs.

Cassandra had the wry thought that in the events of the past few days she had abandoned all claim to discretion, and now informed her brother of their sister's *affaire* with Moreville. Pretended ignorance at this point would have tangled explanations beyond hope of clarity. Like Livia, Harry had guessed at the truth and only commented that it was unfortunate that Sarah had chosen that particular moment to eavesdrop.

But Cassandra had concern for more than her sister's excess of sensibility. She did not intend to leave matters as they were with her brother without saying what she felt. "I understand what you have told me, Harry," she said in a very soft voice to avoid arousing Sarah, "but I will tell you that I cannot believe a word of it. You will probably tell me that I am allowing my feelings to color my judgment, but it is not so. I am not so sure that it is not your dislike of Adrian that colors yours."

Harry was clearly injured. "Cass! Acquit me of that! I *don't* dislike Searle. I've told you that. I simply mistrust his motives in singling out a woman he knows to be promised to another and thereby courting her disgrace."

"I am not disgraced in any fashion," Cassandra said coolly. "If Adrian had not persisted, I might in a month's time have made a mistake which I should certainly have regretted for the remainder of my life."

"If you marry Searle you may have far deeper regrets."

Cassandra moved to the dressing table to find her vinaigrette. "I am sorry, Harry, but I will not listen to you. If you had proof against him, that would be one thing, but all you have is slanderous speculation. Surely some portion of his explanation for his fortune may be checked to discount so base a motive, if only you would do so."

"Cass, I am not insisting that you enter into my suspicions, I'm only asking you not to be too hasty at tying yourself to Searle," he pleaded. "It is only concern for you that has made me speak, or I would have said nothing at all until I had positive evidence."

"You won't find any," Cassandra said with certainty.

"I hope you may be right," said Harry. "I give you my pledge to do all I can to learn the truth, either for or against Searle."

Cassandra applied the vinaigrette to her sister's nose and Sarah revived almost at once, setting up such a dreadful keening wail that Cassandra wished she had left her unconscious. They managed between them to quieten their distraught sister, but Cassandra felt she would deal better with Sarah by herself and asked Harry to leave them, which he did with undisguised relief.

Sarah had been weeping softly but her sobs began to increase in frequency and volume until her sister advised her that if she set up a wail again she would box her ears.

"You are completely unfeeling," Sarah said, sniffing and hiccuping. "The man I love better than any in the world is dead, and not by a sad chance of fate, but by the hand of a murdering monster."

"Don't be absurd," Cassandra advised her. "That is complete nonsense and you know it."

"I heard what Harry said about Lord Adrian."

"It is the merest speculation, which he himself admits."

Sarah took the handkerchief that Cassandra handed to her and blew her nose with force. "I think it is more. I see now what Hannah was trying to hint to me when I confided my fears to her yesterday."

"Hannah! What has she to say to anything?"

"Freddy is in the Foreign Office and he would know what is being said. When I told her that I feared that Robert's accident might have been the result of a quarrel with Fareland, she said I must not allow myself to be fanciful, and stressed that Adrian Searle was the last to be seen with Robert and that there was no reason to believe that Fareland or anyone else was with Robert after that. I thought at the time that she was only reassuring me that it was an accident."

Cassandra rose from her perch on the edge of the bed and returned the vinaigrette to the dressing table. "If anyone is going to sit for the portrait of murderer, Fareland would be the perfect model. God knows, *he* had motive enough." She had certainly thought of Charles Fareland as the possible murderer of Robert Moreville, but she would never have uttered her suspicion if her brother and sister between them had not upset her with their ready accusations of Adrian. "Just before we came out of the abbey, I noted that Charles had gone off somewhere. He may well have followed Adrian and Moreville and waited until Adrian left to confront Moreville."

Sarah abandoned her languishing posture and sat bolt upright. "Charles would never do such a thing. I could believe that he and Robert fought, and in the scuffle, Robert fell and struck his head, but never that Charles would deliberately murder him. It is very wicked of you to suggest such a thing just to protect your lover."

She saw no irony in her words. Cassandra, though she was angry, maintained her calm. "Don't judge me by your own behavior, Sally," she said with just a bit of edge to her voice. "Adrian is not my lover, but he is going to be my husband, so I think it would be best if *you* did not say wicked things about him."

"You couldn't marry such a man," Sarah cried, aghast.

"I can and I will," she said in a voice too firm to

leave any doubt of her intention. "Therefore, you had best keep your stupid theories to yourself for all of our sakes." Not trusting her check on her temper, she turned and left Sarah to make her own way out of the house.

She went back to the garden and walked briskly along the paths, and since the garden was not large, circuited it several times before her calm returned to her, though to her chagrin it could not be complete. She could not, like her brother and sister were all too ready to do, convict Adrian on such evidence, but the seed of doubt had been planted. Sarah's opinions she could easily dismiss, but Harry was neither a fanciful nor a rash man and his suspicions could not be entirely disregarded, however much she wished to do so.

As well as she could, she examined the facts that she knew without prejudice. At the end of it she was still inclined to disbelieve the circumstantial evidence against Adrian, but could not entirely absolve him. Her heart might do so, but her mind, with its strong pragmatic bent, would not.

When she judged that Sarah had left, Cassandra returned to her room and changed into her riding habit. At such an unfashionable hour, Hyde Park would be virtually free of any members of the *ton*, so she could enjoy a bit of exercise that would hopefully serve to exorcise her suspicions. She remained out until after the hour for luncheon, and when she rode up to the house she saw Adrian leaving it.

He came up to her as she halted before the door. "I wasn't sure I believed you were out. I fear I mistrust you, beauty," he said, laughing. He sobered as he caught something in her expression. "What is it? Are you having doubts?"

She shook her head and smiled. What he had seen was her reaction to his confession that he mistrusted her. With all of her heart she wanted to trust him, but the fact that she could entertain Harry's suspicions against him for even a moment proved that she still did not.

"Come out with me," he said abruptly, nodding toward his curricle, which was being tended by a groom.

"I can't," she began, and then suddenly changing her mind said, "No, I shall. Can your groom take my horse to the mews?"

Within a few moments, without ever going into the house, Cassandra found herself beside Adrian driving through the crowded street, headed not toward the park, but out of the city. Even though the groom had been dispensed with, their conversation was commonplace and desultory while he negotiated the difficult traffic of the city.

As she sat beside him, her fears and suspicions withered away like pulled weeds exposed to the sun. She studied him covertly through her lashes as he skillfully maneuvered his horses through the busy streets, and thought him the most beautiful creature she had ever beheld, though now she did not count it against him. Becoming aware of her scrutiny, he cast her a sidelong glance and a quick ethereal smile, which overwhelmed her heart with happiness—though she knew it was absurd that such a simple thing should do so.

As they reached the outskirts of the city, traffic eased considerably and he dropped his hands, letting his team out at a brisk trot. "Are you abducting me, my lord?" she said, amused. "I thought we were merely going for a drive."

"We are, but not where we shall have half our acquaintance gawking at us. As you've reminded me, the world still thinks you betrothed to Bourne. Has Tilton sent notice of your withdrawal to the papers yet?"

Cassandra started guiltily. In the discussion that had followed her announcement to her brother, she had entirely forgotten to ask him to do so. "I am not certain," she hedged. "When we return I shall remind him."

They were clear of the city and had the road virtually to themselves. He slowed his horses again and regarded her with an expression that was inscrutable. "Did you tell him, Cass?" he asked quietly.

"Yes," she said more sharply than she intended. "I wish you would not doubt me so."

"And yet I think you still doubt me. What is it, Cass?" he asked, certain that more was troubling her than her earlier anxieties about their future. "Don't say it is nothing, for I saw it in your face as soon as we met."

Cassandra did not know whether to be pleased or dismayed that he read her so accurately. He stopped the carriage entirely on the side of the road and turned to her. As she looked into his eyes, she knew that he could indeed be a dangerous man. Against all the force of her considerable will, he had made her love him, and so completely that she was prepared to defy her family and the world, if necessary, to be with him. She essayed a smile that was not entirely successful. "It was a difficult interview. You know that Harry doesn't approve of my jilting Matthew in favor of you."

"Is his approval so necessary to your happiness?"

"Harry and I have always been close," she said, her tone soothing in response to his, which was coldly defensive. "But if you mean will I marry you with or without his approval, the answer is yes. I think, though, it might be best to say nothing of our promise to each other to anyone else for the moment."

There was no sign at all of the customary smile in his eyes, and his manner was guarded. "You make it sound like we are covering up some shameful scandal," he commented. "Why don't you tell me what is really troubling you, Cass? If you love me, trust me enough for that."

Cassandra was stung by his words, for she had had no intention of telling Adrian of Harry's suspicions. She knew he was right. If she loved him she had to trust him; the first could not continue without the second. "Harry has been very concerned by what occurred at Caver," she began, having no idea what she would say to him.

"As we all are," he said, and she didn't think she imagined the watchfulness in his expression.

She looked directly into his eyes as she spoke. "He is afraid you may have been involved in some way."

"I know," he replied, completely nonplussing her.

"How could you?"

"It isn't only Tilton that thinks it. Oh, it is not general gossip," he assured her, seeing her expression of horrified dismay. "I think there was some suspicion immediately, probably because Caverstone recalled that I went off alone with Moreville while we were in the abbey. There was a degree of coolness and restraint when I returned to the abbey with the litter. When they questioned all of us before we left, it was clear the bent they were taking when they started asking me questions about Alistar as well."

Cassandra actually felt a little sick to think that it was more than just a theory of her brother's. "Harry mentioned Alistar too," she admitted wretchedly. She then told him all that Harry had said to her, even to his comment that Adrian was suspected of collaborating with the French in some way for money.

He listened to her gravely, though for the most part she told him nothing he did not already know. But at the mention of the Porutguese foreign minister, he laughed with genuine amusement. "Oh, yes, there was a definite connection between me and Araujo. We were both chasing after the same woman, the wife of an aide to Strangford. My motives were purer, though. Araujo wanted to use her as an informer; I only wanted to sleep with her."

"Who succeeded?" she could not prevent herself from asking.

"Why, both of us, I think," he admitted readily enough. "I abandoned the field to Araujo after a bit, though. He outranked me, after all, and she was too fond of garlic."

"I would be a fool to marry you," she said with

mock severity, but his nonsense had made her laugh and broken the spell of melodrama.

He smiled in that way that always melted her heart. "You would be a fool not to. My wild oats are sown. I shall be a very tame husband now, with no fear of later regrets." In his mercurial manner, he turned suddenly serious again. "Do you think I am a murderer?"

"No," she said, but with a minute pause before she spoke, which robbed the word of conviction.

It was not sufficient to satisfy him. He gave a dry little laugh. "Hedging your bets, love?"

"No," she said more firmly, and angrily.

"Then marry me now. At once," he said, seeking more positive reassurance. "I can procure a special license by morning. The devil fly away with your family and with the rest of the world as well. We'll go at once to Dunwhittie and spend the summer there. The place is the size of a small village. We need never even see Gerald or Annabelle if we wish for our privacy."

"I've no wish to be married in any helter-skelter fashion."

"Do you wish to be married at all?" he asked pointedly. "If your brother is right, I will visit a ruin upon you almost as great as upon myself."

She was not sure why, but she hesitated. She certainly had no intention of marrying him out of hand, knowing full well that his suggestion was made out of anger and hurt at her hesitation, but she had no wish to make him suppose that she doubted his innocence.

As she did not respond, he supposed he understood her and said, "I see. If you wish to be free of your promise to me, I free you. It is best to do it now, before it is generally known. Not even the rich Miss Tilton's reputation could survive a fourth jilting."

He spoke jeeringly, but Cassandra could not blame him because she knew she had given him pain. "I love you. I don't believe anything could change that."

"I meant what I said, Cass. Marry me tomorrow."

"You know perfectly well that I can't do that," she

said crossly. "Please just let us go on as we said we would and be married in August."

"I am almost afraid to let you out of my sight for so long."

She put her hand on his shoulder and lifted her face to kiss him lightly, a gesture of reassurance rather than passion. "I did my best to resist you," she admitted, "but now that I have surrendered, I am yours. For better or worse. Forever." At these words he appeared to be easier, and she found herself soundly kissed. It was nearly time for her to dress for dinner before he set her down again at Tilton House.

Neither Harry nor Livia commented on her day-long absence, and Harry did not again allude to his suspicions of Adrian. When she spoke with him after dinner that night about sending notice of her ended betrothal to Matthew to the paper in the morning, he agreed with perfect amiability.

It was on the day following the next that the announcement appeared, and Cassandra felt the repercussions immediately. When she walked into the ladies' robing room at a rout party that night, all conversation stopped with an embarrassing abruptness, and Lady Bourne, who was amongst the guests, gave her the cut direct.

Cassandra wished that Adrian were there, for his impudent smile would have lifted her spirits at once and removed her fears that she was casting herself and her family into a mire of gossip and scandal. But her practical side was equally glad that he was not there, for she feared giving any hint just yet that the end of her betrothal to Matthew was the result of her attachment to Adrian.

Matthew was not in town and Livia told her that she had heard he was at Bourne Hall. Cassandra could only be glad of it. The day would of course come when she would have to meet him again, but she did not look forward to it.

For all that she saw of Adrian, he might as well have been away as well, and when she did see him it was invariably in company. He did call, but with Livia usually present, and often other callers as well, it would have looked very singular for them to have engaged in private conversation. She did not give much thought to his feelings in the matter, for she assumed that he understood her reasons for this temporary distance between them and was as secure of her love for him as she felt of his love for her.

At a ball given by Lady Beresford a sennight after the notice had appeared ending her betrothal to Matthew, she even hesitated when he asked her to stand up with him. "I am not sure that it would be a good thing to do."

"To dance with me?" he asked, a faint incredulous smile touching his lips. "Dear God, Cassandra. Not even the sharpest tongues could find anything in that."

"I just want everyone to accept my jilting of Matthew before it becomes obvious that we care for each other," she said, but allowed him to lead her onto the floor.

"Don't you think your preoccupation with what people will say and think a bit excessive?" he suggested dryly.

"It is not for my sake that I care," she retorted. "I *would* marry you tomorrow, but by jilting Matthew, I have set tongues wagging again, and with Harry still concerned over this matter with Moreville, I don't want to do anything to make it worse, or which might upset him and Livia. It is only for a very short time, after all," she added, chiding him a little. "We shall be married before the summer is out."

"Shall we?" he said, and then they were parted by the dance. When they were together again, he asked her to meet him in one of the anterooms, but she refused. "Tomorrow, then," he suggested. "In Green Park. I still have Menina for you."

Cassandra was tempted, but was determined on her course of circumspection and found an excuse to put him off for this as well. She knew his expressions well, and though to the world there appeared to be no creases to mark his brow, she knew he was angry with her. "You are being unreasonable, Adrian," she insisted when once again they were brought together. "I thought you understood."

"I am beginning to be afraid that I do," he said gravely, and from then on, when they spoke at all, it was of generalities.

One member of Matthew's family who did not cut her was Hannah McInnes. Surprising Cassandra at a card party on the following night, Hannah actually sought her out to tell her that she was quite sorry that matters had not worked out between Cassandra and her stepbrother. "I had hoped to call you sister one day," Hannah told her, "and indirectly then, my dear Sarah as well. She has been most distraught since poor Robert's death, I know. I do not see her tonight, which may be just as well. She is looking so hagged that people are beginning to comment on it, and you know, once people start casting about for a reason, it doesn't take them long to discover it. It is wise for that same reason that you are not seen to be too much with Lord Adrian."

Cassandra eyed her coolly. "I understand you, Hannah, but I assure you I am in no way avoiding the company of Lord Adrian. You presume too much, I fear."

As usual, Hannah was impervious to the snub. "I can't really blame you, of course. It is the only prudent way to go on, in light of what is being said."

Cassandra knew she was encouraging the other's impertinence, but she could not help herself asking, "Is being said of whom?"

"Of Lord Adrian, of course," replied Hannah with obvious surprise. "You must not pretend with me, Cassandra, for Sally has confided the whole in me. In any case, everyone has already guessed that there was something wrong about Moreville's death and that Lord Adrian is suspected of being in some way involved. There are no open accusations against him, but Freddy told me they are laying bets on his guilt or innocence at some of the clubs."

"That is horrid!" Cassandra said, outraged.

"It would certainly be uncomfortable for you if it were known that you contemplated marriage to him," Hannah informed her before going off to join friends for a game of whist.

In light of these words, and the knowledge that what she had supposed were the private suspicions of a few men were now *on-dit*, Adrian's attempts to receive some assurance from her and her refusal to give this assurance was put in a different light. Suddenly Cassandra understood his odd comments when she had demanded his understanding of her feelings. He must think that she was coming to condemn him as well, but perhaps had not yet the courage to face him with her suspicions. He had already accused her of hedging her bets.

That night when she returned home, she deliberately waited for her brother to come in, though the hour was well advanced when he did so. Harry was not particularly fond of wine or spirits, so she had no fear that his faculties would be impaired for the important discussion she wished to have with him.

He was a little surprised to find her waiting for him in the upstairs hall, but readily followed her into her sitting room and made himself comfortable in an armchair near a window, as if it were three o'clock in the afternoon rather than three o'clock in the morning.

Cassandra told him plainly what Hannah had said to her, adding her own fears that much of the gossip was being caused by Sarah's loose tongue. "I fear it may be so," he agreed. "Perhaps Sally is being indiscreet because of a need to avenge herself on the man she feels may be Moreville's murderer, or it may be nothing more than self-protection should her own husband be suspected. It has, of course, crossed my mind, in consequence of what you have told me, that Fareland would have an excellent motive for ridding himself of his rival and may even have had the opportunity to do so. The only thing lacking is evidence. There is not the least thing to connect him with Moreville that afternoon."

"Beyond the fact that Lord Moreville was last seen speaking with him, I don't see that there is any better evidence against Adrian," Cassandra remarked tartly.

Harry had the grace to look a little uncomfortable and said, "Well, you know there are other factors as well. I admit that I am very dismayed that such damaging *on-dit* against Searle should have gotten about because of my own indiscretion in telling you what I did and having Sarah overhear us. Our further investigations have achieved nothing, and in fact there is some evidence that Searle came by his present fortune exactly as he claims to have done. In any event, his fortune is quite genuine; he has a very substantial amount invested in the five-percents, and that, I gather, is not the whole of it. I honestly don't know if Adrian Searle had anything to do with Moreville's death. If he is innocent, I have done him a grievous wrong, but I fear it has gone too far to be corrected. He will just have to brave it out, I think, though the going will be rougher before it is smoother."

She was pleased that Adrian was proven not to be a fortune hunter, but anxious that Harry foresaw more trouble for Adrian in the future. "In what way?" she asked, only too aware of her own part, however indirect, of the responsibility for the harm that was being done to the man she loved.

Harry sighed and regarded her in silence for a few minutes, obviously weighing what he should say to his sister. "I am about to be indiscreet again, I fear, but perhaps it will in a small way mitigate any injury I may have inadvertently caused by my first indiscretion." He stretched out his feet to make himself more comfortable and said, "I think you know that one of the matters being discussed at Caver was whom we should find to replace Alistar, whose position in the Foreign Office, because of recent events in Portugal, was crucial. It is true that Searle has stated a number of times that he has no desire to return to active service in the

Foreign Office, but it was thought by nearly everyone involved in making the decision that he was the ideal man for the post. While we were at Caver he was sounded out about it and in the end he did indicate that he might be persuaded to take the position. We left it that he would think on it for a fortnight or so and then inform Canning and Portland of his decision."

"Adrian said nothing to me of it." Though in the circumstances, she reflected, he had scarcely had the opportunity.

"No. He would not. We asked him to keep the offer to himself until he made a decision, to avoid the sort of pointless political maneuvering that goes on whenever there is an unexpected change in any of the ministries. The point is, Cass, that with all the public speculation concerning this wretched business with Moreville, it has been decided to withdraw the offer."

"Then they do think him guilty," Cassandra cried, dismayed. She got up and began to move about the room in agitation.

"No, I don't really think it is that," Harry said slowly. He smiled grimly. "Rather it is a precaution to avoid embarrassment to the government in the future, should it come to something."

"Then Hannah did not exaggerate," she said dully. "Is Adrian aware of how matters stand?"

"That is where the reparation comes in. Canning told me this only today. The reason they will give is Portland's failing health, which is not expected to last out the summer. They will offer him some blather about a possible change in government and not making any important decisions on personnel just at the moment, but he will not be deceived."

"No. Do you mean to warn him then?"

"It would be unethical of me to do so in the circumstances," Harry said, raising his head to look up at her, for she had stopped her restless movement and was standing beside his chair. "But you might do so if you wish."

Cassandra nodded unhappily and went back to her

chair. "Livy is going to visit her aunt near Richmond tomorrow morning. I will send a message to his lodging to come here and we may be alone." She saw Harry raise his brows and said crisply, "What would you have me do, Harry? Further his humiliation by informing him of his disgrace in front of others? What is so dreadful about it is that it is so undeserved."

Harry stood up. "I hope it is undeserved," he said cautiously. "I know that Moreville was murdered, and frankly, there is no one with better opportunity than Adrian Searle to have done it. The same is true for Alistar, whose death was accepted as the work of footpads, but which also had elements that made that solution open to doubt. Has it occurred to you that it would even follow that if Adrian were about to return to the Foreign Office he would be in even greater fear that Moreville might find out about any possible collaboration if that was what occurred?"

Cassandra rose again as well. "I have told you, Harry, that I don't believe that and won't listen to it."

Her brother lightly kissed her forehead. "I want you to be right, Cass. Believe that. But I am glad that you have had the sense not to get yourself talked about with Searle. It is seldom discretion that is responsible for regret."

But that was not how Cassandra felt. She felt she had not stood by Adrian when he needed her most, though she had done so out of ignorance rather than intent. She knew she might remedy this now, but she was wretchedly torn. Her heart told her that he could not be guilty of such heinous crimes, but her brother, whom she had all of her life trusted completely, seemed all but convinced of Adrian's guilt, and she had to acquit Harry of malice in any form. Her traitorous intellect could not absolve Adrian beyond all question, and all her doubts about making yet another unhappy choice assailed her.

She had a note sent to his lodgings even before she had breakfast, so it was not surprising when Adrian presented himself quite soon after Livia had left for Richmond, almost indecently early for a morning call.

As soon as she set eyes on his beautiful, beloved face, she was ashamed of having allowed herself to indulge in dead-of-night horrors and allowed him to embrace her as soon as the door was closed behind him. This, she realized at once, was another sort of mistake, for his touch was incendiary and it was with a pounding heart that she insisted that they sit while she told him her difficult news.

It turned out not to be news at all to him, but it assuaged some of his concern that she cared enough to warn him. "I have already had the hint from Canning," he said, not betraying any emotion at all. "I might blame him as a man for convicting me on unfounded conjecture and gossip, but I can't fault him as a politician. To take me into his office and then have me taken up as the murderer of one of his own undersecretaries would be political suicide."

"What is going to come of all this?" she asked. His only reply was to shake his head, and she went on, "Please believe me, Adrian, I had no notion that talk was so rife until last night when Hannah McInnes told me of it."

"La McInnes? I thought that the Bournes had all cut you. I can guess the source of her information."

"I could murder Sarah myself," Cassandra said, red spots of anger in her cheeks.

Adrian got up from the chair and came to sit beside her on the sofa. "Answer me plainly, Cass. Has this affected us? Do you still feel as you did when we first returned from Caver?"

"You shouldn't have to ask me," she said, but the memory of her shameful doubts robbed her words of the conviction they should have possessed.

"But I do."

"Would I be willing to marry you if I thought you capable of murder?"

"There are women who like a man to be dangerous."

"Not that dangerous," she said baldly.

He bent his head and kissed her gently. "If you won't marry me at once, at least come to me."

"As your mistress?" she said, withdrawing from him a little.

"As the woman I love, who loves me equally."

She would have gotten up from the sofa, but he took hold of her hands and held her still. "Why are you being this way, Adrian? When we agreed to be married, you said you understood the doubts and fears that I had for us and that you would never importune me as Ned did."

"And I have told you before that I am not Ned," he replied with an edge in his tone. He could not understand her hesitation now that they had openly declared their love for each other, and was inclined to mistrust it. "Things have changed considerably since that night. What to you is importuning, to me is a wish for reassurance that is tangible. At this moment, I need more than empty assurances that all is still well between us, because I feel as if it is not. If we are to be married in a little more than a month, it can't matter."

"It matters to me."

"It wouldn't if you loved me as you say you do."

She was very close to tears of anger and chagrin. She was furious with him for trying to force her into a physical commitment to him and yet she understood his need for it. "That is unfair," she said unsteadily, and pulled her hands away from him. She got up quickly and moved to the other end of the room. Physical distance was always the only sure way she had of resisting him.

He rose more slowly and advanced toward her, thwarting her purpose. But she would not move away in undignified retreat. She let him come quite close to her and merely raised her face to meet his eyes. "You don't think it unfair to keep me on a leash like a pet dog if your feelings have changed toward me?" he asked without inflection.

"They haven't," she cried almost with despair. "But

if you are going to behave so horribly, they very well may."

He, too, was angry now, and careless of what he said, though he only half-believed his words. "You love me, but you will await developments before you make it irrevocable. I am not a bully, Cass. I need to know that you care enough for me to send the world and its conventions to the devil. Instead you put me off at every turn and avoid me when you can."

"That isn't true," she said in a quiet voice.

"I think it is. Perhaps you were right from the beginning. Maybe it is only physical attraction after all."

Once again he swept her into his arms, but not gently in his usual manner. Her back was against the wall and he pushed himself tight against her so that she could feel every contour of his lean, hard body. His lips didn't merely seek her response, they demanded it. She was as angry as she was afraid, and she willed herself not to respond to him, but her own desire played her false. When he withdrew from her he was nearly panting and her breath came in small sobs. Without consciously willing the action, her hand came up and dealt him a ringing blow to the face.

"It is obvious, my lord, that we were mistaken in one another," she said with icy control. "Perhaps Hannah or your other lightskirts welcome such rough embraces, but I do not." A tremor appeared in her voice on the last few words, and determined not to dissolve into vulnerable tears before him, she swept past him and out of the room. But once in her room, she cried as if her heart were breaking, as indeed it was.

# 11

THOUGH Cassandra presented her usual smiling countenance to the world for the days that remained until they were to leave for Cheltenham, inside she was almost sick with unhappiness. Livia, more sensitive to her moods than most of her friends, noted the strain Cassandra was put to to behave with no hint of her inner turmoil. In this state, Cassandra was too weak to resist her persuasions and confided in her sister-in-law that she had ended her short-lived betrothal to Adrian as well.

"I think I am destined to be on the shelf," Cassandra said with a watery laugh as she dried her tears. She sat on Livia's bed with her sister-in-law's supporting arm about her. "I cannot think there has ever been another woman so stupid as to choose four men to marry her and end by sending each of them away."

"Once all the whispering is done, you will both be in better frame to know what you really wish," Livia said with quiet confidence that did much to ease Cassandra's feelings of hopelessness. "It is hardly wonderful that both of your tempers have so easily flared. I think it is a horrible thing that a man can be virtually condemned on nothing but gossip. He is still received everywhere, but I have heard that more than one acquaintance, unsure of which way the wind will blow, has crossed the street rather than meet him or be forced to cut him."

"What if the whispering is never done?"

"It is already fading, I think," Livia said reassuringly. "I know Harry had a talk with Sarah and I think no more fuel will be added to the gossip from that quarter. Harry only wants to know the truth and to protect you if it should prove against Adrian. But if you are certain of Adrian's innocence, then there is nothing to fear."

"I am sure of it," Cassandra said emphatically, "but at times I cannot prevent a question or doubt from coming into my mind."

"Which is quite natural. You must not tease yourself so, Cass," Livia said, squeezing her hand. "When you have both had a little time apart to reflect, you will be able to make up your quarrel. If you love each other, I am certain of it."

But Cassandra was not. She did not mention it to Livia, but she had a new thing to trouble her. The very night that she had quarreled with Adrian, at an assembly both attended, it seemed to her that every time she saw him, he was in company with Hannah. Her first response was to suppose that he was spiting her for her stinging words to him before she had run from the room, but in the days that followed, she saw them together frequently: riding toward Hyde Park, dancing at a ball, sitting together at a musicale. The worst part of it was that she blamed herself for all but suggesting that he seek out Hannah for comfort. Cassandra had no doubt at all that the dashing matron, with a series of lovers behind her, would not be overnice in her notions of propriety and would give Adrian that "assurance" that he had so craved.

Matthew had returned to town, but so wrapped in her own troubles, Cassandra had no thought to spare for him, and their eventual meeting, though it was cool, was not particularly self-conscious as she had feared it would be. By the night of the fete to be held at Carlton House which, as Adrian had said, would mark the end of the London Season, Cassandra was glad that she would be going to Cheltenham on the day after next, where she at least hoped she would find peace of mind away from Matthew, Hannah, and most important, Adrian. Since there was to be no wedding either to Matthew or to Adrian, the Tiltons had decided to remain in the house they hired in Cheltenham annually until nearly September, when they would then go to Tillings for the remainder of the time until Harry returned to his government chores in October and the Little Season began.

Cassandra had half-decided to cry off from attending the fete with her brother and sister-in-law, but a night spent alone with no company except for her own unprofitable cogitations was not an attractive alternative. Dressing for the evening, she chose a gown of fine-spun ivory gauze that was a bit daring in cut and which set off her figure to tantalizing perfection. She did not consciously dress with Adrian in mind, but meeting him almost as soon as she was shown into the receiving saloon, she saw his eyes flicker over her breasts and bared shoulders and felt a tiny prick of satisfaction at the expression she surprised in them.

"I hope to find you well, my lord," she said with a cool formality as she offered him her hand.

But time and separation had made him more able and willing to understand her difficulties and restored as well his usual equable humor. A faint ironic smile touched on his lips, and his eyes held that intimate spark of humor which she knew so well and loved so dearly. "No. I have not been well, Miss Tilton, as *you* well know," he said in the same civil tone she had used.

Spontaneously responding to his smile, she knew that in this man reposed all her delight, and her fears once again evaporated as if exposed to the sun. She looked about to see who might be listening, and said with sudden impulse, "Do you still wish to be married on the morrow?"

"Yes," he replied without hesitation.

She took a deep breath. "If you can procure a special license tomorrow, I will wed you before the day is out."

His habitual slow smile spread into a grin. "Actually, I am not certain that I am free tomorrow," he said with chagrin. He saw the change in her face and added quickly, "I am quizzing you, my love. I have had the license since we returned from Caver."

Her happiness restored after one of the most wretched weeks she had ever known, she remained at his side, not caring if it was remarked. Harry held no truck with being fashionably late, and the rooms were still a bit sparse of company. Enjoying this while they could—for the Prince of Wales's elegant saloons would soon fill well beyond capacity—they strolled about the room, pausing occasionally to speak with friends. It was while they were speaking with Roger Caverstone that Hannah McInnes came into the room on the arm of her husband.

Cassandra, in the flush of her returned happiness, had forgotten her, and now she felt again a little stab in her heart. In the circumstances, she could not really blame Adrian for seeking comfort there, but it had to be settled between them that the liaison would not be continued. When they moved on again, she said, "What of Hannah McInnes?"

He seemed genuinely puzzled. "What of her?"

"Please, Adrian. Let us have no more fencing. I saw how much you were together in the past sennight."

"And you think I have mounted her as my mistress?" He laughed outright, not displeased by her display of jealousy, for he had passed more than one uncomfortable hour imagining her in the arms of Matthew Bourne. "You would be well-served if I had, for suggesting that she would find my advances more to her taste than you did, but I did not." There was such a ring of sincerity in his voice that she chose to believe him.

As greater numbers arrived, they were eventually parted and she did not see him again until she went upstairs to the music room with Mr. Armitage, an admirer of long standing, electing to hear a brief concert presented by a chamber orchestra that the Prince, an accomplished musician himself, was sponsoring in the *ton*. Since music of this nature was not to the taste

of everyone, many remained in the card rooms and
saloons, preferring conversation to entertainment.

Adrian was not seated in one of the small chairs set
out for the guests, but was propped against the wall
near a door at the far side of the room, so Cassandra
saw him as soon as she entered. She wished they might
sit together, but her escort steered her to two vacant
chairs at the end of a row on the opposite side, and
her breeding would not allow her to object.

As she had suspected, music and musicians were
both superb, and for a time she lost herself in the
enjoyment of the music. But during a pause she glanced
at the place where she had last seen Adrian and discovered that Hannah McInnes had joined him. In
spite of his assurances and her wish to believe them,
she had a suddenly hollow feeling. Cassandra looked
away, not to be caught out staring at them, but her
pleasure in the concert was ruined. She could not
prevent herself from looking up again, and this time
saw that Hannah had taken a nearby seat again, which
would have alleviated her anxiety if Adrian had not at
that moment unobtrusively slipped out of the door
that he stood near.

Though Hannah appeared not to have noticed his
departure, Cassandra had no doubt that the other
woman was only too well aware of it. In a few more
minutes, Cassandra was certain, Hannah would rise
again, perhaps complaining of the warmth of the room,
and leave by the other door, to meet with Adrian for a
prearranged assignation. Doubtless he wished to inform his mistress of his pending change in status.
Cassandra felt almost sick with disappointment and
self-condemnation for being such a complete fool.

She had to know the truth of it. Using the very
excuse she had attributed to her rival, she left Mr.
Armitage, insisting that he remain for the rest of the
concert. Carlton House was large and riddled with
saloons of varying size and anterooms of every de-
scription. And their meeting place might have been in
any one of these. Standing in the corridor, which was

quite empty except for the two footmen who stood in the doorway of the music room, Cassandra forced herself to ordered thinking and decided to enter the room next to the music room. It proved to be a large saloon, not unlike the ones downstairs where the Prince's guests were assembled. But she found what she sought. At the opposite side of the room was a door similar to the one in the music room. She approached it without hesitation.

The passageway on the other side of the door was narrow and ill-lit. At one end there was a door opened to reveal an equally narrow stairway, and the other end of the passage led to a blank end. Cassandra had no doubt that the stairs led ultimately to the kitchens and servants' hall. It was the only way that Adrian could have gone, so, hoping she would not find herself in an awkward meeting with any of the Prince's servants, she negotiated the steep, narrow stairs.

At the bottom, Cassandra found herself in a similar but shorter passage, which led into a large hall off which were a number of closed doors. She heard the dim sounds of laughter and conversation and supposed that some of the doors must lead to the saloons where the party was in progress. The hall was better lit than the passageways had been, but not to the point that guests would be encouraged to traverse it. It was, of course, possible that Adrian had simply returned to the principal saloons, and she was creeping about like a fool bent on melodrama, but she didn't really believe it. If returning downstairs was his only purpose, there was not the least reason for him to do so by means of the servants' passages.

Taking her courage in hand, she walked into the hall in the opposite direction from the noise of the gathering and opened the first door she came to. She opened it quickly and completely, allowing the light from the hall to penetrate. The room was completely empty. So was the second. Cassandra felt a small surge of hope, but her anxiety was far from assuaged. Only two doors were left, and then she would know;

the whole of her future hung upon what she found or did not find behind these.

As she opened the next door, even before she was able to see into the darkened room she knew she had realized her fears. A hand reached out of the darkness and grasped her own, leading her into the room. She was gathered into a strong embrace and was kissed with conviction. But the embrace ended almost as soon as it began. He uttered a smothered exclamation and drew back from her.

"Cass?"

"You were expecting Hannah McInnes, I collect," she said calmly, though her heart was hammering in her chest.

"Good Lord!" He muttered another expletive under his breath and then said, "What the devil are you about? No. Don't tell me now, there isn't time." He gripped her shoulders hard. "Trust me, Cass, this is not what you think it is. I give you my word on it. I am expecting Hannah, but not for the purpose you are thinking. My interest in her has nothing to do with lovemaking, however it may seem."

Cassandra gave a short disdainful laugh. "I suppose next you will say that you knew it was me when you grabbed me and kissed me."

"No. I at first thought you were Hannah, but you kiss better," he added provocatively. Then, serious again, "Please just trust me, Cass. I'll explain everything to you before the night is out. Go back to the music room. Hannah will be here in a moment and she mustn't find you here too."

In spite of the evidence of her senses, she could not bring herself to condemn him without a fair hearing. Certainly she wanted to believe him. "I don't know what I should think," she said slowly.

"Think nothing—just for the next hour," he pleaded. "Damn!" he said suddenly and in a very different voice. "Someone has come into the hall. You'll have to go out throught the next room." Without waiting for her reply, he half-led, half-dragged her across the room that was lit only by what dim light spilled into it from the hall, to a door at one end connecting it with the next room. It was unlocked and he opened it. He then caught her to him and kissed her very quickly. "Try not to fall over anything in the dark. If there is any noise, you might scare her off." He very nearly pushed her inside the room and shut the door on her.

Cassandra just stood in the dark facing the closed door for several minutes. She felt completely bemused. She had found her betrothed apparently about to embark on an assignation with another woman and she had allowed him, with absurdly little explanation, to persuade her to leave him to his plans. She didn't know if she was being nobly forbearing or a damned fool. She did not hear Hannah come into the room; the only sound she heard at all was the pounding of her own heart. But she could not just return to the music room, as he suggested. Quietly and cautiously she cracked open the door connecting the two rooms.

The door into the hall was not quite, but nearly closed, so that room was as dark as her own, but her eyes were well-adjusted to the dark and the draperies were not drawn in these unlit, unused rooms and there was just sufficient moonlight for her to make out their figures near to a sofa in the middle of the room where she herself had stood with Adrian only a few minutes earlier.

She felt absurdly relieved that they did not appear to be making love, as he had promised, and she was about to close the door again when one of Hannah's hands snaked across Adrian's back and he suddenly pulled her down with him onto the sofa. His body covered Hannah's and Cassandra heard the small sounds and quick breaths of lovemaking. It was more than she could bear. She could not continue to stand and watch until the inevitable occurred, but no more could she simply close the door and go away, knowing that the man she loved was lying with another woman. She advanced into the room, heedless of the inevitable scene she would create.

The sounds from the sofa intensified. The breathing of one, or perhaps both, came almost in gasps. Cassandra felt her knees turn to water, but clutching at the dark shape of a chair, she steadied herself, rage at her betrayal spurring her on. When she reached the sofa, she realized at last that they were not making love but engaged in a struggle. Her eyes caught a little metallic flash of light and she saw it was the glint of moonlight on a blade. She involuntarily caught at her breath.

This sound or some movement caught Hannah's eye, and her concentration, which was the only thing preventing Adrian's superior strength from prevailing, wavered. She let out a small sharp cry, and the knife fell with a soft thud on the carpet behind the sofa. There was a wild scramble while she tried to free herself from Adrian's grasp, but all her strength, which was not inconsiderable, had been sapped resisting his attempt to take the knife away from her, and at last she lay still under him, her breath coming in rasps.

Adrian, satisfied that his adversary was subdued at least for the moment, looked up at Cassandra. Even though she could not see his face clearly in the darkness, she knew he was smiling. "It really isn't what you think," he said, mocking her.

"So I perceive," she said coolly, but sitting in a chair next to the sofa as she spoke, because her knees were still shaking. "But what is it?"

"Shall you tell her, fair charmer, or shall I?" he asked Hannah, whom he still pinned with his body.

"Get off me!" she hissed. He did not move and she said, "Where would I run to now?"

"I don't mean to give you the opportunity," he said, but he sat back, merely retaining a firm hold on her arm. "See if there is a tinderbox on the mantel," he said, addressing Cassandra. "I've had enough melodrama for one night."

Cassandra had recovered a little of her composure and she did as he bid her. She went to the mantel and carefully moved her hand in and around the objects that were on it, searching for the tinderbox.

While she did so, Adrian spoke. "It was all for McInnes' benefit, I suppose," he said to Hannah, who did not reply, "and indirectly and more importantly, your own. You thought your husband was certain to succeed Alistar because he worked more closely with him than anyone else and had even been to Lisbon with him before the exile. McInnes was the logical choice for the position. But Moreville, to his undoing, was immovably opposed to him. With Moreville so against it, Canning would never recommend your husband. Did you know that I had been approached for the position? Is that why you did what you could to foster suspicion of me, or was it simply because I resisted your rather too freely offered charms?"

Hannah sat quite still, staring at some fixed point on the carpet, and still said nothing. Cassandra finally located the tinderbox and lit several candles on the mantel. The room was far from well-lit, but at least some of the shadows receded. "You should have let speculation run its course," he continued, "instead of trying to direct it, for it tipped your hand. I had no more than intellectual curiosity about Alistar's death or Moreville's first accident, but when I became directly involved this time, I had a powerful motive to discover the truth. McInnes, who might well have benefited from both Alistar's and Moreville's deaths, was a logical suspect, but I couldn't imagine him possessing the *sangfroid* to pose as a footpad or highwayman to achieve his end. But brigands may be hired, sometimes for the price of a pint of gin. Hiring bravos requires neither strength nor insouciance. In fact, it occurred to me that even a woman, if she had sufficient strength of purpose, might do so. Suddenly everything seemed much more logical. Your husband is not the fool some people think him, but he is a drunkard, and whatever ambitions he may have had when he entered government service have long since drowned at the bottom of a bottle. But your ambitions are unchanged, I think, and if McInnes wouldn't help himself get ahead, you would do what you could to accomplish it for him."

"This is ridiculous," Hannah said, speaking for the first time. She obviously had regained her composure, and in full measure, for her tone was annoyed, haughty, and faintly amused. There was not the slightest hint of trepidation in her words or voice. "Your insinuations would be insulting were they not so absurd. There is nothing in the least to connect me with either Alistar or Moreville, and it is only your word against mine. Given what is being said about you, I rather think my word will be given credit over yours."

"And mine as well?" Cassandra said, still standing by the fireplace but now walking toward the sofa. "You forget that I saw your struggle with Adrian, and then there is this." She stooped and retrieved the small stiletto from behind the sofa. "What will you say when we give the authorities this?"

With unexpected speed Hannah reached up to grab the knife away from Cassandra. She did not quite reach it, but Cassandra was so startled by the other's sudden lunge that the knife slipped through her fingers. It did not fall again to the floor, but onto the sofa between Adrian and Hannah, who instinctively sprang apart to avoid being struck by the blade.

For one moment they were frozen in time. Then Adrian and Hannah reached simultaneously for the weapon. Not even sparing a moment to berate herself, Cassandra grabbed the nearest thing at hand, a glass bowl filled with spring flowers, and struck out at Hannah.

She moved quickly, but not quite quickly enough. Hannah, the knife having nearly fallen into her lap, caught the handle of the blade a split second before Adrian grabbed at it. Still in a forward motion, Adrian hadn't time to move defensively and the blade entered him at the same moment that Cassandra brought the glass bowl down upon Hannah's head. Hannah fell into his arms and they both fell backward onto the sofa. Adrian pushed Hannah's sodden, still form off him and took the knife, which she still clutched, from her hand. Then Cassandra saw the dark stain on the blade. "Oh, dear God! She's stabbed you."

"Only a little, near my shoulder," he said, and his voice sounded strong enough to allay her immediate fear. "You won't be rid of me that way."

But Cassandra did not respond in kind. "It is my fault," she said unequivocally. "It was unpardonably stupid to drop the knife, and it is just good fortune that you are not killed. What was she thinking of to attack you again? She couldn't hope to kill us both with impunity."

"I doubt she was thinking at all," he said, and then added more practically, for in fact the wound did pain him, "We can make this the principal topic at the breakfast table for the rest of our days, but for now I think we had better fetch someone to help us with our, ah, burden."

"Whom shall I fetch?"

"Colonel McMahon, the Prince's equerry, of course, and you might ask him to bring Canning, if he is still here. I would say McInnes as well, but more likely than not, he is already part foxed. Perhaps Lady Bourne would be a better choice. If you can find her." Cassandra didn't like having to approach Matthew's mother, but she accepted the necessity of doing so.

As it happened, Lady Bourne was almost the first person Cassandra saw as she came out of the hall into the principal corridor leading to the saloons where the party was in progress. Cassandra approached her and spoke quickly before that lady could snub her again, explaining only that her daughter had need of her. She did not wait for a reply, but continued on into the first saloon until she found Colonel McMahon and gave him a brief *sotto voce* account of what had happened.

When he left to find Mr. Canning, Cassandra left the saloon to return to Adrian. She was a little more conscious of the rest of the company this time, and she noted that the people about her seemed to look at her quizzically, as if they were aware that something was amiss. When she had almost reached the side hall, she was caught up by her brother, who linked his arm in hers without comment and led her into the hall.

He gripped her arm as if he expected her to try to escape him. "What the devil are you about now?" he said, clearly exasperated. "Don't you ever tire of creating *on-dit*?"

It was impossible that he could know what had occurred. "I have not slipped off to meet my lover, if that is what you are thinking," she said caustically.

He regarded her at arms' length, his expression quizzical. "If you did, I can only say you have deuced odd tastes."

He was staring at her gown, and Cassandra looked down at herself and saw for the first time that the ivory gauze had a great wet stain all down the front, and caught in the gathers under her breasts were a few loose petals and leaves. Her sense of the ridiculous kindled, she laughed, a combination of relief and appreciation of the absurdity of it, making her brother's expression become even more censorious. "Oh, Harry, you are quite right. This will give them something to talk of for months. But at least this time I am not the one in disgrace. It is Hannah McInnes. She is the one behind the killing of Alistar and Moreville, because she wanted Alistar's position for her precious Freddy. It was Adrian who suspected her, and he has brought her to book."

Harry looked stunned for a moment and then fired several quick questions at her, which she apparently answered to his satisfaction, for he gave no appearance of doubting her word. He insisted, however, that she take him to the saloon where she had left Adrian and Hannah McInnes. When they arrived there, they found Colonel McMahon and Mr. Canning speaking quietly at one end of the room with Adrian, and Lady Bourne attending a now conscious and hysterically weeping Hannah. Standing beside the two women, looking thoroughly discomposed, was Matthew, who had apparently accompanied his mother.

Adrian looked up when she entered with her brother, and his smile was reassuring. McMahon looked dismayed at their entrance, but a few words from Mr. Canning reassured him. After exchanging a few words with Harry, McMahon said, "The most important thing at the moment is not to create a stir. His royal highness abhors fuss from any cause. There is a service hallway almost across from this room, and I will have a carriage brought to the back of the house to take Mrs. McInnes away from here. Has McInnes been told yet?"

Mr. Canning offered to take on that task, and he and the colonel left together.

Not caring what the others would think, Cassandra nearly cast herself into Adrian's arms, but then, remembering his injury, sprang back with an exclamation of dismay. "It's all right," Adrian assured her. "Lady Bourne found me a bit of linen to stanch the blood. It has bled rather a lot, but it is the merest scratch."

Considering Cassandra's odd appearance and Adrian's blood-soaked shirtfront, Harry suggested dryly that it might be best if they, too, left in a quiet way, and then went over to sit beside Lady Bourne until McMahon returned, leaving Cassandra alone with Adrian. But they were not permitted their privacy. Matthew came up to them, saying, "I suppose this will just about finish Freddy. I only hope they will permit him to resign without disgrace." He lacked his usual self-assurance as he spoke. "What do you suppose will happen to Hannah?"

"Given the delicate state of our foreign affairs at the present," Adrian replied, "I would think that they will want the matter kept as quiet as possible."

Matthew visibly relaxed at these words, but Cassandra was outraged. "You can't mean that they will let her go free just to avoid a scandal? It would be infamous!"

Adrian smiled wryly. "Righteous indignation, to be

sure. But it won't come to that. She will be dealt with quietly and privately. Bedlam, perhaps, or a private asylum."

"She is mad, of course," Matthew said quickly. "Lady Bourne was a Stokey, and there has long been a taint in their breeding. I hope this may be kept quiet. I will do what I can for my stepsister, of course, but I need to be careful of my own position." Adrian flicked him a disdainful glance, but Matthew did not seem to notice it. Turning to Cassandra, he essayed a thin smile. "I do wish you well, Cassandra. We would never have suited one another. It is only a pity that we neither of us realized it from the beginning. I fear you have suffered most from the talk about us."

"If I have, I have only my own history to blame," she said, adding, "I was done more good by our brief time together than harm, Matthew. I wish you well also."

Matthew bowed to her, nodded at Adrian, whom he still could not quite face with complete equanimity, and left the room.

Cassandra turned to Adrian and insisted that he open his coat and show her his wound. He did so, and she exclaimed at once when she saw the extent of the bloodstain on his shirt. "It is not nearly so bad as it looks," he insisted. A small pad of cloth was stemming the bleeding and he put it back in place and buttoned his coat again.

"It *must* pain you."

"A little," he admitted.

The colonel returned and he and Harry escorted Lady Bourne and Hannah McInnes out of the room. McMahon paused to inform them that he would return for them as soon as a carriage was gotten ready to take them to their homes. This was accomplished with far greater speed than either would have supposed possible, and there was no time at all for Adrian and Cassandra to discuss in what manner all that had occurred would affect them and their immediate plans for their future. Perhaps for the sake of propriety, or to keep them apart, Harry had had his own carriage readied for Cassandra, and Adrian was conveyed home by one of the Prince of Wales's own town carriages.

Exhaustion that was more emotional than physical overtook Cassandra almost as soon as she arrived at home, and she was asleep almost as soon as she lay on her bed. It was not until the following morning that she recalled her promise to marry Adrian that very day. With all they had been through, she could not quite keep at bay vague anxieties that some other untoward event or misunderstanding would part them again. As the morning wore on and he did not call or send any word, she would not allow her imagination to run completely away with her, but neither did she know any peace of mind or heart.

Completely unaware of the disquiet he was engendering in his beloved's breast, Adrian slept later than his usual hour and permitted his concerned valet to send for Dr. Knighton to attend to his wound to avoid possible infection. When he had satisfied both the doctor and his anxious servitor by his cheerful mien and hearty appetite that he was not about to fall into a fever, he was permitted to dress for the street, and then was further delayed from going to Tilton House by the arrival of Mr. Canning and Mr. Perceval, who came to see how he had fared from his misadventure and to discuss with him what would be the official arrangement of the previous night's events.

It was approaching noon, therefore, when he finally left his lodgings and walked the short distance to Tilton House. Cassandra, sitting by the window, unashamedly on the watch for him, saw him as soon as he turned the corner into Berkeley Square. She drew back a little so as not to be observed, but watched until he disappeared into the house. She arranged herself on the sofa and waited for him to come to her, but he did not come, and unable to maintain her equanimity, she all but ran down the stairs and into the hall. The butler informed her that Adrian had indeed called but had asked for Lord Tilton. Cassandra was surprised, but not dismayed. Harry might not entirely approve of her jilting Matthew to wed Adrian, but he would never stand in the way of her happiness, and if Adrian had decided to offer for her in form, she had no doubt that Harry would at the least inform him that Cassandra was her own mistress and might marry where she pleased. Yet, she could not return to the saloon at the front of the house where she had watched for him and wait placidly for him to come to her. She informed the butler that she would be in the garden if needed, and went outside, though the day was a bit overcast and a little chill.

She was sitting on a stone bench at the edge of a flagged terrace with her back resolutely to the house to avoid staring at the door. When she heard someone approaching, she refused to allow herself to turn and did not look up until Adrian sat down beside her. His expression was not grave, but neither was there the spark of a smile in his expressive eyes.

They regarded each other for a long moment and then he said evenly, "I had no notion I was paying court to so great an heiress. No wonder your brother suspected the motive of a mere second son for wishing to attach you."

She nodded. "In addition to my portion, which is handsome, there is a legacy from a great-aunt."

"But he told me you never suspected me of creampot love." He suddenly dimpled. "It was probably the only thing you did not suspect me of at one point or another." She protested at this but he would not allow it. "I have been cast as everything from a libertine to a murderer, but I flatter myself that Lord Tilton, at least, is now satisfied that I do not mean to ravish his sister, strip her of her fortune, or murder her in her bed once the first two are accomplished."

"Does that mean that you think *I* am not satisfied?" she asked, surprised. "But I have said I will marry you today. Isn't that enough?"

He was only quizzing her, but he saw the spark of anxiety in her eyes and touched her face with the tips of his fingers, running them down to her throat in a loving caress. "I told you I only needed to know that you loved me enough to toss your bonnet over the windmill. We shall wait a bit and be married with all propriety and the blessings of your family and mine."

It was what she had wanted, but she was plainly disappointed. "In August, as we first said?"

"By the end of the week," he said, and his smile grew to a grin as he saw that his words pleased her. He tried to take her into his arms, but she would not permit it.

"We must be careful of your injury," she insisted. "There will be time enough for passion."

"Then it is as well we are not to be married today," he said dryly.

She rested her head against his sound shoulder. "You must not mind my anxiety for you," she said. "When I saw the knife go into you I thought Hannah had killed you." Her voice shook a little at the memory.

"I told you I am not so easily disposed of," he said, but absently, as he recalled a matter he wished clarified. "What did you mean when you said that your betrothal to Bourne did you good?"

"If I hadn't been betrothed to a man of such steady, upright character, I should never have known how little such a match suited me."

He moved back from her. "You prefer your men to be of shaky, questionable character?" he asked with dismay. "Then I have persevered in virtue to no advantage. I wonder if Lady Oxford is at home?"

She refused to be drawn by his nonsense. "Matthew was a hypocrite as well. He labeled both you and Ned as loose fish, but he apparently saw nothing wrong with continuing his connection with Mrs. Maybrith, though he was betrothed to me."

"Reprehensible!"

"You are laughing at me," she said censoriously, "but it is iniquitous."

"I am agreeing, fair one, not quizzing you." He

moved toward her as if to kiss her, but now she pulled back.

"Infidelity is not a thing I take lightly."

"Nor I," he said quite seriously. He was silent for a moment and then said. "You still expect me to be unfaithful don't you? You didn't believe me when I told you I wasn't sleeping with Hannah."

Cassandra dropped her eyes from his. "I wanted to . . . it is so hard for me."

"I know," he said again. He gently drew her into his arms, and this time she did not resist him, even when he kissed her in a gentle but lingering way. "Are you quite sure you wish to marry me?" he said, releasing her a little. "If you can't trust me, I shall fail miserably at making you happy."

"And I you. I *want* to believe in you. If you can be patient with my fears and my imperfections, I promise to be the best wife that I can to you."

"Your imperfections! They are nothing to mine." He suddenly laughed. "Good Lord. We are descending into melodrama again. In the circumstances, it is forgivable, I suppose, but we are in serious danger of becoming maudlin, and that will *not* do." He kissed her again, and this time the heat between them rose quickly to the surface and it was no longer the gentle embrace of courtship. Hating to bring their lovemaking to an end as much as he, Cassandra was nevertheless mindful of the fact that they were overlooked by half the windows in the house and she gently but firmly freed herself from his arms.

He was mildly exasperated and regretted a little his bow to propriety that had made him postpone their hasty wedding. "Perhaps it would be better if I kept you doubting me at least a little," he said darkly.

She looked up at him, surprised. "Why?"

"My Ice Maiden was remarkably thawed when she was most unsure of me. Perhaps you will only want me when you are uncertain of me."

"That is absurd. You know perfectly well that I've

wanted you since . . ." She stopped speaking abruptly, aware that she had betrayed herself.

"Since when?" he demanded in a silky but insistant voice.

She met his eyes without a blush. "Since the night I met you," she said quickly before her courage could fail her.

His delighted smile quite took her breath away with its beauty. He swept her into his arms again before she could protest. "Adrian," she hissed, "you mustn't . . ." But her words melted away like the last of the ice in her heart.

# COMING IN JULY 1988

### *Eileen Jackson*
A Servant of Quality

### *Mary Jo Putney*
The Would-Be Widow

### *Anita Mills*
The Duke's Double

The New Super Regency
### *Edith Layton*
The Game of Love

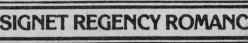

## SIGNET REGENCY ROMANCE